Long Division

PRAISE FOR *LONG DIVISION*

"In a multilayered, allusion-packed, time-traveling plot set in Mississippi, *Long Division* takes us, nesting-doll style, from 2013 to 1985, 1964, and back, engaging complex questions of race, violence, gender, sexuality, and or relationship to history."

—Lucy McKeon, *Boston Review*

"Smart, exciting and energetic...the language romps and roars along through some truly wonderful comic scenes and yet the book doesn't hesitate to comment seriously on questions that matter to human beings everywhere, not just in rural Mississippi."

—Victor LaValle, author of *Big Machine* **and** *Slapboxing with Jesus*

"Laymon does a remarkable job of capturing the moments when you grow up all at once—and cleverly poses a strong case for making sure all teenagers will have the books that help them reach those revelations."

—Alyssa Rosenberg, *Think Progress*

"A curious, enjoyable novel...take[s] relish in skewering the disingenuous masquerade of institutional racism..."

—Publishers Weekly

"The inclusion of something as fantastical as time travel in a book that's primarily about race highlights one of the most singular things about Laymon's writing: his ability to contextualize tragedy with humor.... You can laugh and cry on the same page—a sometimes-strange sensation that allows Laymon to succeed in his main goal: to keep us from forgetting."

—Azeen Ghorashi, *East Bay Express*

"A brilliant young writer...this is a book that sings in the heart but challenges readers to take careful consideration of the power of memory. Like the best of Hurston, Ellison, or Bambara, Laymon's craft flows on frequencies that both honor and extend the traditions those writers established."

—William Henry Lewis, author of *I Got Somebody in Staunton*

Long Division

a Novel

Kiese Laymon

BOLDEN

AN **AGATE** IMPRINT

CHICAGO

The document excerpted on pages 213–214 is from SNCC, *The Student Nonviolent Coordinating Committee Papers, 1959-1972* (Sanford, NC: Microfilming Corporation of America, 1982) Reel 67, File 340, Page 1178. The original papers are at the King Library and Archives, The Martin Luther King, Jr. Center for Nonviolent Social Change, Atlanta, Georgia.

Printed in the United States of America.

Library of Congress Cataloging-in-Publication Data

Laymon, Kiese.
Long division : a novel / Kiese Laymon.
    pages cm
ISBN 978-1-932841-72-5 (pbk. : alk. paper) -- ISBN 978-1-57284-718-7 (ebook)
1. Mississippi--Fiction. I. Title.
PS3612.A959L66 2013
813'.6--dc23

                    2013009054

10 9 8 7 6 5

Bolden Books is an imprint of Agate Publishing. Agate books are available in bulk at discount prices. For more information, visit agatepublishing.com.

"Twice upon a time, there was a boy who died
and lived happily ever after
but that's another chapter."
—André Benjamin, "Aquemini"

...

One Sentence.

LaVander Peeler cares too much what white folks think about him. Last quarter, instead of voting for me for ninth-grade CF (Class Favorite), he wrote on the back of his ballot, "All things considered, I shall withhold my CF vote rather than support Toni Whitaker, Jerome Wallace, or The White Homeless Fat Homosexual." He actually capitalized all five words when he wrote the sentence, too. You would expect more from the only boy at Fannie Lou Hamer Magnet School with blue-black patent leather Adidas and an ellipsis tattoo on the inside of his wrist, wouldn't you? The tattoo and the shoes are the only reason he gets away with using sentences with "all things considered" and the word "shall" an average of fourteen times a day. LaVander Peeler hates me. Therefore (I know Principal Reeves said that we should never write the "n-word" if white folks might be reading, but…), I hate that wack nigga, too.

My name is City. I'm not white, homeless, or homosexual, but if I'm going to keep it one hundred, I guess you should also know that LaVander Peeler smells so good that sometimes you can't help but wonder if a small beast farted in your mouth when you're too close to him. It's not just me, either. I've watched Toni Whitaker, Octavia Whittington, and Jerome Wallace sneak and sniff their own breath around LaVander Peeler, too.

If you actually watched the 2013 Can You Use That Word in a Sentence finals on good cable last night, or if you've seen the clip on YouTube, you already know I hate LaVander Peeler and you're probably wondering about my feelings for that short Mexican girl from Arizona who kicked me in my knee.

The Can You Use That Word in a Sentence contest was started in the spring of 2006 after states in the Deep South, Midwest, and Southwest complained that the Scripps Spelling Bee was geographically biased. Each contestant has two minutes to use a given word in a "dynamic" sentence. The winner of the contest gets $75,000 toward college tuition if they decide to go to college. All three judges in the contest, who are also from the South, Midwest, or Southwest, must agree on a contestant's "correct sentence usage, appropriateness, and dynamism" for you to advance. New Mexico and Oklahoma won the last four contests, but this year LaVander Peeler and I were supposed to bring the title to Mississippi.

At Hamer, even though I'm nowhere near the top of my class, I'm known as the best boy writer in the history of our school, and Principal Reeves says LaVander Peeler is the best boy reader in the last five years. Toni Whitaker hates when Principal Reeves gives us props because she's a better writer than me and a better reader than LaVander Peeler, but she's not even the best girl reader and writer at Hamer. Octavia Whittington, this girl who blinks once every minute, is even better than Toni at both, but Octavia Whittington has issues with her self-esteem and she doesn't talk or share her work with anyone until the last day of every quarter, so we don't count her.

Anyway, LaVander Peeler has way too much space between his eyes and his fade doesn't really fade right. Nothing really fades into anything, to tell you the truth. Whenever I feel dumb around him I call him "Lavender" or "Fade Don't Fade." Whenever I do anything at all, he calls me "White Homeless Fat Homosexual" or "Fat Homosexual" for short because he claims that my house is a rich white lady's garage, that I'm fatter than Sean Kingston, and that I like to watch boys piss without saying "Kindly pause."

LaVander Peeler invented saying "Kindly pause" in the bathroom last year at the end of eighth grade. If you were pissing and another dude just walked in the bathroom and you wondered who was walking in the bathroom, or if you walked in the bathroom and just looked a little bit toward a dude already at a urinal, you had to say "Kindly pause." If I sound tight, it's because I used to love going to the bathroom at Hamer. They just renovated the bathrooms for the first time in fifteen years and these rectangular tiles behind the urinal are now this deep dark blue that make you know that falling down and floating up are the same thing, even if you have severe bubble guts or constipation.

Nowadays, you can never get lost in anything because you're too busy trying to keep your neck straight. Plus, it's annoying because dudes say "Kindly pause" as soon as they walk in the bathroom. And if one dude starts it, you have to keep saying it until you have both feet completely out of the bathroom.

But I don't say "Kindly pause" and it's not because I think I'm slightly homosexual. I just don't want to use some wack catchphrase created by

LaVander Peeler, and folks don't give me a hard time for it because I've got the best waves of anyone in the history of Hamer. I'm also the second-best rebounder in the school and a two-time reigning CW (Class Wittiest). Toni said I could win the SWDGF (Student Who Don't Give a Fuck) every year if we voted on that, too, but no one's created that yet. Anyway, it helps that everybody in the whole school hates LaVander Peeler at least a little bit, even the teachers, our janitor, and Principal Reeves.

When LaVander Peeler and I tied at the state contest, the cameras showed us walking off the stage in slow motion. I felt like Lil Wayne getting out of a limo, steady strolling into the backdoor of hell. In the backdrop of us walking were old images of folks in New Orleans, knee deep in toxic water. Those pictures shifted to shots of Trayvon Martin in a loose football uniform, then oil off the coast drowning ignorant ducks. Then they finally replayed that footage of James Anderson being run over by those white boys over off Ellis Avenue. The last shots were black-and-whites of dusty-looking teenagers from the Student Nonviolent Coordinating Committee holding up picket signs that said "Freedom Schools Now" and "Black is not a vice. Nor is segregation a virtue."

The next day at school, after lunch, LaVander Peeler, me, and half the ninth graders including Toni Whitaker, Jerome Wallace, and strange Octavia Whittington walked out to the middle of the basketball court where the new Mexican seventh graders like to play soccer. There are eight Mexican students at Hamer and they all started school this semester. Principal Reeves tried to make them feel accepted by having a taco/burrito lunch option three times a week and a Mexican Awareness Week twice each quarter. After the second quarter, it made most of us respect their Mexican struggle but it didn't do much for helping us really distinguish names from faces. We still call all five of the boys "Sergio" at least twice a quarter.

Anyway, everyone formed a circle around LaVander Peeler and me, like they did every day after lunch, and LaVander Peeler tried to snatch my heart out of my chest with his sentences.

"All things considered, Fat Homosexual," LaVander Peeler started, "This is just a sample of the ass-whupping you shall be getting tonight at the contest."

He cleared his throat.

"African Americans are generally a lot more ignorant than white Americans, and if you're an African-American boy and you beat not only African-American girls but white American boys and white American girls, who are, all things considered, less ignorant than you by nature—in something like making sentences, in a white American state like Mississippi—you are, all things considered, a special African-American boy destined for riches, unless you're a homeless white fat homosexual African-American boy with mommy issues, and City, you are indeed the white fat homosexual African-American boy with mommy issues who I shall beat like a knock-kneed slave tonight at the nationals." Then he got closer to me and whispered, "One sentence, Homosexual. I shall not be fucked with."

LaVander Peeler backed up and looked at the crowd, some of whom were pumping their fists, covering their mouths, and laughing to themselves. Then he kissed the ellipsis tattoo on his wrist and pointed toward the sky. I took out my brush and got to brushing the waves on the back of my head.

It's true that LaVander Peeler has mastered the comma, the dash, and the long "if-then" sentence. I'm not saying he's better than me, though. We just have different sentence styles. I don't think he understands what the sentences he uses really mean. He's always praising white people in his sentences, but then he'll turn around and call me "white" in the same sentence like it's a diss. And I'm not trying to hate, but all his sentences could be shorter and more dynamic, too.

The whole school year, even before we went to the state finals, LaVander Peeler tried to intimidate me by using long sentences like that in the middle of the basketball court after lunch, but Grandma and Uncle Relle told me that winning any championship takes mental warfare and a gigantic sack. Uncle Relle was the type of uncle who, when he wasn't sleeping at some desperate woman's house and eating up all her Moon Pies, was in jail or sleeping in a red X-Men sleeping bag at my grandma's house.

What Uncle Relle lacked in money, he made up for in the way he talked and taught the ratchet gospels. The sound of his voice made everything he said sound right. When he opened his mouth, it sounded like big old flat tires rolling over jagged gravel. And he had these red, webbed eyeballs that poked out a lot even when he was sleeping. I could tell you crazy stories about Uncle Relle's eyeballs, his voice, and his sagging V-neck T-shirts, but that would be a waste of time, especially since the detail you just couldn't forget about, other than his voice, was his right hand. The day after he got back from Afghanistan, Uncle Relle lost the tips of three fingers in a car accident with our cousin, Pig Mo. Now, he had three nubs, a pinky, and a thumb. You would think that if you had three nubs, a pinky, and a thumb, you would keep your hand in your pocket, right? Uncle Relle always had his right hand out pointing at folk or asking for stuff he didn't need or messing around with weed and prepaid cell phones. He told everyone outside the family that he lost the tips in Afghanistan.

Grandma said Uncle Relle lied about his nubs because he wanted everyone to know he was a damn survivor. In private, in a much thicker voice, she said, "A real survivor ain't got to show no one that they done survived." Grandma was always saying stuff you would read in a book.

"Lavender Peeler," I told him while brushing the sides of my head and looking at his creased khakis, "Oh, Lavender Peeler, my uncle and grandma thought you would say something wack like that. Look, I don't have to consider all things to know you ain't special because you know 'plagiarize' is spelled with two a's, two i's, and a z, not an s, especially since if you train them XXL cockroaches in your locker, the ones that be the cousins of the ones chilling in prison with your old thieving-ass brother, Kwame, they could spell 'plagiarize' with ummm,"—I started to forget the lines of my mental warfare—"the crumbs of a Popeyes buttermilk biscuit, which are white buttery crumbs, that stay falling out of your halitosis-having daddy's mouth when he tells you every morning, 'Lavender, that boy, City, with all those wonderful waves in his head, is everything me and your dead mama wished you and your incarcerated brother could be.'" I stepped closer to him, tugged on my sack, and looked at Octavia Whittington out of the corner of my eye. "That's one sentence, too, wack nigga, with an embedded quotation up in there. And your fade still don't fade quite right."

Without even looking at me, LaVander Peeler just said, "Roaches can't spell so that sentence doesn't make any sense."

Everyone around us was laughing and trying to give me some love. And I should have stopped there, but I kept going and kept brushing and looked directly at the crowd. "Hell, Lavender Peeler can be the first African American to win the title all he wants, y'all," I told them. "But me, I'm striving for legendary, you feel me?"

Even the seventh-grade Mexicans were dying laughing at LaVander Peeler, who was closest to me. He was flipping through one of those pocket thesauruses, acting like he was in deep conversation with himself.

"Shoot," I said to the crowd. "I'm 'bout to be the first one of us with a head full of waves to win nationals in anything that ain't related to sports or cheerleading, you feel me?"

Toni Whitaker, Octavia Whittington, and Jerome Wallace stopped laughing and stared at each other. Then they looked at both of us. "He ain't lying about that," Toni said. Octavia Whittington just nodded her head up and down and kept smiling.

The bell rang.

As we walked back to class, LaVander Peeler tapped me on the back of the neck and looked me directly in my eye. He flicked his nose with his thumb, opened his cheap flip phone, and started recording himself talking to me.

"I'm not going to stomp you into the ground for talking about my mother, my brother, and my pops because I don't want to be suspended today, but this right here will be on YouTube in the morning just in case your fat homosexual ass forgets," LaVander Peeler told me. "I do feel you, City. I also do feel that all your sentences rely on fakeness and magic. All things considered, I feel like there's nothing real in your sentences because you aren't real. But do you feel that a certain fat homosexual is supposed to be riding to nationals tonight in my 'halitosis-having daddy's' van? I do. All things considered, I guess his mama don't even care enough to come see him lose, does she?"

LaVander Peeler got even closer to me. The boy smelled like fried tomatoes, buttered cornbread, and peppermint. I held my arms tight to my body and counted these twelve shiny black hairs looking like burnt curly fries curling their way out of his chin. I scratched my chin and kept my hand there as he tilted his fade don't fade down and whispered in my ear, "You know the real difference between me and you, City?"

"What?"

"Sweat and piss," he told me. "I'm sweat. All things considered, sweat and piss ain't the same thing at all. Even your mama knows that, and she might know enough to teach at a community college in Mississippi, but she ain't even smart enough to keep a man, not even a homeless one who just got off of probation for touching three little retarded girls over in Pearl."

LaVander Peeler closed his flip phone, said, "One sentence," and just walked off.

All Clean.

Turns out LaVander Peeler commenced to tell our principal, old loose-skin Ms. Lara Reeves, that I called him a "nigger"—not "nigga," "negroid," "Negro," "African American," or "colored." I figured it was just LaVander Peeler's retaliation for someone turning him in two months ago for calling me a "faggot." I know who snitched on LaVander Peeler, and it wasn't me, but after he got in trouble for calling me a "faggot" he started calling me a "homosexual," because he knew Principal Reeves couldn't punish him for using that word without seeming like she thought there was something wrong with being a homosexual in the first place.

I guess you should also know that no one else at Hamer or in the world ever called me a "faggot" or "homosexual" except for LaVander Peeler. I'm not trying to make you think I've gotten nice with lots of girls or anything because I haven't. I felt on Toni's bra in a dark closet in Art and she twerked on my sack a few times after school. And I guess I talked nasty with a few people who claimed they were girls on this website called WhatYouGotOn-MyFreak.com, but really that was it. Truth is my sack stayed dry as hell, but I don't think you're supposed to feel like a case about sex unless you make it through tenth grade with a dry sack. The point is that even if LaVander Peeler caught you watching him piss once, I don't think that should really qualify you as a homosexual.

Anyway, I sat in Principal Reeves's office waiting to tell her that I didn't call him a "nigger," but that I did bring my wave brush out after lunch by mistake.

In Principal Reeves's office, next to her huge bookshelf, was a big poster with a quote from Maya Angelou. The backdrop of the poster was the sun and in bolded red letters were the sentences, "Bitterness is like cancer. It eats upon the host. But anger is like fire. It burns it all clean. Courage is the most important of all the virtues, because without courage you can't practice any other virtue consistently."

I hated sentences that told me that my emotions were like something that wasn't emotional, but I loved how those red words looked like they were coming right out of the sun, red hot.

Ms. Lara Reeves had been a teacher since way back in the '80s and she became the principal at Hamer about four years ago. The worst part of her being the principal was that she was also my mama's friend. My mama was known for having friends you wouldn't think she'd have. Mama had me when she was a sophomore at Jackson State fourteen years ago. She's old now, in her early thirties, so you would expect her to have only black friends in her thirties, but she had black friends, white friends, African friends, and super-old friends like Principal Reeves.

Mama taught over at Madison Community College and Principal Reeves took a politics course from her. When I first heard that my principal was my mama's student, I thought I'd get away with everything. But it was actually harder for me to get away with anything since whenever Principal Reeves didn't do her homework or answered questions wrong, she liked to talk to my mama about how I was acting a fool in school.

On Principal Reeves's desk, you saw all kinds of papers flooding the bottoms of two big pictures of her husband, who disappeared a few years ago. No one knows what happened to him. Supposedly, he went to work one morning and just never came back. If you looked at pictures of Principal Reeves back in the day, you'd be surprised, because she looked exactly the same. She had the same curl at 62 that she had at 31, except now the curl was lightweight gray.

Principal Reeves also kept a real record player in her office. In the corner underneath the table were all these Aretha Franklin records. Mama loved Aretha Franklin, too, but she only had greatest-hit CDs, which she'd play every time she picked me up.

I invented calling Principal Reeves "Ms. Kanye" behind her back because even though she asked a lot of questions, you really still couldn't tell her nothing. She asked questions just to set up her next point. And her next point was always tied to teaching us how we were practically farting on the chests of the teenagers on the Student Nonviolent Coordinating Committee if we didn't conduct ourselves with dignity.

Before Principal Reeves stepped her foot in the door of her office, she was saying my name. "Citoyen..."

"Yes ma'am."

"Take this test," she said, and handed me a piece of paper. "Don't look at me with those sad red eyes. Just take the test."

At Hamer, they were always experimenting with different styles of punishment ever since they stopped whupping ass a few years ago. The new style was to give you a true/false test if you messed up. And the test had to be tailored to what they thought you did wrong and what you needed to learn to not mess up again. The craziest thing is that it was usually harder understanding what the test had to do with what you did wrong than taking the actual test itself.

Name _____ Year _____ True/False — Underline one

1. Desperation will make a villain out of you.

True/False

2. Only a fool would not travel through time and change
their past if they could.

True/False

3. You were brought to this country with the expectation of
life, liberty, and the pursuit of happiness.

True/False

4. If you push yourself hard in the direction of freedom,
compassion, and excellence, you will recover.

True/False

5. Loving someone and loving how someone makes
you feel are the same thing.

True/False

6. Only those who can read, write, and love can move
back or forward through time.

True/False

**7. There are undergrounds to the past and future for
every human being on earth.
True/False
8. If you haven't read or written or listened to something
at least three times, you have never really read, written, or listened.
True/False
9. Past, present, and future exist within you and you change
them by changing the way you live your life.
True/False
10. You are special.
True/False
Bonus
11. You are innocent.
True/False**

After I finished the stupid test, Principal Reeves put it on top of a stack of tests she hadn't graded yet and started going in on me. "Citoyen, do you know who the great Brenda Travis is?" she asked me.

"Umm…"

"No. You do not know. Brenda Travis was a fifteen-year-old high school student from right up the road in McComb," Principal Reeves said, and popped what looked like some boiled peanuts in her mouth. "That young lady canvassed these same streets with the SNCC voter-registration workers 50 years ago. She led students like you on a sit-in and, for the crime of ordering a hamburger from a white restaurant, the girl was sentenced to a year in the state juvenile prison."

"Just a regular hamburger?" I asked her. "Not even a fish sandwich or a grilled cheese? That's crazy."

"That contraption holding your teeth in place, that's the problem." Principal Reeves sat at her desk and started ruffling through papers.

"I don't get it," I told her. "What contraption?"

"Your mouth, that contraption. It is going to be the death of you or somebody else," she said. "Today is the biggest day of your life, Citoyen. You want to waste it calling your brother LaVander Peeler a 'nigger' and using a wave brush on school property? You know we don't bring wave brushes to school at Hamer."

The problem was that at Hamer, you used to be able to use your wave brush until the second bell at 8:05, but ever since Jerome Wallace beat the bile out of this cock-eyed new kid, Roy Belton, with a Pine wave brush during lunch, you can be suspended for something as simple as having a wave brush on school property.

"LaVander Peeler ain't my brother," I told her, "and I didn't think I was wasting it. I'm ready. You'll see."

Principal Reeves just looked at me. I tried to look away toward the bookshelf so I wouldn't have to look at her face.

"What's that?" I asked her. "That's so crazy."

"It's just a book," she said.

"I thought you said we were never supposed to say 'just a book' about a book."

Principal Reeves made that rule up last year. She had every book in her bookshelf placed in alphabetical order but on the floor underneath the shelf was a book called *Long Division*. There wasn't an author's name on the cover or the spine. I couldn't tell from looking at it if it was fiction or a real story. The cover had the words "Long Division" written in a thick black marker over what looked like the outside of this peeling work shed behind my grandma's house.

"Who wrote that book?"

Principal Reeves ignored my question and just looked at me.

"Please stop looking at me, Principal Reeves."

"I'll stop looking at you when you start looking at you. You've got to respect yourself and the folks who came before you, Citoyen. You," she paused. "You know better. Didn't your mother, you, and me sit right here before the state competition and talk about this? What did your mother tell you?"

"She said, 'Your foolishness impacts not only black folks today, but black folks yet to be born.' But see, I don't agree with my mama…"

"There are no buts, Citoyen," Principal Reeves said. "You are history. Kids right around your age died changing history so you could go to school, so you could compete in that contest tonight, and here you are acting a fool. The day of?"

"Is that a question?"

"Fifty-one years ago, black students took responsibility for the morality and future of this country," she said. She was so serious. "They organized. They restrained themselves. They put themselves in the crosshairs of evil. They bled. And when the cameras were on, they were scared. But they stepped up and fought nonviolently with dignity and excellence, didn't they?"

I just kept looking down at *Long Division* and started to smell the french fries coming from the cafeteria.

"Nevermind that book, Citoyen. Is it too much to ask of you to respect those students today?" she asked. "Look at me. Those that are still alive are watching. You know that, don't you?"

"You mean tonight?" I took my eyes off the book and looked at Principal Reeves. "Tonight, they'll be watching?"

"Yes. Tonight, they'll be watching, along with the world. But they're always watching, so you must behave and compete accordingly. This is just another test. I'm not gonna suspend you or tell your mother. However, if you act a fool one more time this semester, I have no choice but to reach out."

I hated when folks used the word "however" in regular conversation. You knew that the person you were talking to was so much wacker than you thought as soon as you heard that word. "I know," I told her.

"One more thing," she said and closed the office door. "I hear from LaVander Peeler and a few other teachers that you're spending a lot of time alone in the bathroom stalls."

I looked down at the stains on my brown Adidas.

"Have you been—"

"What?"

"Touching yourself inappropriately at lunch time?"

"Lunch time?"

"Yes. I've heard that after many of the boys go into the bathroom to yell 'Kindly pause,' that you go in there and … listen. We don't want to halt natural human functions at Fannie Lou Hamer, but that activity might be better suited for home, possibly before you go to sleep or maybe even when you wake up."

I raised my eyes to Principal Reeves.

"Do you understand what I'm saying, Citoyen?"

"I'm good," I told Principal Reeves. "You're telling me not to get nice with myself on school property. I hear you. Wish me luck tonight." I started walking out of her office, then turned around. "Wait. Can I borrow that book? I'll bring it back tomorrow. I just never really seen a book with a cool title like that and no author before."

Principal Reeves slowly reached down and handed me the book. "I haven't finished it yet," she told me. "Be careful with that, Citoyen."

"Why?"

"Just be careful," she said.

Principal Reeves had acted weird before, but this was the first time she was acting like she was sending me off to Syria. "Some books can completely change how we see ourselves and everything else in the world. Keep your eyes on the prize."

"I'm good," I told her before walking out. "Don't worry about my eyes. And that prize is mine."

At 3:15, LaVander Peeler and I waited on the curb for his father to pick us up. I had *Long Division* in my hands. LaVander Peeler had on these fake Louis Vuitton shades and he kept looking down at my book.

"What you looking at?" I asked him.

He asked me if I had figured out the difference yet between sweat and piss. I looked up at LaVander Peeler and noticed two continent-sized clouds easing their way through the sky behind his fade that didn't fade. I thought to myself that a lot of times when you looked up at the sky, you'd see nothing but bluish-gray shine, and a few seconds later continent-sized clouds would slowly glide up and take every last bit of shine out of the sky.

I didn't like the drippy ache in my chest that I was starting to feel, so I opened up *Long Division* and read the first chapter while LaVander Peeler and I waited for his father, LaVander Peeler Sr., to drive us to the Coliseum.

...

Special Game...

...I didn't have a girlfriend from kindergarten all the way through the first half of ninth grade and it wasn't because the whole high school heard Principal Jankins whispering to his wife, Ms. Dawsin-Jankins, that my hairline was shaped like the top of a Smurf house. I never had a girlfriend because I loved this funky girl named Shalaya Crump. The last time Shalaya Crump and I really talked, she told me, "City, I could love you if you helped me change the future dot-dot-dot in a special way."

Shalaya Crump was always saying stuff like that, stuff you'd only imagine kids saying in a dream or on those R-rated movies on HBO starring spoiled teenagers. If any other girl in 1985 said, "the future dot-dot-dot," she would have meant 1986 or maybe 1990 at the most. But not Shalaya Crump. I knew she meant somewhere way in the future that no one other than scientists and dope fiends had ever thought of before.

Shalaya Crump lived down in Melahatchie, Mississippi across the road from Mama Lara's house. A year ago, she convinced me that plenty of high school girls would like me even though my hips were way wider than a *JET* centerfold's, and the smell of deodorant made me throw up. The thing was that none of the ninth-grade girls who liked me wore fake Air Jordans with low socks, or knew how to be funny in church while everyone else was praying, or had those sleepy, sunken eyes like Shalaya Crump. Plus, you never really knew what Shalaya Crump was going to say and she always looked like she knew more than everybody around her, even more than the rickety grown folks who wanted other rickety grown folks to think they knew more than Yoda.

It's hard to ever really know why you love a girl, but all I know is that Shalaya Crump made me feel like it was okay not to know everything. You could feel good around Shalaya Crump just by knowing enough to get by. That's what I loved about her most. Sometimes, she asked these hard questions about the future but she didn't treat you like chunky vomit when you didn't get the answer right.

It's hard to explain if you never been around a girl like that. It's just that no other girl in my whole life made me feel like it was okay not to know stuff like Shalaya Crump did. The worst part of it is that even after all we went through yesterday, I still have no proof that I ever made Shalaya Crump feel anything other than guilty for leaving me with Baize Shephard. I'm not just saying that to sound like something you'd read by a broken-hearted white boy from New York City in a dumb novel in tenth-grade English. If you want me to be honest, everything I'm telling you is only half of what made the story of Shalaya Crump, Baize Shephard, Jewish Evan Altshuler, and me the saddest story in the history of Mississippi. And it's really hard to have the saddest story in the history of a state like Mississippi, where there are even more sad stories than there are hungry mosquitoes and sticker bushes.

It really is.

Shalaya Crump claimed she could love me three months ago, depending on how you count. It was January 3, 1985, the last day of my Christmas break. I was about to leave Melahatchie and head back to Chicago. We were sitting under a magnolia tree in a forest we called the Night Time Woods, sharing the last bit of a can of sardines. I was just tired of not saying all of what I wanted to say to her, so I licked the sardine juice off my fingers, picked up my sweat rag, and asked her what I'd been waiting to ask her the whole break.

"Shalaya Crump!" I said, "Can you break it down for me one more time. What I gotta do to make you love me?"

Shalaya Crump laughed and started digging into the red dirt with her dark bony thumbs that were covered in these Ring Pop rings. Right there is when Shalaya Crump wiped her greasy mouth with the collar of her purple Gumby T-shirt and said, "Why you gotta be so green light lately, City?"

"Green light?"

"Yeah, you never stop. All you do is spit game about 'love this' and 'love that.' I already told you that I could love you if you found a way to be..." Shalaya Crump stopped talking, looked me right in the eyes, and grabbed the fingertips of my hands. "City, just listen," she said. "Look, if we could take a spaceship to the future, and we ain't know if we'd ever come back, would you go with me?" Shalaya Crump was always changing the subject to the future at the craziest times.

I swear I tried to come up with something smart, something that would make her think I could be the skinniest, smartest boy she'd ever want to spend the rest of my life with. "Girl, in the future," I told Shalaya Crump, "when we take that spaceship, first thing is I think that Eddie Murphy is gonna do a PG movie. And umm, I think that Michael Jackson and New Edition are gonna come together and sing a song at our wedding, but ain't nobody at the wedding gonna care because everyone at the wedding is gonna finally know."

"Uh, finally know what?" She stopped and let go of my wrists.

"Finally know, you know, what that real love looks like, baby."

"City! Why you gotta get all Vienna sausage school bus when you start trying to spit game?" She paused and actually waited for an answer. I didn't have one, so she kept going. "Just stop. You stuck on talking about love but I'm talking about *the future*. Can we just talk about that? What happened to you? One day you were just regular and we were playing Atari and hitting each other in the face with pine cones. Then, just like that, you get to stealing Bibles to impress me and wearing clean clothes and talking about love and getting jealous of Willis whenever we watch *Diff'rent Strokes* and asking me all these questions about what senior I have a crush on. Can't you just be yourself?"

"I am being myself," I told her. "I don't like how you look at Willis." I knew that making Shalaya Crump love me wasn't going to be easy, so I didn't let her little speech throw me off. "You talk all that mess about me, but you the one who didn't always talk about the future like you do now." I looked in her eyes, but she was looking at the ground. "No offense, girl, but you talk about the future way more than I talk about love."

"But I'm not just talking." She wiped sardine grease off my lip. "That's the difference. I'm asking about what you'd do with me in the future, like in 2013. For real! Would you come with me if I could get us there?" I just looked at Shalaya Crump and wondered how she could say I was being all Vienna sausage school bus and all green light when, seriously, she was the one always wondering about life in 2013. No kid in 1985 admitted to thinking about life in the '90s, and definitely not in 2013, not even after *Back to the Future* came out.

"Never mind," she said. "You don't get it."

"I do get it," I told her. "I get that I might not be the one for you. In 2013, I'ma be like 42. When I'm 42, you'll still think my hairline is too crooked and my sweat'll still stink like gas station toilets." I looked up and hoped she would interrupt me. She didn't. "Anyway. You could never love me even if I was the skinniest, smartest boy in the South. I truly know that now."

Shalaya Crump finally laughed and looked me right in my mouth. "City, I'ma ask you one more time to stop being so *Young and the Restless*. Don't never ever say 'truly' around me again. Never!"

Shalaya Crump was the queen of taking a show or a person, place, or thing and using it like an adjective. No one else in Jackson or Chicago or Melahatchie or TV could do it like her. If she told you not to ever use a word around her, you knew it was a word that should never have come out of your mouth in the first place.

Shalaya Crump took her eyes off my mouth and started looking at my hips. "Look, City," she said. "I could love you the way you want me to, really. I could if you found a way to help me change the future in, I don't know dot-dot-dot a special way."

"Dot-dot-dot? I thought you were done with that read-your-punctuation style. You don't think you played that out last summer?"

"Just listen. I need to know if you'd come with me, even if we couldn't ever come back."

Shalaya Crump was always saying weird stuff like that and trying to create new slang. One day, she called me on the phone long
distance during the school year and said, "City comma I realized
today that I hate Ronald Reagan. When I'm president comma I
wanna make it so you never have to be in a classroom with more
than ten other kids from Head Start all the way through 12th grade.
I think I might wanna make it illegal for parents to leave their kids
with their grandma in Melahatchie for more than three days at a
time if the grandma don't have cable or good air. What you think?"

I waited for her to laugh after saying that, since my ma was
always sending me to stay with my Mama Lara for weeks at a time.
Mama Lara didn't have good cable or air either, and neither did
her grandma, but Shalaya Crump didn't laugh, so I fake laughed
for her and said, "You love you some English and Civics classes,
don't you?" A few seconds later, when no one was saying a word,
she started laughing all late into the phone. Only Shalaya Crump
could laugh all late into the phone and not care about using up
her grandma's long distance to talk about hating Ronald Reagan.
It was stuff like calling me long distance and telling me stuff that
didn't make sense and laughing all late at my jokes that made me
think I could tongue kiss Shalaya Crump.

Anyway, I had a lot of questions about how to change the future and be special to Shalaya Crump, but my Mama Lara drove in
front of her trailer right after she said that thing about coming to
the future with her. Mama Lara told me that it was time to take the
bus back up to Chicago. I left Shalaya Crump that Christmas break
without a kiss, a hug, or anything, but I did tell her, "I'm coming
back to fly to the future with you for spring break, baby. And when
I do, you better love me. Or at least like me a lot."

"I already like you a lot," she told me as I got in the car. "Don't call me baby no more, though. Just be yourself and come back in March. Please. I need you, City."

I promised myself right then and there that I'd never call Shalaya Crump "baby" if it meant that she'd be my girl, and that I'd find a way to be special and change the future when I came back down to Mississippi for spring break. In the meantime, no matter where I was in my dreams, I always found a way to kiss Shalaya Crump. Sometimes I'd be in a blue jungle or a raggedy glass airplane, but there would always be a phone hanging out of a tree or underneath a seat. I'd find a phone and dial 1-4-1-1. When the operator answered, it was always Shalaya Crump and she always gave me the best directions to get to her. Once I got to where she was, every single time we kissed with a little tongue and pressed our fronts together until I woke up sore.

In real life, between January and March, I thought of all kinds of ways to show Shalaya Crump I was special. I wrote every plan down in this thick college-lined notebook I should have been using to take notes in English class. The notebook was called *GAME* in bold capital letters. Sometimes I would think I had the perfect plan but after a few days, I knew that whatever *GAME* I came up with wouldn't be good enough for her. Then, on the first day back down to Melahatchie for spring break, I got lucky.

GAME found me...

CHITLIN CITY.

"Sphincter," LaVander Peeler's father said from the driver's seat. "Use it."

"Sphincter," LaVander Peeler started. "A tightened sphincter can be a sign of—"

The Astro van started veering over to the side of I-55 and LaVander Peeler Sr. clicked the emergency lights on. "Boy, what I tell you?" He smacked LaVander Peeler right below his heart and grabbed a fistful of Izod. "Don't matter if you think you know the word. That's what the white folks think you supposed to do. Don't be too doggone eager. Act like you got some sense."

LaVander Peeler cut his wet eyes to me in the backseat.

"Don't worry 'bout that boy," he told him. "Y'all play too much. This is bigger than both of y'all. I want you to do exactly like them winners."

LaVander Peeler Sr. sat back in the driver's seat and placed his hand on his son's knee. "Ask for the pronunciation. Ask for the etymology just like the Indians do. Say the word back to them as proper as you can. Say, 'I am going to use "sphincter" in a sentence now.' No gon' or gonna. You are 'going to' or you 'shall.' And then you say the sentence as slowly as you can. I'm talking about a whole second in between each word, LP.

"Smile, too. If you wanna talk with the doggone judges, don't break no verbs. Just say, 'Well, all things considered,' then say what you got to say. Toss some composure and thoughtfulness at they ass, too. And hold your doggone head up." He grabbed LaVander Peeler by the chin and tilted it up. "LP, listen to what I'm telling you. They think you were lucky to get here. Both of y'all."

LaVander Peeler Sr. looked at me like I said something wrong.

"These folks think they so slick, trying to decorate the contest with a little color. You didn't come here to lose, son," he said. "You are better and more prepared than all these folks put together because you had to be. Listen to what I'm telling you. This is bigger than you. You understand?"

LaVander Peeler didn't answer. I closed *Long Division* and watched still water flood the gutters of LaVander Peeler's eyes.

The trip to the Coliseum took about 20 minutes and all 20 minutes, except for LaVander Peeler Sr. nicely greeting me, was filled with him testing LaVander Peeler and getting mad at every little thing he did wrong. But it wasn't hateful mean. It really wasn't. It was loving mean, at least to me. If Mama drove me to the contest, it's exactly the loving mean I would have wanted her to share with me, just not in front of LaVander Peeler. That would've been too shame.

"You left your brush," LaVander Peeler Sr. said as I got out of the van. He handed it to me and shook his hand side to side. I told him thank you, and felt sorry that I had to crush his son in front of millions.

But I also felt something else as I walked into the Coliseum. There was something wrong with *Long Division*, the book I'd borrowed from Principal Reeves's office. Even though the book was set in 1985, I didn't know what to do with the fact that the narrator was black like me, stout like me, in the ninth grade like me, and had the same first name as me. Plus, you hardly ever read books that were written like you actually thought. I had never read the words "chunky vomit" in the first chapter of a book, for example, but when I thought about how I'd most not want to be treated, I thought about "chunky vomit."

I'm not saying the City in that book was exactly like me. I hadn't read enough of *Long Division* to know for sure. Still, though, I just loved and feared so much about the first chapter of that book. For example, I loved that someone with the last name "Crump" was in a book. Sounds dumb, but I knew so many Crumps in Mississippi in my real life, but I had never seen one Crump in anything I'd read. And you know what the scariest part of the book was? Near the beginning of the first chapter, the name "Baize Shephard" appeared.

A girl named Baize Shephard lived right next to my grandma's house in Melahatchie, Mississippi, and she had gone missing three weeks ago. Folks made it a big deal because she was an honor student and a wannabe rapper. Baize did this rhyme over this Kanye beat about Trayvon Martin and James Anderson called "My Hood to Your Hood," which got around 18,000 hits. When Obama visited Mississippi after his re-election, he said we needed to treat all our missing children with the same care and vigilance. Ever since then, you'd have a Baize Shephard update every day on the news and my Grandma and her crew started their own country investigation. I understood it could have been coincidence that my name and Baize Shephard's name were in this book with no author, but it still made me feel strange and lightweight afraid to keep reading, especially since my mind should have been on winning that contest.

Walking to the green room in the Coliseum was crazy, just like Uncle Relle said it would be. Grown white folks were looking at us like we were giving out $400 shopping sprees at the new Super Target by Northpark Mall, and LaVander Peeler was eating it up, saying "All things considered" and moving his hands too much when he talked.

When we got to the green room, a lanky woman with an aqua fanny pack around her waist and the name "Cindy" on her left breast came up to us.

"We've heard so much about you two and your ordeal with Hurricane Katrina. And good Lord, all that oil y'all had to deal with on the coast," she said. "It was God's will that you're here with us and we're gonna take great care of you. Eat all the fruit salad and cornbread y'all want before the event. Get good and full."

I looked at LaVander Peeler and just started brushing my hair. Long front strokes. Short side strokes. "You know we're from Jackson, right?" I asked her. "Not the coast. Where you from?"

"Oh, we heard about that." She ignored me and pointed at the brush. "So cute. But there will be no props beyond this point either." She held out her hand for my brush. "We can't change the rules just for you, no matter how special you gents are. This might not be the Scripps Spelling Bee, gents, but this is our national competition and we've got one shot to do it right. We will be televised live and seen on digital cable by millions of folks around the globe. The eyes of the world are upon Mississippi tonight and we can't have our special kids up there with brushes, can we?"

"I ain't giving up my brush," I told Cindy as LaVander Peeler and I walked into our personal dressing room.

When we got into the room, LaVander Peeler just looked at me and didn't say a word. He looked and smelled the same, but he wasn't LaVander Peeler from Hamer any more. LaVander Peeler looked older, madder, glowier, and—I guess—realer than ever. "City, I shall keep it one hundred, as you say.

You are embarrassing the fuck out of me," he said in a tone I'd never heard him use. "This ain't school no more. You are really blowing it."

"Blowing what?" I asked him and waited for an answer. He just stood shaking his head side to side. "Why can't you ever just bust jokes like everybody else at school? Why you gotta be so serious and try so hard to bully people?"

"Me? I don't bully nobody. You're the bully."

"How am I the bully?" I asked him. "And what am I blowing?"

"Everything. You blowing everything, but that's what I expected." He started lotioning up his neck. "All things considered, it just would have been nice if you placed in the top ten. I'm winning this shit with or without you, though. I will not lose."

"Then what?"

"Then I'ma beat them in whatever else they put in my way," he said. "Everything. All things considered, I will never lose to these people. Ever. They need to know that. When I'm married to Malia Obama and living in the biggest house in their neighborhood, they need to know they will never beat me."

"Nigga, Malia Obama don't even know you exist," I told him. "What is she gonna want with a wack dude with a fucked-up fade, who talks fake-proper all the time?"

"Whatever," he said. "All things considered, I don't expect you to understand. These people just need to know."

"And you winning this competition is gonna show them whatever it is that they need to know?" I asked him. "Fool, forget white people. Why don't you try to win this for your real people? Because that's what I'm doing. I'm winning this for all the real chubby poor niggas in Mississippi with tight waves and contentious demeanors." He looked at me with lightweight awe in his eyes. "You like that sentence, right? And maybe you could win it for all the tall Mississippi niggas with, you know, good breath, and flip phones and messed-up fades that don't quite fade right. You feel—"

"City," he cut me off. "You and I both know you shouldn't even be here. That's what's so funny about all of this." He turned toward me and smirked. "And you know exactly what I mean," he said. "Think about it. At the school competition, what word did they give you?"

I knew what the word was, but I wasn't about to say it. There had been three of us in the finals. We were all supposed to get five words. If all of us got every word, our school sent three reps to state. Toni Whitaker was who everyone knew was going to win since she had the highest GPA in the ninth grade and never made less than 100 percent in English. Toni got "*coup d'état*" for her last word. We'd all heard the word but had no clue how to use it in what the judges called a dynamic sentence. LaVander Peeler got "infanticide" and I got...

"'Chitterlings,' City?" LaVander Peeler asked. "'Chitterlings'? And you had the nerve to brush your hair while getting all country with it. I'll never forget your dumb ass. You stood up there with no shame, and said, 'My grandma couldn't understand why the young siblings from up North refused to eat the wonderful chitterlings upon finding out they came from the magical bowels of a big-eyed hog named Charles.'"

"I was nervous," I told him. "Wait. I thought I had the hardest word. How many folks know that 'chitlins' and 'chitterlings' are the same word? You didn't know, did you?"

"They knew," he said, "and that's why they gave you that word. I know you see it. Everybody else does. You get them black words every time the championship is on the line."

"I do?"

"All things considered, you can spin your sentences fairly well," he said. "I admit that you're probably the most exciting contestant in this contest."

"You think so?" I asked him.

"Yeah," he said, "'cause your dumb ass will say anything. But you ain't even on a regional level as far as really spinning these sentences go. They want you here. My daddy and Principal Reeves even said it." He turned his back to me and started laughing to himself. "I bet these contest people give you 'hypertension' for your first word tonight."

"'Hypertension'? That's a black word?" That's all I could come up with.

"Exactly. It's so simple and black," he said. "Just like your dumb ass. And, by the way, only simple black people get 'hypertension' and compared to 'capriciously,' they might as well have given you something easy like 'homosexual,' because that's a compound word, too. And, all things considered, that's what you are: white homeless fat homosexual City who is going to get hypertension after he loses this competition to LaVander K. Peeler."

"'Homosexual' is a compound word?" I asked him. "What's the K stand for?"

LaVander Peeler started laughing and humming the beat to the Piggly Wiggly commercial. I put my brush down on my bag and gently went over the top of my head with the palm of my hand. Mama and Uncle Relle had never said anything to me about getting black words or about how the people at the competition wanted me there. I couldn't understand why they needed me if they already had LaVander Peeler.

It didn't make sense.

"Let me ask you one more question, LaVander. Let's say you're right. Why would they need me if they already got you?"

LaVander Peeler looked at me like I was crazy. "What's wrong with you? They think it's all about them, not us. They feel good about themselves just by having us in the contest. But they're in for a surprise."

"Why?"

"Because, like I said, this exceptional African American is not letting these white folks win this contest. They messed up when they let me in. Come along if you want to. All things considered, I have to get my clothes on and start focusing."

LaVander Peeler went over on his knees in the corner with his arms stretched out. Then he acted like I wasn't even in the room by stripping out of his clothes and into his outfit for nationals. I didn't know what I was supposed to do, where I was supposed to look. I glanced up once and saw him butt-booty naked, pulling up his boxers. I didn't get why he brought a change of boxers for the contest. Maybe he was always changing his boxers in the bathroom of Hamer. Maybe changing his boxers at strange times, not just saying "All things considered," was really the weirdest thing about LaVander Peeler.

I didn't want to tell you this, but I think I should. LaVander Peeler's pubic hair was some of the nappiest I'd ever seen in my life. It looked like a black cabbage patch of tight balled-up cabbages. The truth is that LaVander Peeler was skinnier than me by a good 34 pounds, just like every other boy in my grade, but his sack was much rounder, wrinklier, and old-looking, too. I think I had plenty width on him in the privacy area, but I couldn't be sure.

I really couldn't.

We were both in there writing words on paper and practicing asking for the Latinate when Cindy came in without knocking. "Gents, turns out you're right. City, you can have your brush with you as long as you want. My boss understands cultural difference and wants to make you as comfortable as possible. This is going to be a global experience. So you should wear these, too."

She handed us two Rocawear button-ups.

I looked at LaVander Peeler. He looked at me. And for the first time, his look asked me what I thought. All I could really think about was what he saw when he looked at me. I know he saw ashy hands and a wave brush. But I knew in that second that he couldn't hate me. He didn't have to like me, but he definitely couldn't hate me when there was so much work for both of us to do in the next three hours. We had to show everyone, including white folks, chubby jokers with tight waves, and skinny jokers with suspect fades, just what was possible.

As we walked out, Cindy told me to be sure to bring my wave brush.

"Nope. I don't need it," I said and looked at LaVander Peeler. "My waves are tight as they are going to get. Cindy, you know you are looking at the next two winners of your contest, don't you?"

"I sure am," she said.

LaVander Peeler looked at me like I was crazy and started reading a dictionary. "And we are *going* to do it for us, right, LaVander Peeler?"

LaVander Peeler ignored me, so I reread the first chapter of *Long Division* until it was time.

When we left our dressing room, we walked into the general prep room where some of the competitors walked around, talking with each other and mouthing sentences. I scanned the room the same way I do when coming into any room where it is obvious most of the people aren't black and Southern.

Over in the corner were the two white boy twins from Louisiana. They had "Katrina's Finest" airbrushed in brown block letters on the back of these tight dirty sweatshirts. The twins were outside a huge group of white kids huddled in the corner looking at something. The kids at the back were all on their tippy toes trying to see over the cluster of about 15 kids. You could see that the white kids kept fake yawning, and rocking these half smiles. Between white faces and white shirts, I saw a cheek and a neck that was a little less dark than mine. And to the left of that cheek was a folded forearm that was close to LaVander Peeler's color. I started to get a terrible *déjà vu* feeling.

I tapped LaVander Peeler on the shoulder and pointed to the crowd. He walked toward the other contestants, got on his tiptoes, swiveled his head a bit, and started scratching the scalp part of his fade. Then he walked out of the room for almost two whole minutes.

When LaVander Peeler came back in, he looked at me, exhaled, and shook his head again before walking to the other corner of the room and slumping in the corner. I got to rubbing the top of my head with the palm of my hand and followed him.

"What is it?" I asked him. "What happened?"

LaVander Peeler looked up at me, eyelids half covering the brown of his eyes, bottom lip just hanging. "They got us," he said on volume two, when he'd just spent five minutes talking to me on volume seven.

"Why?" I looked over at the crowd again.

"They got us."

The Cindy lady came in and told us to get in line. As the crowd broke up, they taped our respective states on the back of our shirts. "LaVander Peeler, look," I said, and pointed to these two Mexican kids and the tags on their shirts. Both the Mexican boy and girl were really from Arizona, the state where the governor made a rule that Mexican kids couldn't learn Mexican history in high school and another rule that said you could try to arrest Mexicans as long as you thought they were Mexicans. During one of our Mexican Awareness weeks, Principal Reeves taught us that Arizona was becoming the Mississippi of the Southwest, whatever that meant.

LaVander Peeler got in line as he was told. He didn't pout or whine. LaVander Peeler's eyes had that slick mix of shock and shame. I can't say that he was crying because tears didn't pour down his face, but I swear that he had more of that same water cradling his red eyeballs than I'd ever seen in the face of someone who wasn't actually crying.

"Your eyeballs are sweating. Or is that piss?" I asked him, trying to make him laugh. "What's wrong, man? What did you see?"

LaVander Peeler ignored me. Still water flooded the bottoms of his eyes from the time he got his Mississippi tag until we reached the stage, the crowd, and those white-hot lights.

WORDS, WORDS, WORD.

I sat on the left side of the stage, third seat from the aisle, and LaVander Peeler sat in the same seat on the other side of the stage. At the end of my row was the one Mexican girl. At the end of LaVander Peeler's was the one Mexican boy. I looked at their names for the first time. Jesse Cruz and Stephanie Cruz were the names on the tags. And the words "Jesse" and "Stephanie" were in quotations.

I thought to myself that if ever there was a time to bring my Serena Williams sentence game to the nation, this was it. With all that still water in his eyes, LaVander Peeler was in no shape to win, or even compete. I figured he'd miss his first sentence, or maybe he wouldn't even try, and then he'd have to sit on that stage for two long hours, with drowning red eyeballs, watching me give those fools that work.

"We'd like to welcome you to the Fifth Annual Can You Use That Word in a Sentence National Competition," the voice behind the light said. "We're so proud to be coming to you from historic Jackson, Mississippi. The state of Mississippi has loomed large in the history of civil rights and the English language. Maybe our next John Grisham, Richard Wright, Alice Walker, William Faulkner, or Oprah Winfrey is in this contest. The rules of the contest are simple. I will give the contestant a word and he or she will have two minutes to use that word in a dynamic sentence. All three judges must agree upon the correct usage, appropriateness, and dynamism of the sentence. We guarantee you that this year's contest will be must-see TV.

"Before we begin, we'd like our prayers to go out to the family of Baize Shephard. As you all know, Baize is a young honor-roll student who disappeared a few weeks ago in the woods of Melahatchie, Mississippi. We will be flashing pictures of Baize periodically throughout the night for those of you watching live in your homes. If you have any information that might help in the investigation, please alert your local authorities. Let us take a moment of silence for Baize Shephard."

"LaVander Peeler," the announcer resumed, "is our first contestant. I'm sure most of you know that LaVander tied for first place in the state of Mississippi competition with our second contestant, Citoyen Coldson." Seemed weird that we were going to be first and second. "LaVander Peeler, your first word is 'lascivious.'"

LaVander Peeler stood up with his balled fists at his side. He stepped to the microphone and looked down at his feet.

"If lascivious photographs of Amber Rose were found on Mr. White's office computer," LaVander began, *"then the odds are higher than the poverty rate in the Mississippi Delta that Mr. Jay White would still keep his job at the college his great-great-grandfather founded."*

LaVander Peeler walked right back to his seat, fists still clenched. No etymology. No pronunciation. The crowd and the contestants started clapping in spurts, not understanding what had just happened. I was clapping the skin off my hands when they called my name. I stepped to the microphone, pumping my fist and looking at LaVander Peeler, who still had his head tucked in his chest.

"Citoyen, we'd like to welcome you, too."

"Thanks. My name is City."

"Your first word, Citoyen, is… 'niggardly.'"

Without uttering a syllable, I ran back to our dressing room and got my brush.

"I just think better with this in my hand," I told the voice when I got back.

"No problem. 'Niggardly,' Citoyen."

"For real? It's no problem?" I looked out into the white lights hoping somebody would demand they give me another word—not because I didn't know how to use it, but because it just didn't seem right that any kid like me should have to use a word like that, not in front of all those white folks.

"Etymology, please?" I asked him.

"From Old Norse *nigla*."

"*Nigla*? That's funny. Am I pronouncing the word right? 'Nigga'dly.' Pronunciation, please."

"Nig-gard-ly," he said. "Citoyen, you have 30 more seconds."

I kept squinting, trying to see out beyond the lights, beyond the stage. "Okay. Y'all have time limits at nationals, huh? I know the word, but it's just that my insides hurt when you say that word," I whispered into the mic. "And I wish it didn't but it does."

"Is that your sentence, Citoyen?" the voice asked.

I sucked my teeth and sped up my brushing. "You know that ain't my sentence."

"Citoyen. You have ten seconds."

I slowed my brushing down and angled myself toward LaVander Peeler. "Um, okay, *I hate LaBander Veeler*," I said.

"Is this your sentence, Citoyen?"

"No. Um, *I truly hate LaBander Veeler sometimes more than some of y'all hate President Obama and I wonder if LaBander Veeler should behave like the exceptional African-American boy he was groomed to be in public by his UPS-working father, or the, um, weird, brilliant, niggardly joker he really is when we're the only ones watching.*"

I brought the brush to my waist.

The judges looked at me for about ten seconds without moving before they turned toward each other. The head judge covered the microphone and started whispering to the other judges.

"Noooo, Citoyen," he finally said. "We are so, so sorry. That is not the correct, appropriate, or dynamic usage of 'niggardly' in a sentence. An example of correct, dynamic usage would be, *Perspiration covered the children who stared incessantly at the woman in the head wrap since she insisted on being so niggardly with the succulent plums and melons.* Please have a seat."

I started brushing the skin on my forearm, then pointed my brush toward the light.

That's all I could see.

I walked toward my seat, then turned around and headed back to the microphone. "I mean, even if I used the word right, I still would've lost. You see that, don't you?" The buzzer went off again. I threw my brush toward the light and the buzzer kept going off. "That's messed up, man," I told them. "What was I supposed to do?" I saw Cindy offstage to the right, motioning for me to sit down.

"Forget you, Cindy! Look at LaVander Peeler over there crying. I hate that dude. Naw, I mean really hate. I be sitting at home sometimes praying that someone will sew his butt hole tight so he could almost die from being so backed up. I'm serious, but look at him over there with tears in his eyes, looking crazy as hell on TV. It don't make no sense.

"Now look at them Mexicans." The buzzer went off again. I turned around and looked at the Mexican girl on my row. "You think it's hard for y'all in Arizona? Look at us. Look at us. They do us like this in our own state. Ain't nothing these white folks can do to make you feel like me and LaVander Peeler feel right now. They scared of y'all taking their jobs. They scared of us becoming Obama. I mean, do y'all even call yourself Mexican? Ain't this a competition for Americans? Peep how they made slots for Mexicans but you don't see no slots for no Africans or no Indians. Where the Indian and African players at? Shit."

Stephanie stood up, stretched her back, walked right up to my face, kicked me in my kneecap, and said, "Please sit your fat ass down." She whispered in my ear, "I'm trying to help you out. Seriously. You have no clue how you're playing yourself right now."

The buzzer went off again.

I put one hand on top of my belly blubber and started going over the top of my head with the palm of my other hand.

Short, fluid strokes.

"I ain't playing myself. Shoot. What was I supposed to do?" I said to everyone one more time. "Bet you know my name next time. And I bet you won't do this to another black boy from Mississippi. Shout out to my Jackson confidants: Toni, Jannay, Octavia, Jerome, and all my country niggas: Shay, Gunn, and even MyMy down in Melahatchie just trying to stay above water. I got y'all. President Obama, you see how they do us down here? You see?"

With that, I walked off, right past my chair, past the Mexican girl who kicked me, directly into the backstage area. Then I turned back around and walked back to the middle of that stage.

"And fuck white folks!" I yelled at the light and, for the first time all night, thought about whether my grandma was watching. "My name is City. And if you don't know, now you know, nigga!"

CLICK THAT.

During the first mile of the walk home, I flipped-flopped looking at the cover of *Long Division* and watching my feet miss most of the huge cracks in the asphalt on Capital Street. Every time I stepped on a crack, I thought of all the folks in Mississippi and the Southern Region who saw the contest live on TV and all the people around the globe who might see it later. The second mile I walked on the sidewalk down North State Street, and every time I missed a crack, I thought of the folks who would hear about what I did on the internet. I figured that everything I did would be sent in Facebook links with messages like, "Jade, clink that link girl. I just can't."

Everyone I knew would see what I did. Worst of all, Grandma would see it and be completely embarrassed when she went to church next Sunday. Everyone would look at her and say stuff like, "It's okay, Sister Coldson. Your grandbaby ain't know no better."

I walked in the apartment and sat down on the edge of Mama's bed. I wondered if Mama made it to the contest or if someone called her cell and told her what happened. Either way, Mama was probably on her way home to give me a legendary back beating. She would cry while doing it, too, I figured, and think she failed. But maybe for a second, I thought, Mama would understand that I was completely stuck on that stage.

One way to curb the back beating I was going to get was to write down my version of what happened. If I wrote about it, Mama would think I learned something from it. The only problem was that Mama took our used laptop to work with her, so I wrote on a blank page in *Long Division*.

If you watched the edited version of the 2014 Can You Use That Word in a Sentence on YouTube last night, you know that I hate LaVander Peeler and I have a head full of waves that could drown you and your barber. Public Speaking isn't even in my top eight pleasures, but I still tied for first place in the Fifth Annual State of Mississippi Can You Use That Word in a Sentence contest.

After writing for about 30 minutes, I went back in the garage and glanced at the clock. It was 8:50. The competition was supposed to be over at 9:00. I didn't want to but couldn't help turning on the TV.

One of the Katrina twins was on his way back to his seat and the crowd was doing that under-excited clapping which meant he couldn't appropriately use the word he was given in a sentence.

"Great try, Patrick," the voice said. "You've represented New Orleans, city of refugees, exquisitely tonight, and you can place no worse than third if our final two contestants get their words right."

With that, the Mexican girl walked onstage.

"Stephanie," the voice said, "if you can use this next word correctly in a dynamic sentence and our last finalist misses, you'll be our new champion. Thank you for blessing our stage with your presence."

The camera panned the rest of the competitors sitting in the background who were looking either sad and salty or just happy to be there. And sure as shit, there was LaVander Peeler to Stephanie's right, head still down, fists still balled up.

"Stephanie, your word is 'cacodoxy.'"

Lord have mercy.

I'd never heard that word before. And when the spelling popped up on screen, I felt terrible for her. Stephanie went through etymology and pronunciation.

She held her hands behind her back. Then she started tugging on her ponytail and tapping her left foot on the front of her right foot. She stood still with her hands right on her hips and started looking up at the ceiling.

"Fifteen seconds, Stephanie."

"You people really do think you're slick," she said loud enough so we could hear it, and started her sentence. "*The man behind the desk is not only annoying, he also suffers from keen halitosis and severe cacodoxy, causing him to make my brother and me put our names in some quotations.*"

The buzzer sounded. "No, Stephanie, I'm sorry. 'Cacodoxy,' a noun, is an erroneous doctrine, like 'Up with hope and down with dope.'"

"Are you serious?" she asked without leaving immediately. "You won't even use it in a sentence?" She sat down with her arms folded tight against her tummy, and you could see her mouth the words "That was so fucked up" before tucking her head into her chest.

Work, I thought. *She gave them that work!*

"Our last competitor is, surprise, surprise, LaVander Peeler," the voice said.

LaVander Peeler walked up to the microphone the same way he had before his first word, "lascivious." "You can do it," I said to the screen. "I'm sorry I left you."

"Seems like a lifelong dream might actually come true for this special young man," the voice said. "LaVander Peeler, if you use the next word correctly, Mississippi will be proud to call you our National Can You Use That Word in a Sentence champion. LaVander Peeler, your final word is…"

LaVander Peeler raised his head and looked right into the light.

"…'chitterlings.'"

In the background, Stephanie shot her head up, too. LaVander Peeler didn't blink at all. Again, he asked for no etymology. He balled his fists tighter and watched the light. I could not believe what was happening. "Don't do it," I said to the screen. But I wasn't sure what it was I didn't want him to do. And neither was LaVander Peeler.

He opened his lips slightly and stood there in front of the light. Watching his parted lips shaking made me think I understood what LaVander Peeler was feeling and doing on that stage. Since the first day I met LaVander Peeler in eighth grade, he made it clear that he would always *consider all things*—including ways of being an exceptional African American, ways of winning all contests, and ways of using language to shield him from being just another black boy. Considering all things prepared him to win the regional contests, but it didn't prepare him for what it would feel like to not be given a chance to really lose. I didn't get it until that second. It wasn't at all that we were there just for decoration, like LaVander Peeler Sr. said. LaVander Peeler and I, or LaVander Peeler or I, were there to *win the contest*. They'd already decided before the contest even began that one of us needed to win. The only way they could feel good about themselves was if they let us win against the Mexican kids, because they didn't believe any of us could really compete. Yeah, we were all decoration in a way. But it was like LaVander Peeler, specifically, was being thrown a surprise birthday party by a group of white people who didn't know his real name or when his birthday actually was.

Maybe LaVander Peeler thought I understood we were all being given an unearned birthday party, and that I did what I did on stage to show other chubby black Mississippi boys with contentious demeanors that dignity and pride and keeping it one hundred were more important than being decoration.

But it wasn't.

That's what I realized, looking at LaVander Peeler shaking on that stage. In order to be the first Mississippi black boy with a head full of waves to win a national contest in anything, you had to actually *win*—not make a speech about why the contest wasn't fair after you lost.

"'Chitterlings,'" he began. LaVander Peeler paused again and looked behind him, then hard to his right, then turned hard to his left. He looked back into the light, tears finally streaming down his face, and said, "*Citoyen's grandmother couldn't understand why the young sibling from up north refused to eat the wonderful chitterlings upon finding out they came from the bowels of a big-eyed hog named Charles.*"

No bell went off for a good eight seconds. Then, out of nowhere, balloons fell from the top of the stage. Popguns went off! That "Harlem Shake" song played. Blizzards of confetti fell in front of the eye of the camera as Cindy and two of the judges walked onstage with their hands over their heads.

The voice behind the light screamed, "LaVander Peeler, you have done the unbelievable! Times are a-changing and you, you exceptional young Mississippian, are a symbol of the American Progress. The past is the past and today can be tomorrow. LaVander Peeler, do you have anything to say?"

Would you like to thank your state, your governor, Jesus Christ, or your family for this blessing?"

"...*who entered the kitchen like a monster and asked*," LaVander Peeler said, "*'Why are y'all eating all my children?'*"

The music completely faded out and the balloons and confetti stopped coming down. Cindy held the trophy right next to LaVander Peeler and he said it all again: "*Citoyen's grandmother couldn't understand why the young sibling from up north refused to eat the wonderful chitterlings upon finding out they came from the bowels of a big-eyed hog named Charles who entered the kitchen like a monster and asked, 'Why are y'all eating all my children?'*" he said. "I'm saying that 'chitterlings' are the children of hogs. All things considered, I'm saying it literally, too, not metaphorically. Chitterlings are the children of hogs."

"But you already used it correctly, LaVander Peeler," the voice said. "And you did it quite dynamically, I might add."

"All things considered, I'm saying that chitterlings are the children of hogs." With that, he closed his teary eyes and tucked his head into his chest. The crowd gasped. And I did, too.

But now what was going to happen? Would there be a three-way tie? Would the three finalists have to spell again? Cindy slyly did the glide off-stage with the trophy. LaVander Peeler went and sat back in his seat. The camera stopped focusing on LaVander Peeler and instead just panned all the competitors.

Then out of the left side of my screen, LaVander Sr. marched out and yanked his son by the crease of the elbow off that stage. A few seconds later, a woman I assumed was Stephanie's grandma came up onstage and started pointing at Stephanie and telling her to get up and go. Eventually, Stephanie got up on her own, with her arms still folded, her head still tucked in her chest, looking at the ground. She walked off the stage, but not before she threw a finger sign right at the camera.

A few seconds later, the voice behind the light walked right across the front of the camera and onto the stage. The voice bent and whispered something in the ear of the twin from New Orleans who was also in the finals. A few seconds later, one of the twins was holding LaVander Peeler's trophy over his head with one hand, and the other twin joined him with both of their backs to the crowd. The twins let everyone know that as crazy as the night had been, the trophy was definitely in the hands of its rightful owners, Katrina's Finest.

I turned the television off and sat on the floor of the garage with one of Mama's old brushes. I wanted to get nice with myself at the thought of something I knew. But there was too much I didn't know, like when Mama was coming home, how hard I'd get my back beat, if LaVander Peeler would be my best friend now, how folks would talk to us all around Jackson, what made me say those things to the Mexican brother and sister, and how La-Vander Peeler collected the courage to go from Fade Don't Fade to that adolescent black superhero on stage.

I knew I could never ever hate LaVander Peeler again after that night. And crazy as it sounds, that was enough to make me feel good about throwing the brush under the bed, getting nice with myself like a true champ, and writing my story until Mama came home to tell me why what I did was wrong for me, wrong for black people yet to be born, and wrong for the globe. Mama would tell me this, I figured, while crying and giving me the legendary back beating of my life.

And after the back beating, I'd tell her not to cry. I'd tell her that I understood why I deserved the welts on my arms and back. And when she was quiet and gently rubbing the welts up and down, I'd turn around and say, "Mama, all things considered, I feel like I love LaVander Peeler."

But when Mama finally came home, none of what I thought would happen really happened. I didn't get beaten. Mama didn't even tell me what I did wrong. Quiet as it's kept, she barely said a word to me. She just folded up in her bed and kept crying on the phone to my grandma, saying, "I'm so sorry, Mama. I'm so, so sorry." And since Mama didn't whup my back, I didn't tell her I felt like I loved LaVander Peeler, not just because it might make her remember that she didn't whup my back, but because I didn't actually know what I meant. I didn't think my body wanted to kiss or even grind up on LaVander Peeler. But I also knew that no one on earth could make me happier or sadder than that boy either.

That felt like love to me.

The phone kept ringing the next morning and Mama told me not to answer it. I wanted to ask her why it was ringing so much and why I couldn't answer it but I'd made it this far without a back beating and I didn't want to chance it.

Forty minutes later, we were headed to the bus station. Mama didn't say a word to me the whole trip. She bought my ticket when we got to the bus station and waited in her car until I got on the bus.

Then, just like that, Mama left.

No "I love you." No "See you later." No "Behave yourself." I was headed to Melahatchie, Mississippi, for four days to stay with Grandma.

I walked all the way to the back of the bus and person after person, no matter whether they were old, young, black, brown, clean, or dusty, was messing with their cell phones and bootleg iPods. Some folks were talking. Some folks were listening. But most were texting. I walked to the back of the bus hating all the sentences I imagined those folks writing, hearing, and reading, and I pulled out *Long Division*.

Five minutes after the bus took off, I got a tap on my right shoulder. I turned around and one of the girls who had been two seats in front of me was now sitting right next to me, and her friend was sitting in the seat in front of me. Both were looking me dead in my face. They were cute up close, but cute in two different ways.

The cuter one was slightly sleepy-eyed. I liked that. She looked at the cover of *Long Division* and said, "Who wrote that book?"

"I'm not sure," I told her.

"We going to Waveland," she said. "Where you going?"

"Melahatchie, to stay with my grandma."

"You heard of that girl they call Baize Shephard?" she asked me.

"That's her real name," I told her. "They don't just 'call' her that. She lives next to my grandma."

"You the boy from the game last night, right? The one with the brush who was cutting up on them white folks?"

"Yeah, I guess."

Sleepy Eyes looked at her friend in front of us. "Told you that he was the one with the brush," she said. "The one from that private school."

I almost forgot the new brush was in my hand. I started brushing to help me with my nerves. "Fannie Lou Hamer ain't no private school," I told her.

"This girl right here," she pointed to her friend, whose eyes weren't sleepy at all. Truth be told, her eyeballs were so large and round that when you looked at her you wondered how she could ever sleep. She was wearing this muscle shirt that would've fit just right except her pregnant-looking belly made it cut off too soon. The girl had plenty of stretch marks on her stomach, too. As someone who had plenty of stretch marks himself on his biceps and waist, I always liked stretch marks on girls, even if it was on the front of their bellies.

"She told me that she wants you to holler at her," Sleepy Eyes said. "She tweeted on her phone this morning that she think you was smart and fine, even if you heavy."

"No, I don't," Stretch Marks said laughing. "I'ont think you fine. I don't even know him. Stop lying, V!"

Sleepy Eyes just looked at Stretch Marks for a full eight seconds without saying a word. Then she looked back at me. "She told me that she wishes she could take a video with you for her Facebook with you saying one of your sentences."

"Okay," I told her and got next to Stretch Marks while Sleepy Eyes taped us. "My name is City," I said into the camera phone, "and meeting these two cute girls right here on the way to Melahatchie made a day that started off sour as warm buttermilk into a day destined to taste something like a banana Slurpee." I looked at Stretch Marks's face and she was giggling her ass off.

"Can we touch your brush?" Sleepy Eyes said to me and put her phone in her pocket.

I handed it to her. "That's a different brush than the one I threw at the contest." She smelled the brush and she handed it right back.

"I get why you said what you said to that Mexican girl," she told me. "It was funny. I just don't think she had nothing to do with it, though. I don't mean to drop no shade. I'm just wondering how come you didn't go off on her brother like you went off on her."

"I don't even know," I said. "That's a good question. I said what I said because she was there, in my row, and I wanted her to feel worse than us. But..."

"But you don't know what that girl was feeling. You just didn't even care."

"That's true," I told her. "And after I left, she put in that work."

"I would never be in one of those games but if they did me like they did you, I would have done the same thing you did," she told me. "I would have gone off on the brother though. That would be wrong, too, but that's what I would do. I woulda called him a li'l Mexican bitch."

"I don't know about all that," I told her.

"Why you don't know. That's pretty much what you did. You just snapped. I saw it. Would you do anything different if you could do the game over?"

That was one of the best questions anyone ever asked me. "I guess I would have been more prepared for what they were gonna throw at me. And no matter what, I shouldn't have never left my boy, LaVander Peeler, up there by himself."

"Shoot. At least you internet famous now," she said.

"Is he internet famous, too? LaVander Peeler, I'm talking about."

"I don't think so," she said. "He was too serious to be internet famous."

I tried to look smooth and real-life famous as Stretch Marks and Sleepy Eyes walked back to their seats. They kept looking back at me and smiling every few minutes. Sleepy Eyes's smile made me embarrassed for her, but it also made me want to go in that stanky bus bathroom and get nice with myself.

I picked up *Long Division* and was reading when three white boys who looked like they were in college came from the front to the back of the bus with their camera phones ready.

One of the boys put his phone in his pocket and sat next to me. "Sorry if we're bothering you, big guy," he said. "It's just that was some funny shit you did last night, man. Could I record you saying, 'The Ron, I hate you more than LaVander Peeler?'"

"I guess I could say that," I told the boy, and looked up at Sleepy Eyes and Stretch Marks, who were still watching me.

"Cool," the white boy said. "And if you wouldn't mind, could you say your name after you tell me you hate me?"

It felt like a weird thing to do, especially given what I had said about white folks at the contest, but as soon as he got his phone ready, I put my internet-famous arm around his neck, looked right into the phone held by his friend, and said, "The Ron, I hate you more than LaVander Peeler. My name is City."

I kept looking up from *Long Division* on the way to Melahatchie, but Sleepy Eyes and Stretch Marks didn't turn around and smile at me for the rest of the trip. Not even once.

...

Baize...

On Old Ryle Road, folks like to bathe, eat, and put on clean clothes before sitting on the porch. When I woke up, I ate a fried-egg-and-cheese sandwich with some old Miracle Whip. Then I sat out on the porch in some faded cutoff jeans and the Magic Johnson Converse Weapons Mama Lara got me for Christmas. I called my grandma "Mama Lara" because everyone else did. Mama Lara said that boys weren't supposed to call or knock on girls' doors until they were seniors in high school, so my plan was to wait on the porch all day if I had to until Shalaya Crump came outside. That's when I'd drop my new *GAME* on her.

Mama Lara's husband was a man named Lerthon Coldson. I never knew him. Shalaya Crump's granddaddy and Lerthon Coldson were best friends way back in the day. They disappeared 21 years ago in 1964 in this place we called the Shephard house. The Shephard house was in the middle of the Night Time Woods, and it was the only real house on Old Ryle Road. Every other house was a trailer or shotgun house lifted off the ground by some cinder blocks. The Shephard house was built right from the ground up, and it had lots of grass that looked like veins growing up all over the house. The house was huge and it was all one level, but it didn't just look like a box. It looked kinda like a tic-tac-toe board from the outside, with a huge roof in the middle.

Neither Shalaya Crump or me knew our granddaddies, but sometimes we'd wonder about how two grown men could go inside a house one day, then never come back out. That wonder brought us together in a way. But even if our granddaddies didn't disappear, we still would've been close. We'd been friends ever since I could remember having friends.

When Mama Lara came out to talk to me on the porch, she told me how her girlfriends were mad because they got group-rate tickets to see *The Price Is Right* and she decided at the last minute not to go. Mama Lara claimed she would've gone to California with her friends except she didn't like driving with church folks in close spaces for more than one state. To tell you the truth, she only liked to travel on the weekend because she hated to miss the stories on CBS during the week. Plus if she would have gone, I wouldn't have been able to come down for break.

While I was out there on that porch, Mama Lara hugged me and held her hands on my hips. "Jesus, my baby boy is a fat little man who is two points away from that honor roll," she said. "Your granddaddy would not believe how fast you sprouting out."

I sat there waiting for her to explain what she meant with my arms folded across the top layer on my stomach.

"Oh," she said. "Unfold your arms. You ain't gotta cover them fat breasts. What I'm saying is that your mind, your mouth, and your heart finally working right. You finally sprouting out."

"You making me feel funny saying I got 'breasts,' Mama Lara."

"All I'm saying is that you ready to move," she said and looked me right in my eyes. "Yeah, you ready in mind, body, and soul."

I loved Mama Lara more than any person in my family. She had these scars on her face from an accident when she was younger, and she'd do everything possible to cover them up when she left the house. It was cute to me how she was old and cared so much about a few scars on her face. But Mama Lara was also a little on the shady side, to tell you the truth. She was always leaving the house at the strangest times and coming back smelling like outside.

I ignored Mama Lara and looked across the street at Shalaya Crump's trailer. Shalaya Crump was on spring break just like me, but I knew that she wasn't going anywhere because her grandma had to work. She had actually never gone anywhere for break. Not once. She blamed it on her parents giving her away to her grandma as soon as she was born. Shalaya Crump never met her real parents, but she thought they would have wanted to at least travel to New Orleans or Alabama if she lived with them. She had only been out of the county one time, and that was for the state science fair finals in Jackson. And even then, her grandma didn't let her spend the night.

Shalaya Crump looked so happy to see me and I tried hard not to look as happy as I was to see her. I started pulling my dingy Izod up over my mouth and fake yawning. She offered me a saltine and a sip of cold drank. Then she gave me the kind of full body hug that made me taste melted Jell-O Pudding Pops.

I don't know how to say this without making you hate me, but Shalaya Crump smelled like she'd just come back from about six recesses right on top of one another. And at every recess, she must have been swimming naked in a sea of cube steak gravy. I didn't mind her gravy funk, though, for three reasons: #1 — I hated the smell of deodorant. #2 — Shalaya Crump's funk smelled better than most girls' best stale perfume. #3 — I loved me some cube steak.

"How you been?" she asked me.

"What's wrong?" I asked her.

"You really want to know?"

"I do, my queen. Tell me what's on your mind."

Shalaya Crump shook her head and said, "Oh God," before grabbing both of my hands and walking toward the Night Time Woods. The Night Time Woods separated Old Ryle Road from Belhaven Street, where most of the white folks lived in their trailers. Grown folks always told us that no good could come from getting caught in those woods after dark because of this crazy family called the Shephards. I had heard that the Shephard house got burned down a number of times in the 1960s by the Klan. All the Shephards were dead now except for this one old woman people called the Shephard Witch. I had never really seen the Shephard Witch, but I heard she lived in what was left of the nasty church right in the middle of the woods.

"I'm worried about the future, City."

"Oh. That again." I tried to say it like I was so surprised she was bringing it up. "I ain't thought about it that much, but you think it'll be fresh? Like, I wonder if it's gonna be like moving sidewalks and flying cars. That would make it easier for me to get to my queen so I ain't trippin'."

"No, boy. Please just stop. Like what if there's this huge flood that kills people? Or if the water in the Gulf turn black? Or if we have a black president and..."

"A black president?" I asked her. She threw me off with that one. "And black water? And you say I'm crazy?"

"Just listen, okay? I mean if something you couldn't believe happened, like we got a black president or a flood swallowed the whole town, you would wanna know how that changed your life, wouldn't you? Do you even see what I'm saying?"

Shalaya Crump was really asking me a question, and you know what I was really doing? I was really half listening and half looking at her lips, wondering if they ever got chappy. She had the kind of lips, especially the bottom one, that always looked full of air and shiny, but not too shiny, from all that gloss.

"Well, do you?" she said again.

"Yeah, I think so," I told her. "You wonder what the future has to do with you if all these new things are happening. Like, everybody knows you're extremely super bad right now in 1985, right? But if you saw yourself in 1999, would you be like, 'Oh my goodness. Who is that homely ass girl right there, cleaning the mess out her toes, looking greasy?' Or maybe things happening in the future would make other people so mad that they would want to make you be invisible."

"Yeah, yeah, City!" she grabbed my forearm and looked me in the eyes. "That's exactly what I mean. Kinda. What happens if we disappear in the future?"

It was like the smartest thing I've ever said, and it was the first time I'd used the word "extremely" in a sentence, but the sad part was that I didn't really know what I meant. I just knew it sounded like something Shalaya Crump would want to hear. It was some GAME I'd been practicing for two months in my mama's bedroom mirror. "Hold up, Shalaya Crump. Remember when you said that you would love me? Wait, first—did you mean it?"

"If I said it, I meant it."

"For real? That's good. Well, ever since you told me all I needed to do was be special and say something cool about the future, I kinda..."

Shalaya Crump interrupted me. "City, speed that up. Why you gotta be so long division? For real, you don't have to tell me all the background. The story doesn't have to go on and on and on."

"It doesn't?"

"No," Shalaya Crump said. "Everything with you is long division. You busy trying to show your all your work. Just get in and get out."

"But my favorite part of long division was the work," I told her. Shalaya Crump had thrown my *GAME* completely off. "I hate the answer. I do. We had this conversation already. You said you hated the answer, too."

"That's different. I hate the answer because I don't believe in mastering the smaller steps," she told me. "They never teach you to like, you know, linger in the smaller steps."

"Linger? What's that mean?"

"They just tell you that you gotta master the small steps if you wanna get to the big answer," she told me. "But I wish we could really pause at each step in long division and talk about it."

"Pause and do what?"

"Don't worry about it," she said. "Just get on with it, City. Please!"

"Okay, well, I wanna linger, too. Remember when I stole those Bibles for you over Christmas?"

"Yeah, I do. We already talked about this."

"Do you remember what you said to me when I tried to convince you it wasn't me?"

"I said that I know it's you because stealing Bibles takes a whole different kind of crazy than Melahatchie crazy."

"Right! And you said that you liked that I was Chicago or Jackson crazy. That meant that I was crazy enough to go around stealing pleather green Bibles from other folks' trailers just to impress you. Well, I'm still Chicago or Jackson crazy, baby. Southside! That means I'm crazy enough to fly to the future with you, too..." I acted like my shoes were untied. "But when we land, I wanna know what I get."

"What do you mean?"

"Well, if I flew to 2013 with you, I hope that maybe you'd want to, you know, kiss a nigga."

"City," she started laughing. "Why are you calling yourself 'a nigga'? You don't even talk like that."

"Whatever," I said. "You know, maybe kiss a nigga on the lips! With a little bit of that tongue."

"City, just talk like yourself! Saying 'a nigga' a lot ain't gonna make me love you."

"Aw, girl! I wasn' even tryn' to make you love me," I tried to correct myself.

"Yes, you were. Now you doing it again."

"No, I ain't."

You should have heard the way I said, "I wasn' even tryn' to make you love me." I made "wasn't" and "trying" one syllable each. And I sucked my teeth after I said it and rolled my eyes, too.

"When you first came down here, you didn't even say 'a nigga' a lot," Shalaya Crump said.

"I said 'a nigga' sometimes. Shoot, we say 'a nigga' in Chicago and Jackson just as much as y'all say it down here."

"Yeah, but a little bit is normal. Now when you trying too hard to make me like you, you say stuff like 'hard on a nigga' or 'worrying a nigga' or 'grinding on a nigga's nerves.' I'm not saying that I don't be laughing when you say it..."

"You do laugh."

"I know," she told me. "That's what I'm saying. But..."

"But what?"

"But that just ain't who you are. I know you, City," she told me. "You was all scared of flies and chicken when you first came down here."

"So. What does that have to do with saying 'a nigga' all the time?"

"Nothing, but now, it's weird. You sucking on your teeth and wanting me to 'kiss a nigga'?" She started laughing and walking deeper behind some baby sticker bushes. "Just be you. And I'll just be me."

I knew I should have said okay, but I always had to have the last word, even with Shalaya Crump. "You know what, Shalaya Crump? You don't leave enough room for folks to change. I'm serious. You always gotta control everything. How come no one else can change but you? When I first met you, your breath stayed smelling like a pork chop sandwich. For real. You never brushed your teeth. Now you brush your teeth on the regular and chew gum."

Shalaya Crump was dying laughing but I was just telling the truth.

"Don't try and laugh it off," I told her. "You changed so I can change too. And maybe I changed how I talk from listening to you. You ain't ever think about that?"

"Whatever, boy," she said and got serious again. "The point is I ain't giving out no kisses or no tongue like peppermints. I ain't no gotdamn Candy Girl. Now can you please shut the hell up and let me show you something?"

We stepped into the cold Night Time Woods together. From inside the woods, the purple gray of the road cut through the green just enough that it was the prettiest thing I'd ever seen next to Shalaya Crump's face. Any other color against that green wouldn't have been so pretty, but this purple gray and green was more than pretty. This purple green and gray made me know that Shalaya Crump and me were meant to be kissing soon.

I grabbed Shalaya Crump's hand as soon as we got deep in the woods. In six years of knowing Shalaya Crump, this was the first time I had ever held her whole hand and had her lead me into something. We had held hands before when we were in Sunday school and I tried to tell her that her hands were the sweatiest girl hands in the country. But this time was different. Shalaya Crump held on, and even when I loosened my grip, she held on even tighter. That's always how you can tell if a girl likes you. If you loosened your grip and she loosened hers, you might as well go play football with your boys or something, because nothing is gonna pop off. Anyway, I felt like we were in our own version of "Thriller."

"City, I can't do this by myself anymore. I need you to come with me."

"Need me to what?"

"To come with me."

"Where?"

Shalaya Crump knelt down next to this rusty handle that was covered in pine needles and leaves. The handle looked like the handle of this rusted brown iron Mama Lara used to keep her doors open. When Shalaya Crump pulled the handle, this hole inside the ground opened up. The door to the hole had rusty handles on both sides so someone inside the hole could pull the door shut if they needed to. Inside the hole were these dusty steps that led straight down to red clay. Shalaya Crump stepped half-down in the hole in the ground and looked up at me. All that was left outside the hole was her boobs, her head, and her bony arms. She looked back at me and said, "Please, City. Don't let me go by myself this time. I need to show someone."

If anyone else in the world, including my mama or Mama Lara, were boob-deep into a hole in the ground, asking me to follow them, I would have run away and called the police. But standing right there, watching Shalaya Crump want me to help her so bad, made me ask myself when was the next time I could count on Shalaya Crump inviting me anywhere dark, small, and secret with her. I figured the worst thing that could happen is that we could get covered in worms or maybe it would be too hot in the hole and my sack would commence to smelling sour. But worms don't bite, I told myself, and Shalaya Crump's underarms were already funky as six recesses.

The hole wasn't the easiest to get in if you had wide hips, but after a while, I was in. "Now what?" I asked her. "Does my breath stank like stale Miracle Whip?"

Shalaya Crump grabbed my hand with her left hand and grabbed the handle with the other hand. "Don't let go," she said, "until I open the door again, okay?" Shalaya Crump pulled the secret door closed and darkness swallowed everything you were supposed to see.

"Your eyes closed, Shalaya?"

"Naw," she said. "Yours?"

"Yeah." I kept them closed for about ten seconds and tried to find Shalaya Crump's hand. "What about now? Your eyes still open?"

"Yeah, City. You should open yours, too."

"Mine are open now," I lied. "I ain't scared of the dark."

"Okay," Shalaya Crump said. "Just be yourself when we open it. I need you to be yourself and don't say a word to anyone."

Shalaya Crump pushed the secret door open after about seven more seconds. Just like that, the woods were green like the Hulk's chest instead of green like a lime. It felt hotter when we stepped out of the hole, too. Took a while for my eyes to adjust to the brightness. You could see bigger slithers of dark road from where we were in the woods, like the woods had gone on a diet. The road didn't seem like a road anymore, either. It looked like a tar-black slab of bacon that was way fatter than it was before we went in.

"What's wrong with Old Ryle Road?" I asked her.

"It's new," she said. She looked at my face, hoping that I'd act like I understood. "This ain't the same woods we know, City."

"It ain't new," I sucked my teeth. "How could woods be new in like five minutes?" I looked around and saw the Shephard house. Then I turned and looked at Shalaya Crump, who was watching me watch everything around us. "Why you watching me like that?"

Shalaya Crump didn't answer me. "You smell that?" I asked her and started coughing. The air in the woods was heavier than it had been. I always wanted my mama to get me one of those plastic asthma bottles like some of the white kids on TV, but she said I never needed one. "I think I got asthma, girl. I'm serious."

She looked at me and forced a fake laugh. "What happened to all the trees? And that house," I pointed toward the Shephard house. "What happened to it?"

I started running toward what I thought was the Shephard house and Shalaya Crump ran behind me. It was the same shape as the Shephard house but it read "Melahatchie Community Center" on the iron front door.

"City, calm down. Please. You have to be calm. Don't be so loud. They're gonna hear us."

"Who?"

I looked through the woods toward Old Ryle Road and saw a crazy blue Monte Carlo with the most golden wheels I've ever seen in my life. The rattling of its license plate was in rhythm with a deep boom that sounded over and over again. It was the craziest, best-sounding boom I'd ever heard in my life.

"You hear that? What is it? Is that some new Run-D.M.C. or Herbie Hancock? Who that?"

"Be quiet, City."

"How you gonna tell me to be quiet and you got me going in a hole feeling crazy? What's wrong with you?" I grabbed her by her shoulders.

Shalaya Crump pushed my hands off. "Don't ever push me." She looked me in the eyes. "Ever! I don't care if you feel crazy or not. All we can do is watch, okay? We can't let them know we're here. Shhh. Listen."

We stood there in the middle of what kinda looked the Night Time Woods, looking at what kinda looked like Old Ryle Road. I tried to block out anything other than the sounds of blackbirds chirping and stiff leaves blowing up on our feet and squirrels digging around in trees.

"Yeah, shoatee. Call me," the voice said from the street. "I'ma keep my phone on!" But there was no one with him. The man was talking to himself.

"Is this a dream?" I asked Shalaya Crump. "Is it? It is, right? Well, I'm 'bout to wake up myself up." I took out my sweat rag and started trying to pop myself in the middle of the forehead, hoping I would wake myself up.

Shalaya Crump took my rag from me and told me to shut up. I heard more rattling booms coming from another strange truck with all black windows and white hubcaps. I looked at Shalaya Crump and the confusion made me start tearing up right in front of her face. I tried to wipe my eyes with my sweat rag but it was too late. I was so *Young and the Restless.* Shalaya Crump was right.

"City," she breathed all heavy and acted all weird like she was on a soap opera, "you know how I asked you not to show your work before?"

"Yeah."

"Well, don't ask me to show my work when I tell you this, okay?"

"Okay!" I wiped my eyes and tried to get the boogers out with the same wipe.

"This is 2013, City, and..."

"*What?*"

"Let me finish. I'm scared because, well, I think I'm dead. Can you help me?"

I waited for her to say more, or at least look at me with a goofy grin. But she didn't. Not at all.

"Shalaya Crump, I want you to show *all* your work now. All of it. I don't give a damn if you say it's long division."

Instead of showing her work, Shalaya Crump took me by the hand and led me to the edge of the woods, where the sticker bushes met the shallow ditch that separated the woods from the Old Ryle Road.

"You can't talk to anyone, City. I only come out here at night when can't no one see me," she said. "I keep trying to find myself."

I wanted to ask Shalaya Crump all kinds of questions, but across the street, in what should have been Mama Lara's house, was a girl sitting on the porch with a tiny silver briefcase on her lap. Down the road, I saw that the trailer next door wasn't even there anymore. The girl on the porch had her head down, except for every now and then when she'd raise it to drink from this huge cold drank. Every time she took a swig, she looked toward the woods. It looked like she was talking to herself and playing with a calculator.

"Where did that person get that big ol' cold drank from?"

"All the bottles of cold drank are big around here."

I looked harder at the girl and looked over at Shalaya Crump, hoping she would give me something more than she was giving me. "Well, why is she sitting on Mama Lara's porch?"

"Does that look like your Mama Lara's porch, City?"

"Well, kinda. I mean, not really. I mean it does, but it doesn't. But…" I didn't know how to say what I wanted to say. Shalaya Crump was right that the place didn't exactly look like my Mama Lara's any more. It looked like what my Mama Lara's place would look like if it had been in a few tornados. It made me feel funny that Shalaya Crump didn't say anything about how the girl sitting out on the porch, at least from where we were, looked almost just like her except this girl was thicker with way shorter hair, maybe a bigger nose, and boobs that looked like the balled-up fists of a seven-year-old.

"Who is that?" I asked her.

Shalaya Crump didn't answer, and I got tired of asking her questions she wouldn't answer. I started across the street toward the girl on the porch.

As I got closer to the porch, I could see that the girl on the porch had a strange haircut like a boy. The hair was the shape of Mr. T's hair but there was still hair on the sides, and the top was thicker than his.

The girl on the porch closed the tiny silver briefcase and stood up. She placed this book, with the words "Long Division" on the cover, on top of the briefcase. The silver briefcase was one of those weird things you only see on TV. When she stood up, you expected her to say something. Or you expected me to say something, but I didn't, and she didn't either. I just looked at her for probably ten whole seconds. Then she finally said, "Excuse you! Who you looking for?"

I walked closer and realized that Shalaya Crump had the same eyes and face shape as this girl on the porch, but this girl was a little lighter than her and she had really long legs, and arms like a penguin. Up close, you could see that this girl's forehead was one of biggest and greasiest you've ever seen in your life.

"You might wanna check yourself, mayne, don't you think?" the girl said. "You think you can just walk up on folks because you can dress?"

"Um, I can dress?"

"Where you get them Converse at? I like that little hipster white boy thang you got going on."

"You do? I got these for Christmas."

"What's your name?"

I just looked at the girl and thought of the coolest name I'd ever heard. "Voltron," I told her. "But you can call me T-Ron if you want." I never told white folks or strangers my real name. But usually I alternated between Bobby, Ronnie, Ricky, and Mike, the names of the dudes in New Edition.

The girl rolled her eyes, then opened up her little briefcase and sat back down. "Okay T-Ron, my name's Baize. Baize Shephard," she said before moving the book and opening up the tiny silver briefcase. "Look, mayne, I don't mind you being on my porch, but you gotta quit looking thirsty like you wanna steal somebody's rhymes."

"Rhymes? What kind of rhymes? Girl, what's wrong with you? Why you keep calling me 'mayne'?"

"That's what we say."

"Who? How do you even spell that?" I asked her. "Just be yourself."

"You don't even know me," the girl said. "And I don't know you either. Mayne! But I know how you look. And you look like the type to wanna steal somebody's rhymes off their computer. Can I keep it one hundred?"

"I guess so. What does 'keep it one hundred' even mean?"

"One hundred. Like 100 percent. Listen, if you don't want me to think you jack people, then don't call yourself T-Ron. That can't be your real name," she said.

"Wait—that's a computer?" I asked her.

"Yeah, what else would it be?"

"I thought it was a silver briefcase. Whatever it is, that thing is cold as a mug."

"A briefcase?"

"Yeah, for children."

She laughed loud and hard. "You trying to spit game?" she asked me. "What does that even mean? Show me a child who uses briefcases. I know you've heard of a laptop computer."

"A lab top computer?"

"Lap. *Lap*, mayne. See," she picked the computer up, held it in the air for a moment, and then placed it back on her lap. "This is a computer and this, see this? This is my lap. Stop fronting. Why you playing stupid? You go to school around here, don't you?"

"Um, yeah."

"Then you must've gotten one a few years ago with the last of that Katrina money they sent us after all them tornadoes hit us again. Don't tell me your mama and them sold it on eBay? I was watching this web series, *Confessions of a PTSD*. You heard of it?"

I looked at the book where she'd moved it. I could really see its cover for the first time. On the cover was a husky black boy's body standing in the middle of a stage. The picture cut off right above his shoulder blades so we couldn't see his face. His left hand was in his pocket and his right hand was clutching a wave brush. Behind the boy was another, lankier boy with his head down and both of his balled-up fists dangling between his legs. Near the bottom of the cover were the words "YouTube," "views," and the number "47,197,508." At the top of the cover in bold letters were the words "Long Division."

I was thinking of what to ask her about the book when I heard a man's voice in conversation behind me. I turned to the road as a taller man with a big brown T-shirt was walking down the street talking to himself.

"How come everyone around here likes to talk to themselves?"

"He's on the phone," the girl said. "Why you trippin'?"

"I ain't slow. I can see he's talking to himself."

"Look, you ain't gonna get loud with me on my own porch. You know that's Bluetooth. I know it's played out. They think they styling with the little headsets, just like you think you think you styling with that outfit," she paused, "and that curly shag. Where you from?"

I looked across Old Ryle Road at Shalaya Crump and motioned for her to come on over. "My friend is over in those woods and I want her to see all this. Is it okay if she comes over and sees Katrina's computer?"

"No," she said. "Why didn't she come with you?"

"No?"

"Your 'friend,'" she made these quotations marks in the air, "is a girl, right?"

"Unh huh!"

"She's your girl, right?"

"Um, she halfway my girl."

"Oh, okay," she said. "Yeah, well, no! I been seein' that girl sneaking around here for a while. She looks shade tree to me. I went after her the last time I saw her peeking out of those woods."

"You did?"

"Yep. But she disappeared. I found this, though, after she left," she said and grabbed the book. "You ever heard of this book?"

I ignored her question and walked over beside her and saw that the computer really wasn't a tiny briefcase at all. There was a keyboard and a flat TV screen, and on the flat TV screen were all these colorful dizzy images and boxes and words.

I couldn't blink.

Or breathe.

Or move.

"Don't think I'm hating on your girlfriend over there ,'cause I'm not. I just saw this strange white boy over in those woods yesterday, too, and I let him use my computer. He was dressed like one of those white children who be getting home-schooled up north. You know, the kind whose parents don't let them watch TV or eat sweet cereal? Anyway, I gave him some of my daddy's old clothes."

"Wait, what?" I asked. I heard her but I didn't really hear her. All I could do was watch and listen to my heartbeat as the girl moved her fingers across the letters.

"Yeah, he told me he was looking for more clothes that matched the time."

"Matched the time?"

"I told him to go downtown to the Salvation Army." While she was talking, she pushed something below the little square thing on the computer and in a second, the screen flipped on to what looked like the front page of a newspaper. The headline on the newspaper was "The Obamas Get Another Family Dog Just in Time for the Election Cycle."

"Who is that?"

"Who is who? The dog? I don't think they named it yet."

"Not the dog. The man and the woman and those girls. Who are they? And how come you can watch TV on your computer?"

"Stop playing. You think the oldest one cute? All the boys in my class stay falling out over that girl."

I looked at the bigger girl. "I mean, yeah, she's kinda cute but who are these folks?"

"Dumbness, we cared about funky dogs when the president was white. Why we can't make a big deal about dogs when the president is black?"

"That's the president?"

"Oh my god, dumbness. I just can't."

"And this is a computer and a TV and a newspaper all on that screen?"

"Yes, boy."

"And what is that?"

I pointed to a little rectangle on the side of the newspaper where someone named *@UAintNoStunna815* wrote *@SMH you goin to that Spell-Off #yoassdumberthanyoulook* and someone named *@YeahTheyReal601* wrote *TTYL LOL cute herb on my porch #hatingaintahabit.*

"Twitter," the girl said, "but that ain't none of your business."

"Wait. And people here talk on phones with no hands?"

"Voltron!" It was weird because even though my name wasn't Voltron, it made my insides tingly to hear her call me by what she thought was my name. "Why are you acting like you stuck in the '90s?"

"What year is this?" I asked her. "Be for real."

"2013, crackhead. You got that new swine flu?"

A voice from inside the house interrupted my good feelings. "Baize, come on in here and set this table. We got to practice them words for that Spell-Off."

"That's my great-grandma." Baize looked down at my hips. "She want me to come in and study for the spelling bee tomorrow. It's over in the community center. You going? Want me to ask her if you can eat with us? I ain't gonna lie to you; her cooking is wack, but she getting better at frying some catfish."

As the screen door slammed closed, I got closer to the laptop. Right next to the computer and *Long Division* was this little black thing that looked like some kind of special calculator. If it wasn't sitting next to that computer, I would have been super interested in it, but it was kinda boring compared to that laptop computer.

I didn't know what to focus on when I looked at the computer— the machine carrying the pictures and the words, or the pictures and the words themselves. I had never felt anything like that before. I just wanted to talk to someone who would also understand none of what I was seeing and all of what I was feeling. And that someone was across the road peeking her slow/fast-blinking eyes through green and orange and brown trees.

I picked the laptop computer up with my two hands scooped underneath like it was a tray, placed *Long Division* on top of it, and looked toward the hole. Then I thought about how happy Shalaya Crump would be if I brought her a calculator from 2013. So I put the calculator in my mouth, jumped off the porch, and sprinted back to the woods.

When I reached her, I gave Shalaya Crump the calculator and we both ran toward to the hole. Shalaya Crump got in first and I followed her. With just my head outside the door, I could see Baize sprinting toward us. She was screaming and cussing, talking about, "Naw. Naw. I know you didn't."

It was too late, though. The secret door was closed. The computer, *Long Division*, the calculator, Shalaya Crump, and me were in it and we were headed back to 1985.

When the door opened up, you couldn't see Old Ryle Road at all, but you could see the fuzzy glow of the streetlight. Shalaya

Crump was next to me breathing louder than I'd ever heard her breathe. I had never even seen her tired in all the years I knew her, not even during push-up contests. Shalaya Crump actually had the best wind of anyone I'd ever met.

"Look at this." I angled the screen toward her so she could see the pictures and the newspaper and the black president, but the screen was blank except for little shapes along the bottom. "That girl, she told me this is called a laptop computer from Katrina. I don't know why it ain't working. I swear when I was on the porch there was all this stuff on the screen. And look at this book. That girl said it's the weirdest book she ever read."

Shalaya Crump simply turned and walked off. "I'm going home, City," she said.

"Wait. Why? Why'd you stay in the woods? You talked to that girl before? She said she's seen you before. She's like a fatter version of you with a nappy mohawk but not really..."

"You like her, don't you?"

"Like who?"

"I know you do."

"That girl? Baize?" For some reason, I thought Shalaya Crump was really asking me if I liked the girl as in spit-some-*GAME like*, so I thought about it and told her exactly what I thought.

"I don't *like* her like that, but she didn't get on my nerves like a lot of girls do either. She had these big circle earrings and there was something strange about how she talked. It's like her tongue was too fat, but sometimes it didn't seem too fat. She kept talking about rhymes and 'one hundred' too much. Her face was bumpy, too, especially on her forehead. And then she liked how I dressed. No girl ever told me that. She looked like you, except her hair was way shorter, but I already told you that. Maybe I liked her but not that much. I think she knows more than I know and I guess I think I know more than her about other stuff, too. I liked that she had a laptop computer more than I liked her. You know what I'm trying to say?"

"Bye, City."

Shalaya Crump walked off in front of me out of the woods. I followed her down Old Ryle Road talking the entire time about the girl and the laptop computer and asking her did we really just jump to 2013. We must have looked crazy to anyone who saw us.

When I got in front of Mama Lara's house, I said bye to Shalaya Crump, but she just went to her trailer without saying a word to me. I would have cared if it were any other day.

When I got in the house, I flipped open the computer and moved the little arrow thing around the screen like I'd watched Baize do. In the corner was this little picture with the word "Unfinished" on it. I moved the arrow to the picture and pushed on it. A half-drawn blue, white, and plum-red picture opened up on the screen. At the bottom of the picture was this water with palm trees and a few little boats, but right above the water was a huge face and a cool-looking Klansman with a stick over his shoulder floating in the sky. The face looked like Baize's in a way, but it kinda looked like my face, too, if my hair would have been lined up right. I ran the arrow over all the images in the picture and pushed on them but nothing happened. It was like playing video games except I didn't know how you were supposed to win.

After a while I pushed on something called "Word" and a blank screen opened up. After you pushed "Word" there was the word "File," and at the bottom of "File" were all these sections that said

"Storm Rhyme" and the numbers 1 through 10. When I pushed on "Storm Rhyme #4," writing appeared right in the center of the screen:

...*Not your everyday rapper*
    but every day's a gray haze.
        Who took the moons outta
    June?
        Come take the
        pain outta Baize.

    My big fat beautiful mouth
    was born right here in the South
    where Ma and Daddy, they went swimming,
tryin to find a way out.

But Katrina was hummin
    and my folks got to runnin.
    Ears open for God but she
    ain't telling them nothin.

    Now Melahatchie ain't
    exactly what
    We thought it was.
    Blues for days, dark mayonnaise
and kinda country...
    Uhh...

    You wanna
    touch us?
    Oooh...

You really fucked us!
    Booo...

I had a hunch that you'd try to
crush us
so I grabbed
my tool.

And now you're scared of a dike?
This ain't a brick, it's a mic.
You went for yours, growled a little
and I was scared of you.

Sike...

Matter fact you suck,
and quite wack, you ducked.
Now quack, or cluck,
cuz Baize don't give a...

Sometimes you read the stuff people write and have a hard time thinking the person would write the stuff you read. That's because most people try to write like they're writing for a bad Honors English teacher or a librarian even when there's no Honors English teachers or librarians around. The only honors class I was ever in was English, and Ms. Shivers said everything you wrote had to be believable. It's more important that it's believable than that it's smart, she told us. English teachers like Ms. Shivers were always talking about "the reader." Whoever "the reader" was, it never seemed like she could be like me. How could you make someone you didn't know do things they didn't want to do?

Anyway, even though I couldn't figure out how the words were supposed to sound when Baize rapped them, I could still hear Baize saying the words to "Storm Rhyme #4" in my head. I was

Baize's reader, and I believed everything she said. By the end, I hated that Katrina girl just as much as she did.

But I knew no Honors English teacher or librarian was "the reader" for "Storm Rhyme #4." And it wasn't just because of the cussing or rhymes. It was mainly because of those dots she used. She used dot-dot-dot to start the rhyme, and she used dot-dot-dot in the middle of the rhyme, and she used dot-dot-dot at the end of the rhyme. And it just seemed kinda perfect to me. I'd seen those dot-dot-dots and I'd heard Shalaya Crump say dot-dot-dot before, but I never really knew what they meant or how folks were supposed to use them. I used them once on a test when I didn't know the answer and Ms. Arnold wrote, "Citoyen you better be ashamed before God for trying to trick your teacher." I thought Ms. Arnold should've been ashamed before God for not using a comma after she wrote my name.

Anyway, I had never really even been allowed to spend much time on a typewriter or a big computer either, but typing on a lap- top computer was even better. Whatever you typed showed up on the screen, and if you didn't like what you wrote, you could erase it and rewrite it. After you rewrote it enough, it was like your words were famous. Even if you had the best pencil-writing style in the world like Shalaya Crump, no matter how good the writing looked, it never looked famous. And if you erased too much and the paper was all smudged, you just looked dumb, poor, and messy. But the words on Baize's computer screen looked famous, like words in a book, even if you wrote something that you would never see in a book, like "Storm Rhyme #4."

I started typing a lot and erasing a lot. It took me about ten minutes to come up with: *My name is City. Shalaya Crump says I'm like long division.*

Then, out of the blue, I realized something. Shalaya Crump was jealous of me liking that girl, Baize. I guess I should have known it earlier, but I never thought I could do anything to make Shalaya Crump jealous. Just thinking about her being jealous made me feel so good about myself. If she was jealous, I knew it would only be a matter of time before she was kissing me. My new *GAME* was to keep her jealous for a little bit, then prove to her that I liked her way more than Baize. A few minutes after that, I knew we'd be kissing. Once I got kissing Shalaya Crump back in my mind, I couldn't think of anything else. It was always like that. So I typed and erased about her for hours. At the end of the night, all I had was one good sentence, and I used italics and the dot-dot-dots in it too. It felt like the right thing to do:

I never had a girlfriend because the last time I saw Shalaya Crump she told me that she could love me if I helped her change the future dot-dot-dot in a special way.

Barely awake, I opened *Long Division* and read until I fell asleep.

Thick Parts.

As soon as I stepped off the Greyhound bus in Melahatchie, Grandma hugged my neck, but I was straight zoned out. That *Long Division* book had me feeling weird, new weird, like I was a character in a book or video game and someone was writing or controlling all the craziness around me.

Grandma interrupted my new weird. "My baby's still husky," she said, and kissed both of my jaws. Then she grabbed my shoulders and took a step back. "You look so intelligent. I don't care what none of them folks say."

Whenever I went down to Melahatchie, I always felt younger than I was. Mainly, it was because Grandma had really never talked to me or treated me any different between the ages of five and fourteen. I had to trim the hedges, crack open walnuts, and get the okra out of the bottom of the deep freezer now just like I did when I was five years old.

I threw my stuff in the back of her Bonneville and thought about how besides being the thickest grandma in Central Mississippi, I would have bet my original wave brush that Grandma was probably the thickest, finest grandma in all of Mississippi, Alabama, Arkansas, and Louisiana. I'm not saying Grandma was perfect, either, but even the annoying stuff about Grandma, like how she was completely swinging from the scrotum sack of the Lawd, was—well, kinda…thick.

Grandma was probably six feet tall, and every part of her body and face was so thick that nothing looked thick. But her stuff was symmetrical, too. Sometimes you'd see folks with all thick parts, but half of their body weight was all up in their ass or all in that gut, or one of their eyes was way bigger than the other one, or maybe there was too much distance between their eyes and where their hairline started.

For example, my mother had this rounded, thick, mushroom-style nose and she looked like the early version of Weezy on that old Nick at Nite show, *The Jeffersons*. Mama looked like Weezy, but Mama's lips were kinda… well, I hate to talk about my own mama like this, but Mama had lips like the white folks on *Jersey Shore*. There was no thickness or pinkish hang to Mama's lips. You saw thin poofy lines and you saw teeth. Snake lips, I called the fat beneath her nose. I still don't know how in the hell that happened to Mama since she came out of the vagina of someone as thick and perfect-looking as Grandma. You wouldn't even know Grandma was six feet tall or the finest, thickest Grandma in the region until you walked right up on her.

Anyway, of all the different kinds of people in the world, Grandma was the last person I wanted to watch me act a fool at the contest. But I also knew, even though she couldn't say it, that she was one of the only people who would know what it was like to be up there on that stage and not know if there was a difference between being right and doing wrong.

Grandma had a bag with two pork-chop sandwiches in her hands and her eyes were twitching like a hummingbird while she sat in that driver's seat.

"Them folks is just evil," Grandma said. She never mumbled or slurred her sentences and her voice was deep, heavier than cane syrup. "Plain devilish. You hear me?" Grandma thought the man who worked in the bus station restaurant hadn't given her enough change back on purpose.

"Well, did you tell him how evil he is, Grandma?"

"Naw, City. No telling what that man could've put in our food."

She pulled all the way out of the bus station. "You gotta be careful with them folks if you stay with me the next few days. You hear me?" I nodded. "If you learned anything after messing with them folks on that stage, should be that you don't never know—"she looked me right in the eye.

"Never know what?" I asked her.

"How far they'll go to get you."

Grandma told me that we had to stop by Walmart before we went home. She said Walmart had a sale on her new favorite brand of wig, Wigs4Blax, and that she might as well get the wig today since this was her half-day off.

My grandma had three jobs. She worked as a housekeeper at the Island View Casino. She washed and ironed clothes for three white families in town. And she sold pound cake and fruit salad every other Saturday afternoon.

When we pulled into the lot of the Walmart, a green pickup truck flew past us and damn near knocked the front end off the Bonneville. Grandma stuck out her arm and secured my chest while slamming on the brakes. "Jesus give me strength," she said. "What in the world is wrong with your children?"

It was the middle of the day, so most folks who worked hard and sweated for a living were still at work. Grandma was getting ready to park next to this orange and gray Cadillac sitting on 22-inch rims.

"Young folks ain't got nothing better to spend that money on except long cars and crazy tags?"

"What?"

"What a nigga do in the dark will damn sure come to the light somehow."

"Grandma?"

"Yes, baby."

"I appreciate how it sounds when you say 'nigga' and I'm sorry about acting a fool at the contest."

"Shhhh," Grandma said and parked the car. "And leave your little brush in the car. Folks in here likely to steal everything that ain't nailed down."

The Melahatchie Walmart was always packed. Always. I never had anything stolen the hundreds of times I'd been in there and folks always looked so happy walking around, especially in the electronics section. I walked with Grandma to the wig section of the store and this old white woman with wrinkly skin, a maroon scarf around her pudgy neck, and her hair in a ball came up on us.

The woman's nametag said "Louise Ellsington." She had gold for days draped on the outside of her scarf, and on her fingers were the shiniest rings I'd seen in real life. She walked up onto us lightweight fast, with one hand on her hip and the other on her chin.

"Hey. Hello'ew there!" she said. "We want y'all to know'ew that today, we've got a special on our Wigs4Blax brand." She pointed to the raggedy looking wigs on the sale rack. "We sure do'ew."

I could tell that the lady was from Jackson and had probably worked in the outside malls in Jackson before taking a job at the Melahatchie Walmart. At the outside Jackson malls, all the older white ladies with hair in a ball and penny loafers always said "o" sounding words like "o'ew" sounding words, but in Melahatchie the "o" sounded like "o" no matter who said it.

"So'ew," she said, "if you buy one of those Gary curl wigs, y'all get a free year subscription to the new *Ebony* magazine..." she trailed off, and just looked at me. I tried to look away, then look back, but she was still watching. "Y'all got a talkative little devil there, don't y'all?" she said to Grandma. "Were you the one doing all that talking on TV yesterday?"

"Yes ma'am," Grandma said. "My baby does love to talk. Don't pay him no attention." She patted me on the back. "Now how much did you say the Gary curl wig was?"

I couldn't believe Grandma was talking like that in front of that lady. Her voice, her body, everything shrunk. It was like she wasn't even Grandma anymore. I never heard Grandma say "ma'am" to someone who was younger than her. The rumor was that Grandma actually brought the Jheri (not "Gary") curl to Melahatchie from Milwaukee back in the early '80s. Now she was acting like she couldn't even pronounce it right, all because she was talking in front of a weird-looking white woman who couldn't even pronounce "so" and "do."

Grandma and I held hands as we walked back to the Bonneville.

"If Tom Henry coulda seen you raising hell on TV, he woulda swore up and down that he was looking through his red eyes at himself."

"Why?" I asked her.

Grandma started getting comfortable in the driver's seat chair. I could tell she was about to go into one of her Granddaddy stories. The stories always started different, but every one of them, except the one that ended with him disappearing in Lake Marathon, ended with Granddaddy acting like a demon and destroying something before Grandma intervened.

"I remember one Saturday we got to fighting 'bout money or something like that," she started. "He was tired of me working all these jobs, you know? Anyway, Tom Henry claimed he was going for a walk to get his mind right. I knew that meant he was 'bout to get that damn stuffed monkey and walk off in them woods across the road from the house.

"Anyway, while he was gone, his friends Cherry and Shank come over here looking for him to go fishing. All three of us, we out there on that porch, you know? 'Course I ain't tell Cherry or Shank he was over in them woods with no fake monkey, so I just said he wasn't nowhere to be found. Soon as I said that, here comes your granddaddy prancing out them woods with that monkey in his hands and one of those shit-eating grins on his face. Tom Henry walks up on the porch and tries to hide the monkey behind his back.

"Cherry says, 'Tom, what the hell you doing holding on to a ugly little fake monkey off in them woods, man? Ain't you done outgrown dolls and hide-and-seek?' Like I told you before, I reckon your granddaddy reacts like a demon when somebody stands on his own porch and calls him crazy. So Tom Henry commenced to beat the clothes off of Cherry and Shank. Off! You hear me?" Grandma was laughing hard as she could and smiling ear to ear. "And when the police came, Tom Henry was still beating both of them to the white meat until I calmed him down. He spent two nights in jail for that."

Grandma got busy when it came to her sentences. With Grandma's at-home sentences, it was like there was no screen between her mind and your ears. You got all of her, all of her voice. She could destroy anyone in the region in a sentence contest, including LaVander Peeler and me, as long as the judges were fair. I realized then, though, that Grandma's at-home sentences and her in-the-car sentences were completely opposite of her at-the-mall-sentences.

"Hey Grandma," I said. "Would you tell that story at the mall in front of that white lady, with the same dynamic sentences?"

"First of all, that wasn't no story. And I don't know nothing about no dynamic sentences," she told me. "That's the truth. And the truth ain't got a thing to do with that damn white woman, City."

"Oh. Okay," I said, knowing she was lying through her teeth.

THAT WIRELESS.

Grandma and I walked up on the porch of her house. Hurricane Katrina tore up Grandma's old shotgun house eight years earlier, but within a year, she'd gotten a new shotgun house built in the same spot. The house was raised off the ground about a foot and a half by some cinder blocks. The porch led to the front door, which opened to the living room, and from there, depending on what angle you looked in the house, you could see through the bedroom, the dining room, and the kitchen.

Grandma didn't have a hall, either, like the houses on TV and in books. Grandma's house had a living room with an old floor-model big-screen TV, a glass table with some Bibles and photo albums on it, a played-out stereo that only ever played Mahalia Jackson, and my Uncle Relle's sleeping bag right in the middle of the floor. Uncle Relle stayed with Grandma probably four times a week. Anyway, pictures of our family, the ones live and dead, were all over the living room. Walk ten more feet, there was a dining room with a plastic chandelier over a round wooden table. On one side of the table were two big deep freezers full of dead animal parts and food from her garden. On the other side of the table were a washing machine and a basket filled with the white folks' clothes Grandma washed to make a little more money. Fifteen more feet and there was a tiny kitchen. Four more feet and you were out the back door, under a clothesline, where there was a scary work shed I was never allowed to go in and a chinaberry tree.

I kept looking at Relle's sleeping bag, wondering when he was coming home. I wanted to know what he thought of what I'd done at the contest the night before. I figured he was going to be the only person in my family who was actually proud of me.

"Grandma, do you get wireless yet?"

"Wireless? Wireless what?"

"Internet!"

"Naw, we ain't got none of that mess, and you ain't gonna be hooking up no wireless to my TV."

"It ain't got nothing to do with the TV," I told her. "It's so people can check their email. What does Uncle Relle do if he wants to check his email?"

"He heads up the road to the library like everybody else, I reckon."

I wanted to push it more but I didn't want Grandma getting mad at me. I know Melahatchie was only a bus ride away, but it felt like a time warp. It always felt like it was behind whatever time we were in up in Jackson, but after Hurricane Katrina, it's like time went fast in reverse instead of just slowing down.

"Why you sweating, City?" Grandma asked me. "Go in the bathroom and wipe your face off." I turned to open the screen door and half-stepped in the door when Grandma finished her sentence: "...and go get my switch."

"What!?"

I stared at Grandma's face, not hardcore like I had the power to shoot liquid heat from my eyes, but more like I had X-ray vision and I was looking at the raggedy spinal cord that held the skull, that held the mouth, that held the tongue that formed those terrible words, *go get my switch.*

"You remember where it is, don't you? Go on and get my switch now," Grandma said. "You can't be acting a fool like that in front of them folks. You know we can't have that."

Man, she said it so calm. Like it was only a whupping. Grandma hadn't whupped me in two and half years.

But what could I do?

Nothing except drop my head, walk through the front screen door, through the living room, through the kitchen, out the back screen door, around the side of the house, and under the chinaberry tree. I had just matured to a point where I could get nice with myself in places other than the shower and the bathroom at school, and here I was about to get a beating like a child.

I almost hated this part of the beating way more than the actual beating. The anticipation and fear of all those lashes builds and builds, and then you realize how shameful it is that you're about to get your ass and back beaten by the same switch you're about to pick. And the whole time you're thinking that you don't wanna mess up on purpose and pick a little thin switch. You also don't wanna pick one that's too big to leave welts, because that means Grandma is gonna take her fine ass out there to pick the switch herself. And it didn't matter how deep in that bush the perfect switch was, Grandma would always find it.

I narrowed my choices to a slender one with a lot of leaves on it, or a big one that wouldn't wrap around my fat back too well.

Now, I had to hand it to her.

Should I smile or cry?

Grandma was out on the porch scaling the nasty big fish we were going to eat for dinner when I finally made it back.

Should I smile or cry?

I opened the screen door and waited for her to extend her hand.

"Here you go, Grandma." I acted like I was going to hand the switch to her, but when she reached for it, I dropped it on the ground and took off through the screen door, through the TV room, through the kitchen, and out the back screen door.

And Grandma came flying after me.

I ran on the other side of the clothesline and tried to use one of her yellow fitted sheets as protection. "Boy, put down my damn fitted sheet," she yelled. "Put it down!"

I threw the yellow fitted sheet on the ground and ran and ran. And Grandma ran and ran, too. Then she stopped by my granddaddy's work shed, right next to the chinaberry tree. She threw down that wack switch I gave her and then dove right in the bush and pulled out a switch that looked like a six-foot whip with a handle.

I understood right there that I wasn't simply running away from the greatest whupper in our family. Hell, I was running away from the greatest whupper in the history of Mississippi whuppings.

Grandma started running after me again. When I reached the back of the house, she was in the switch's reach, but she tried to turn the corner too sharp, and slid into a split.

Damn.

I knew Grandma would no longer just beat me for acting a fool at the contest. In the fourteen years that I'd known Grandma, she'd whupped me about six times, and the crazy thing was how she never looked at me like she wanted to rip the spine out of my back when she was whupping. You could tell that it was just regretful work for her.

Five minutes later, I was sobbing and balled up on the ground like a greasy, burnt-brown cinnamon roll with good waves. To tell you the truth, I felt honored to be whupped by Grandma. And I felt proud that during the entire whupping I never let go of my new brush.

After the beating and bath, Grandma prayed for me while I sat on the bed. Then we ate. I got so full off of nasty-looking, good-tasting catfish and fries, sweet iced tea, and thick pound cake that I couldn't breathe. I helped Grandma do the dishes, then we jumped in her bed to take a little nap before *The Bernie Mac Show* and *Meet the Browns* came on. I asked Grandma if it was okay for us to sleep on top of the sheet in our underwear with the fan directly on us.

Even though I was lying there in my underwear, Grandma looked at me in a way that made me feel like I was wearing something top-notch like a leather tuxedo with matching Jordan 6s. And even though my mama had seen me naked way more times, I felt less weird about Grandma seeing me. Grandma had a way of looking at you when you were naked that didn't make you feel terribly fat and soft. Most other folks, especially my mama, looked at me naked and made me feel like the fattest, softest ninth grader out of all the states in the Southeastern Conference. My mama tried not to look like that, but you could tell that she was trying too hard by the way she kept cutting her eyes away from me and saying stuff like, "We should probably start buying Diet Mountain Dew, Citoyen."

But with Grandma, whether I was naked or not, she looked at me the same way. To tell you the truth, if Grandma was trying to get the hem right on my slacks, she could have accidentally bumped into my scrotum sack and I wouldn't have cared because I knew that Grandma wouldn't have cared. If anybody else bumped into my scrotum sack like that, I'd probably act like I was dead or paralyzed until they left.

Grandma just looked at me without talking for about fifteen seconds. That's a long time to look at someone who is right in front of you. She smiled real thick and slung her arm across my chest. "Them folks is millions and millions of miles away from here today, you hear me? Million miles away," she said. "I want you to read the Bible every day you're here. You trying to get free, but you can't do it by yourself. We gotta get you to that water, City. That's why your mama sent you here."

"Wait." I sat up in bed. "That's messed up. Mama really sent me down here to get whupped and baptized for what happened at that contest?"

I waited for an answer, but the lids of Grandma's eyes slowly fell down. Her breathing got all heavy again, and about six seconds later, Grandma was asleep, her thick arm still slung across my chest, protecting me from something she wanted me to believe was millions and millions of miles away.

MyMy, Coach Stroud, and Pot Belly.

I grabbed my book and my brush and decided to go out and see if my Mela-hatchie friends had ever heard of *Long Division*.

I really only had three Melahatchie friends: Shay, MyMy, and Gunn. Gunn lived in the Melahatchie projects. Shay lived right down the road a little. MyMy lived in a trailer in the Mexican trailer park right next to Grandma's house. The only white people in the whole trailer park were MyMy and her mama.

The dirt underneath the Mexican trailer park was like the dirt at a play-ground, except it was darker and redder and filled with lots of perfect rocks. There were paper-sack-colored flat rocks with three or four deep scrapes, rocks the shape of chicken nuggets, black rocks that looked like charcoal, and dirty white ones with sharp edges.

I walked maybe two steps on that dirt when four limping rat dogs start-ing howling and running circles around these two women who were work-ing on this broken-down Explorer.

The women saw me looking at them and they stared at me like I had a smushed little foot growing out of my cheek. I didn't know if they looked at me like that because I had a brush in one hand and that *Long Division* in the other, or if maybe they had seen the contest and heard what I said about those Mexican kids from Arizona.

As soon as I stepped to her door there was MyMy's beady eyes, holding her Magic Slate, and looking crazy as ever. MyMy was ten years old and she was still in that phase where you find a detail about yourself that's different than everyone else and you try to make that one thing "your" thing. Her thing was trying to talk as little as possible, so she always carried this Magic Slate so she could write what she wanted to say. The only time she'd talk was if she was in the woods across the road from her house. She called those woods the Magic Woods.

MyMy's Magic Slate was the old-school kind with the thin plastic over the top, the kind where you wrote with a little plastic pencil and if you wanted to erase it, you had to pull the plastic up. If you met MyMy, you probably wouldn't be surprised that she would communicate through a Magic Slate. Nothing about the girl was regular. Her glasses weren't even regular glasses. They were these cheap greasy magnifying glasses that let you see every little movement her eyes made. Her eyes seemed to be back further in her head than normal. And they were blue. But the black part in the middle of MyMy's blue eyes was big and beady. And even when they looked at you, they kept zooming back and forth way too fast. It made me scared to look at her sometimes. One of the only regular things about her was that she always wore some New Orleans Hornets mesh shorts like the kind I wore to sleep back home.

As soon as MyMy walked down the steps of her trailer, I could tell by the way she held her head that she wanted me to hug her.

I didn't hug her, though. I just said, "MyMy, did you see me on TV?"

She nodded up and down.

"What did you think?" I asked her. "You can be honest." MyMy shrugged her shoulders. "What would you have done?"

She pulled out her Magic Slate and wrote, "You and Baize are Fameus."

"Girl, I know you know how to spell famous," I told her. "Did you even know Baize?"

MyMy just looked at me and didn't say a word. Even before Baize Shephard went missing, everyone in Melahatchie talked about her like she was their best friend. Baize was one of those girls who had thousands of friends on Twitter and Facebook, but she wasn't that close with anyone in Melahatchie except my friend Shay.

MyMy and I were headed to the Magic Woods when we saw these two big green trucks with confederate flags in their back windows. They were parked in the middle of the trailer park.

"Mean white men drive them trucks," MyMy said.

"That 'not talk' thing you do, I'm just letting you know it ain't cute. And how are you gonna call somebody white when you are white as a bleach stain?"

MyMy just laughed and said, "Bleach stain."

We walked in the opening of the woods and I was rereading the beginning of *Long Division* to get a sense of where this hole in the ground was. MyMy snatched the book from me and opened it to the first page.

"Your name is in this book," she said.

"I know," I told her. "Keep reading. Baize is in there, too. You see the name of the second chapter?"

"I don't want to," she said and threw the book down. "I don't like that book."

"Why? You should read it. It's not a hard book to read." She just looked me in the eyes and didn't say a word. "All the time you been in these woods, MyMy, have you ever seen a rusty handle that leads to a hole in the ground in these woods?"

"Why?"

"Have you seen one or not?

"I think so," she said. "I think it's over here."

I followed her and sure enough, hidden by some pine needles, was a rusty brown handle coming out of ground. "Oh shit. You ever pull that handle before?"

MyMy started walking away from me. "I don't think we should open that."

"Why?"

"We don't want to know."

"Girl, please. Who are you supposed to be? We don't want to know what?

"You hear something?" she asked me. I listened harder. We heard some cracked bass and a synthesizer blasting from some tinny speakers.

MyMy snatched my arm and we took off out of the woods and ran back onto Old Morton Road. Coach Stroud was driving the ice cream and watermelon truck our way. No matter where you saw Coach Stroud, he always wore a Titans hat turned to the back.

Coach stopped his truck in front of us.

"Hey, Coach!" I said.

"Hey Wide Load," Coach said while stretching his neck. "How you making it these days? I heard how you lost your mind on TV but I ain't been able to watch it on DVR."

Coach had this lisp that was deep and ringing, more like Biggie's lisp than Mike Tyson's. When I was ten, Mama gave me this slightly illiterate book about how all humans come from Africa. The book had pictures in there of the first man and first woman. The first woman didn't look like anyone I'd ever seen except maybe Michael Jackson, but the first man had a mouth just like Coach Stroud. I'm not saying that I didn't look lightweight ape around the mouth area, but Coach looked pretty much full ape. That was really one of the best things about him.

"That's the little white gal you been running 'round with since you got on TV?" Coach asked and stared at MyMy. MyMy walked up looking all hungry and crazy at the pictures of ice cream on the truck.

"I ain't running around with no white girl. I just got here. People spreading rumors about me running around with white girls?"

"You know how y'all do," Coach said.

I had no idea what he was talking about. "You still suing the city, Coach?"

"Well, we working on it," Coach said. He was one of those dudes who always talked about suing somebody and taking the money he won to the casino to play blackjack. "Always doing something to keep a hardworking black man down. So I gotta handle my business."

Coach Stroud smiled as he scratched the sack part of his tight red coach pants. Everyone in Melahatchie said that Coach Stroud was busting booties with my friend Gunn, and when you hear that a grown coach and one of your friends are busting booties, it makes you want to run your big ass back into the woods when you see him scratch his sack.

I figured that one of the worst things in the world was to have folks think you bust teenagers' booties. Nobody would ever look at you the same after that. Even when you're just doing stuff that everybody else does, like scratching your sack, no one would look at you the same. Coach was a walking "Kindly pause," and that was fine with me. I just hated that I ever even thought I loved LaVander Peeler. No part of me really wanted to touch his sack, but I knew you couldn't tell people that you loved another boy, because as soon as folks heard the word "love" they would look at me the same way I looked at Coach when he had that sack itch. I wondered, for the first time, what busting booties had to do with love. Once I thought I loved Toni Whitaker and Octavia Whittington, but that was because those girls were the only two real people I thought about when I got nice. They were the people who made my privacy the hardest. As much as I thought I loved LaVander Peeler, I can't even say that anything about him made my privacy hard. So if it wasn't love, I just wondered what it really was, and why I felt so much of it when I saw him up on that stage.

Anyway, I was allergic to watermelon, but Grandma seemed so happy when she ate them, so I decided to use the ten dollars Mama gave me for the trip to buy Grandma a gift.

"Coach, lemme get one of them baby watermelons." Coach just looked at me and started rolling his tongue underneath the inside of his top lip. "Gimme one of them baby watermelons, Coach! Why you looking at me crazy?" He still just looked, steady rolling his eyes like he would look if you fumbled in practice or acted scared to hit someone or didn't run a play right.

"Come back here with me, Wide Load." He walked through his truck. I looked at MyMy and walked back with him. "What you doing, man?" he asked me.

"What you mean, Coach?"

"What I mean!? Wide Load, you worse than them ignorant-ass rappers grabbing hard on them dicks, selling that poison, and calling everybody 'niggas.' You don't eat no watermelon in front of no white folks," he told me. "I know them folks in Jackson taught you better. Don't look at me like that, boy. I don't care of she is just a little white gal. Like I told y'all during the season. Practice makes perfect. You play the game the way you live your life."

"White folks don't like watermelon, Coach?"

"Naw, Wide Load. That ain't it. It just some things you just don't do. I swear before God that I don't know what's wrong with y'all little young boys in this generation. Black men like me fought so—"

"Oh Jesus," I said.

"Now you blaspheming his name? We did our best so y'all could have equal opportunities and some of whatever the white man got. We got a black president in that White House fighting to stay alive and here y'all go trying hard to act like niggas in front of the white man's woman." He stopped and looked at me like he'd just asked me a question. "What if Obama acted like that? You don't see how they love seeing us do things like fighting and acting a fool on TV and dancing and eating on watermelons?"

"That's stuff I like to do anyway, Coach," I told him. "Plus, I like to do other stuff, too."

"Shhh. Wide Load. Shut the hell up. I'm asking you how you think that makes us feel?"

Coach was waiting for an answer, but you know what's crazy? I'd never thought of Coach Stroud as being any part of the "us" he was talking about. The only time people talked about Coach Stroud was when they talked about Melahatchie's biddy ball team. And the only time folks really talked about Melahatchie's biddy ball team was when they were saying we might not need to be coached by someone who liked to bust booties.

"You ain't answer me, boy."

I opened my mouth, but he interrupted me. "It's like this, Wide Load. I'mo say it to you one more time. White man see you acting a nigga, he liable to think we all still niggas. Niggas are *less than* white folks in they eyes. Look what they did to that young brother, Trayvon. If they think you less than human, you don't deserve no respect. Period. You are a smart young man. I know you understand."

"You done?"

"See, that's your problem, Wide Load. You play too much. White man see your big ass acting a fool on TV, and he gon' have a reason to take away the rights we done worked so hard for. Y'all gotta learn how to manage that freedom we got for y'all. You see what I'm saying. Ain't enough to be free. What you gon' do with the freedom?"

Coach was pissing me off even more than Principal Reeves when she gave that wack freedom speech. "Coach, you know something?" I was about to call him a half-ape, half-faggot in too-tight coach pants.

Instead, I said, "You probably should just give me the watermelon before I say something to hurt your feelings," and went back around to the side of the truck.

He leaned close to me. "You act like a li'l head-buster, but don't never forget, City, that you got a head, too." Coach leaned back, blinked a few times, and swallowed some spit. "Here you go, boy. That'll be six dollars."

He really had a look in his eyes that told me he wanted to elbow me in the jaw. I thought about how since my friend Gunn was known as the best young fighter in Melahatchie, there really was no telling how effective Coach Stroud was with his hands, but still I wanted him to know something.

"Coach Stroud." I looked down at MyMy and thought about not saying this in front of her. "You pissed me off in the back of your truck a few minutes ago, but I guess I really don't think you be busting Gunn's booty. I don't. I just think he's too young to have a grown boyfriend or girlfriend. And I thought about calling you a 'faggot' back there, too, but then I remembered how you were damn near a ninja," I told him. "I also kinda remembered that 'faggot' sounds like some kind of balled-up monster made of ground-up dookie chunks, razor blades, and rotten muscadines. You ain't no monster, Coach. Not to me."

I looked at Coach and I grabbed MyMy's hand and got a little distance from the truck. "I hear what you saying back there, but can I give you some advice? Fuck white folks," I told him. "For real! Their eyes ain't gotta be everywhere you are. Y'all are too old to care about them so much. They can only do as much harm as you let them, and all y'all oldheads are letting them do way too much."

Saying that made me feel like Satan in a way because I knew that Coach Stroud couldn't go up in anyone's house in Melahatchie, including Grandma's, and tell on me. Everybody in Melahatchie would allow Stroud to walk on their porch. And they'd sit down with him and they'd laugh loud and talk louder about the weather, the Saints, white folks, or some trifling heathen who wasn't there to defend himself. But I didn't know of one grown person in Melahatchie who would let him all the way in their house. Not one.

Coach Stroud drove his truck on down the road and MyMy and I were on our way out of the woods when that green truck that was parked in the trailer park drove slowly toward us.

It stopped in front of us. Four men were squeezed into the cab. They were blasting that old Ricky Rozay song, "I'm Not A Star." One of the dudes had crossed eyes, dimples, red hair, and a pot belly that looked far too old for his face. I had a baby watermelon in one hand, my brush under my arm, and *Long Division* in the other.

"You the boy who was on TV yesterday?" Pot Belly asked. "The one with that brush who done all that talking?"

"Yeah, that's me," I told him. "My name is City."

"City?" He looked down at me. "What's a boy named City doing out here in the country?"

"I don't know. I'm just visiting my grandma," I told him. "City is just a nickname."

"I see," he said. "Let me ask you this. You fast as you is smart?"

"For my size, I'm alright."

"You faster than this man right here?" he asked and pointed to the only boy in the truck, who wore a V-neck shirt with the arms cut off.

"That's a boy," I told them. "He ain't no man."

"City love to sass, don't he," Pot Belly said to the other men in the truck. "You had plenty of sass yesterday on that TV, didn't you?"

Pot Belly whispered something to the round-face white boy. The kid jumped out the back and stood next to me. The truck was right in front of us.

"Now, we gonna say go," Pot Belly said, "and I want y'all to run after the truck 'til we say stop."

"Naw, I'm good," I told the man. "I'm tired of running. I don't even know y'all like that." I put the watermelon down and started brushing my waves. "Plus, my wind ain't that good 'cause I just raced."

"That's alright, Chucker. We ain't going that far."

"My name is City," I told him and kept brushing my hair. "You know what? I don't like the feeling of this situation, so we're finna go on about our business."

"Mind if I look at your brush, Situation?"

"Why?"

"Never seen one up close," he said. "Just wanna look at it."

"Naw," I told him. "I'm good."

"You don't wanna race. You don't wanna share your brush. What you wanna do, Situation? Use some sentences. How you practice for something like that?"

"My name is City," I told him again. "Not no Situation."

All the men in the truck were laughing so hard at this point. One of them said, "Situation, you wanna use 'brush' in a sentence?"

"I can do that," I told him and started walking toward them. "The next funky-ass white boy to ask me for my brush is going to get knocked out Deebo-style, and if his friends jump in and try to help, they might get a few licks off, but I'm gonna get my revenge with my Jackson army one way or another. Let's go, MyMy." I grabbed her hand.

"Here," the man said, and threw a comb on the ground. "You are so talented, Situation. I'll let you see mine if you let me see yours."

The comb wasn't like the heavy plastic black combs Mama and them used sometimes. It had smaller edges and a thin handle. I reached down to pick it up and hand it to him, when out of nowhere, I felt a heavy foot in the center of my back. My solar plexus smashed into the ground and my lips kissed the asphalt right as my brush popped out of my hand. Then I felt another kick in my ass.

I looked up. One of the men picked up my brush and threw it to Pot Belly, and they all jumped in the truck. I spit the little rocks, dirt, and blood from my lips and looked at the eyes of the other men in the car. "Use that in a sentence, you nigger son of a bitch," Pot Belly yelled. Red dirt started pouring out of the back of that truck and they slowly rolled away. I sat there on the ground swallowing the taste of rocks. It felt like someone was tickling the back of my tongue with one of those square batteries.

I went in my pockets, grabbed those right-heavy rocks, and tried to break out their back windows. MyMy ran with me. She was beside me throwing rocks. Pot Belly's voice was still back there laughing, pointing, teasing, watching me. The young boy that he had called a man was recording it all, too, on a cell phone. "Hey girl, hey," Pot Belly yelled as the boy recorded it all. "You best don't grow to be no nigger-lover. Leave Situation alone."

I turned around in the middle of the road, wiped the dirt off my face, and walked back into the woods. "Move, MyMy," I told her, and spit a bloody piece of the inside of my bottom lip on some sticker bushes.

My mother had beaten me probably over a hundred times in Jackson, but no man and no white person had ever put their hands on me. Ever. I had lost some battles at school with LaVander Peeler and felt like I had lost on that stage a few days earlier, but in those situations, I always thought I could fight back. Even if I lost, I knew that the other person or other people fighting me knew that they had been in a fight.

This was completely different.

All I could do after getting my chest smashed into the ground and being called a "nigger" by those white men was hope it all stopped hurting. That was it.

MyMy started trying to wipe the dirt off my face. "Don't get dirt all on your clothes," I told her and wiped my face again with my own shirt.

"They called me 'nigga' too, City."

"MyMy, you ain't no nigga," I told her. "And don't say it again."

"How come?"

"Because it hurts when you say that word." I turned back toward the road behind us. "And I know it doesn't really hurt you when you hear the word. You feel me? It's because no one can treat you like a nigga."

"It does hurt me," she said and kept trying to look me in the face. "I didn't like it when they said it."

"It didn't really hurt you, though. It's like the word 'bitch.' My principal said boys shouldn't ever say that word because we never have to deal with being treated like a bitch. She's right, too. Or..." I started thinking about how I treated that Mexican girl at the contest. The only bad word I knew to call Mexicans was "spic." Really, I should have just called Stephanie a "spic bitch" because that's how I treated her and that's how I wanted her to feel.

"But you just said it," MyMy interrupted my thought. "You said 'bitch.'"

"I was making a point," I told her. "Don't say that word either. You too young to say words like that."

"City," MyMy tugged on my shirt. "What does that word really mean?"

"Which word?"

"'Nigga.'"

"Damn, girl. Didn't I just tell you not to say that word? Look. I know that I'm a nigga. I mean...I know I'm black and—" I thought for a few seconds of what Mama told me the word meant when I was in Jackson—"but 'nigga' means below human to some folks and it means superhuman to some other folks. Do you even know what I'm saying? And sometimes it means both to the same person at different times. And, I don't know. I think 'nigga' can be like the word 'bad.' You know how bad mean a lot of things? And sometimes, 'bad' means 'super good.' Well, sometimes being called a 'nigga' by another person who gets treated like a 'nigga' is one of the top seven or eight feelings in the world. And other times, it's in the top two or three worst feelings. Or, maybe…shoot. I don't know. I couldn't even use the word in a sentence, MyMy. Ask someone else. Shoot. I don't even know."

"City," MyMy interrupted me. She kept moving side to side, tearing leaves off of little lilac clovers. "I think we can kill them. They made you sound crazy on TV."

"Naw, girl. We could try to kill a few, but they had rifles in the back of their truck and they were taller than us and they could kill us a lot quicker than we could kill them. Plus, if I kill a white person, they would throw everyone in my family under the jail," I told her. "Me and you can do bad things, hood-rat things, but we can't ever kill white folks. How do you not know that?"

We started walking out of the woods when MyMy stopped and looked at me with those crazy eyes. "City, I have a brown thing on my hand. See?" MyMy held out her left hand and showed me a little brown dot in the middle of her palm. Looked like a big freckle. "I wish this thing was white and the rest of me was the color of my birthmark."

"Don't be dumb. Just be happy that you are whatever you are," I told her. "At least the way you are, ain't nobody kicking you in the back and making you use 'niggardly' in a sentence. It's not that you're dumb, MyMy, but you're kinda dumb compared to me. You feel me?"

"City?" MyMy said.

"What?" I could tell she was flipping subjects again.

"I don't know what n-i-g-g-a is," MyMy was talking her ass off now. "And you do not know what n-i-g-g-a is, but we can say I'm not n-i-g-g-a and you're not n-i-g-g-a and Baize is not n-i-g-g-a."

"MyMy, we can say that if you really want us to, but I'm pretty sure I'm a nigga for life," I told her. "And you might wanna stop talking about Baize since you didn't even know her. Because I'm almost positive Baize would tell you that she was a nigga for life, too." We started walking again. "I swear that white folks need to just shut the hell up sometimes. Y'all make it hard for everybody."

We started walking out of the woods. "MyMy, watch out for them sticker bushes," I said.

I had *Long Division* in my lap when Grandma came out on the porch and asked me what was wrong. I told her that I was sad because I didn't want to get baptized and I wished she had internet so I could see what people were saying about me.

"What happened to your lip, baby?" she asked me.

"I just fell in the woods. Why?"

Grandma went in the house and came back out on the porch with some peroxide and a washcloth. "Don't ask me why," she said. "Tell me what happened to your lip, City."

"Grandma, do white folks like watermelon?"

"I reckon they do."

"More than black folks?"

"I don't reckon they do." She started laughing.

"Well, Coach Stroud didn't want me to buy a watermelon in front of white folks. That's what he said.

"Baby, Coach Stroud was just trying to protect you."

"From what, Grandma?"

"From life, City," she said. "Stroud ain't all the way right, but he just want you to survive. Keep your guard up, because you don't never know."

"Never know what, Grandma?" I was getting anxious and a little mad at the goofy answers Grandma was giving. "How far they go to get you? That's what you said when I got off the bus. But what if I do know how far they'll go? I know. I do!"

Grandma didn't say a word.

"Well," I said, "if someone was tired of hearing about white folks, do you think they should say, 'Forget white folks,' or 'Forget what white folks think'?"

Grandma looked at me harder. "I think the fool probably ought to ask himself why and what it is they want to forget. I ain't forgetting nothing they did to us. Nothing! I spent my whole life forgetting. Shit." Grandma started rubbing her wrist really hard. "City, what ain't you telling me?"

"I'm telling you everything," I told her, when her phone rang. I could tell it was Uncle Relle by the way Grandma's face dropped and her eyes starting twitching. Grandma handed me the phone and walked out to give me privacy. She was really good about doing that.

"You did it, li'l nigga," Uncle Relle said over the phone.

"Did what?"

"You made that move."

"What move?"

"You got folks playing what you did on the internet everywhere. Now you 'bout to make that TV money. They ain't tell you?"

"Tell me what?"

"Listen," he said, sounding way too giddy, like Funkmaster Flex. "Don't tell Mama I told you this, but they want you to be on a reality show."

"Who?"

"*You*, City. Your mother don't want you to do it but we got to find a way to make it work."

"Me?" I asked him. "Why?"

"Because of what you did," he said. "You got over two million hits on YouTube, damn near a million views on Worldstar, and it ain't even been 24 hours since it happen. They know that they can make some money off you. I'ma tell you all about it tomorrow. BET and VH1 trying to do a *Black Reality Stars of YouTube*."

"Stop lying."

"I ain't bullshitting you, baby boy," he said, sounding completely sincere. "They want you, and that corny tall one who won."

"LaVander Peeler?"

"Yeah."

"But he didn't win."

"That's what I say, but don't hate," he said. "Look, I'ma be there tomorrow morning. I gotta record you going through your day. Shit might be worth something someday."

"But you don't have a camera."

"City, I got about six phones with cameras. Don't worry 'bout me. Just do you. And don't say nothing to Mama."

"Uncle Relle?"

"What?"

I didn't want to say what I felt but I needed to tell someone. "I don't believe you," I told him. "Bad things are happening to me too fast. You know what I mean? Everything is happening too fast. I'm reading this book called *Long Division* and there's a character in it from the '80s named City. It's hard…"

"It is what it is," he interrupted me. "Fuck a book. Ain't no one reading no books in 2013 unless you already a star or talking about some damn vampires and wolfmen. Like Jigga said, every day a star is born. Not a writer. A star, nigga! Today that star is you."

"Bye, Uncle Relle," I said, not really understanding how much of what he said was truth but knowing Jigga didn't really have anything to do with it. I went out on the porch and looked across Old Morton Road at the Magic Woods. They didn't seem nearly as magical as the woods I'd been reading about in *Long Division*.

Boom Boom Boom.

Grandma's screen screeched open around 8 p.m. *Boom Boom Boom.* Grandma looked at me and grinned. I grinned back so she wouldn't feel as stupid as she looked. *Boom Boom Boom.* After knock number three or six, depending on how you count, Grandma's door opened and, in slow motion, in walked our boy, Ufa D, in a head-to-toe camouflage outfit with two DVD collections under his arms.

Ufa sat his big self on the couch next to Grandma. They half-smiled, touched feet, and tossed goofiness at each other like grown folk did on good cable after they got done doing it.

Ufa looked over at me on the floor and just started laughing his ass off. I would've been more pissed but Ufa had a burning sweet tobacco smell about him. The smell had its root in his mouth, but somehow it spread all over his body.

Ufa always brought one episode of *The Dukes of Hazzard* and one episode of *Dallas* over to Grandma's on Friday nights. Ufa and Grandma realized a year ago that you could buy the box sets of old shows at Walmart. Ever since then, Friday was *Dallas* and *Dukes of Hazzard* night just like I guess it was for them way back in the 1980s. After bringing in the box sets, they would go back out to his truck and get the fried fish or chicken platters and cold drank that he left there.

When folks came to Grandma's house, they parked in this little rocky sand patch to the right of the porch. But Ufa D went way past the patch and parked on the grass next to the work shed, damn near in the back of Grandma's house, under a magnolia. We walked back and looked in the back of his orangey-red pickup. On top of lots of dry pine needles and lots of long stalks of sugar cane were three big burlap sacks filled with orange drank, donuts, fried chicken parts, and potato logs from Jr. Food Mart. Even though my chest still hurt from what happened earlier with Pot Belly, and even though my insides felt super sour, I couldn't wait to eat as much greasy food as soon as possible. For a second, I thought about this skinny speaker they brought to Hamer to talk mainly to the girls in my grade. This skinny dude kept talking about how black girls loved to eat their feelings when things were sad for them. I acted like I wasn't paying attention, but I really wanted to ask that skinny dude so many questions. Anyway, I wondered if I was trying to eat my feelings after what had happened to me over the past two days.

By the time we got in the house, I didn't wonder about anything except how much greasy food I could force down my mouth in the shortest amount of time. If I was eating my feelings, it felt so good while it was happening.

I was hours into a chicken-fat-and-orange-drank-induced coma when Grandma tapped me on the booty.

"Get up, baby," she said. "Time to go to bed."

I waddled back into Grandma's bedroom and lumped myself into her bed. I still had chicken crumbs and cold drank stains all over my shirt.

A little while later, Grandma came in our room. She took off her clothes and put on her gown, but kept on her wig. As long as I knew Grandma, before she went to bed, she'd turn on that damn Mahalia Jackson song, "Precious Lord." Then she'd start humming and writing in a tablet. Usually, I'd be in the bed reading some book or something and Grandma would be on the floor humming.

"I'll be right back," she said.

I was in that bed for about four minutes thinking about all kinds of stuff, and then I heard the screen door open.

I kept listening for the door to close. I didn't hear anything else except the chunky buzz of bullfrogs. I tiptoed over to the door of our bedroom, put my greasy hands on the edge of the door, and peeked around the corner.

Layers of Grandma's booty were spilling over the fingers of Ufa's paws. And Grandma had her arm wrapped around him, too. Their arms made a long, off-center X on the side of their bodies.

All I could think about was Grandma's hand behind Ufa's back, probably cupping his tobacco-smelling booty, too. It's one thing to think of your Grandma's booty being cupped, but when you think of her cupping someone else's booty it makes your insides rot and tangle, especially if that someone is probably married and named Ufa D. It makes you think that the person who fed you and talked to you and listened to you and laughed with you and bathed you when you were young was really some super freak you didn't even know.

Ufa's head was to the side and he and Grandma were standing in the doorway, kissing and hunching like some young white fools on wemakexxxvideos.com. Ufa had his hat off so I could see his face and raggedy eyebrows pretty good. As soon as I saw the white of his eyes, I ran my ass back to the bed, covered my head with the covers, and faced the fan in Grandma's window.

The screen door closed and Grandma stomped back into the bedroom.

"City, you meddling in grown-folk business again, ain't you?" I didn't say a damn word. I figured my best bet was to fake sleep until Grandma tapped me on the booty.

"I know you woke," she said.

I didn't move an inch. Didn't shake. Didn't even smile like I usually did when I fake slept. Even with my greasy head under the covers, I felt the heat of Grandma coming near me. I thought she was going to try to kiss me, so

I made sure my face was tucked tight. But even under the covers, I could still smell Ufa on her.

I needed to throw up.

"Know that I love you, baby," Grandma said, rubbing my back with her fingertips. "You gotta wake up early to go to the library with Relle. G'night."

When Uncle Relle and I walked into the library Saturday morning, I was surprised at the shampooed-carpet-and-cornbread smell of the place, especially since the floor was linoleum. Looking at all the slightly wack books in the library made me grab *Long Division* tighter. I hadn't been in a real library for so long and this one didn't really feel real either. It was more like a mobile home with a lot of bookshelves in it. Every bookshelf in the library was its own section. You had your colorful kids' books section, your Bible section, your John Grisham and William Faulkner sections, and then you had a Classic section filled with books that were thick, dark, and spinach-green and had that rich gluey smell.

I was too old for the kids' books and to tell you the truth, all the Bible stuff I'd heard didn't seem interesting for too long. For less than two pages, you'd get something interesting about naked Adam and Eve eating on apple cores and grabbing snakes by the throat, and then three hundred pages later, you'd get some boring stuff about jokers named Isaac and Ham. But the Bible was better than those other spinach-colored Classic books that spent most of their time flossing with long sentences about pastures and fake sunsets and white dudes named Spencer. I didn't hate on spinach, fake sunsets, or white dudes named Spencer, but you could just tell that whoever wrote the sentences in those books never imagined they'd be read by Grandma, Uncle Relle, LaVander Peeler, my cousins, or anyone I'd ever met.

If you didn't want to read books at the Melahatchie library, you could read magazines or get in line for one of their two computers. The only problem was that the computers were usually used by dusty oldheads sneaking looks at big-booty porn sites.

I sat down at one of the computers and saw that someone had been googling "long division."

"Can you come here?" I asked Uncle Relle.

There was nothing about the book I'd been reading for the past two days, so I typed a sentence from *Long Division* and googled it: *I still have no proof that I ever made Shalaya Crump feel anything other than guilty for leaving me with Baize Shephard.*

There was still nothing on the screen that had to do with the book.

"What you doing copying sentences out of that book?" Uncle Relle said. "Thought you wanted to find out about yourself. You messing around?"

"You think it's possible to have a book and not have it appear anywhere on the internet?" I asked Uncle Relle.

"Who wrote the book?"

"I don't know."

"What you mean you 'don't know'? Who wrote the shit? Look up his last name."

"For real," I told him. "I don't know who wrote it. It could have been a boy or a girl."

"Well," he sat next to me and poked me in the chest with his nubs. "If it ain't no author, it ain't no gotdamn book, is it? Unless it's one of them pamphlets that niggas be calling a book. That shit be embarrassing to me. And even some of them pamphlets be on the internet, City. Now, can you please look up that other shit so we can go? I got a meeting in 20 minutes."

I knew Uncle Relle didn't have a meeting, but I went to YouTube and typed, "City, Can You Use That Word in a Sentence" anyway. The YouTube clip of my speech already had four million hits. It was called "The Wave Brush Rant." It had been linked to by over 80,000 people on Facebook. Another clip, the one of me trying to understand the word "niggardly," had two million hits and was called "City Spells Niggardly." The clip of me telling that white boy on the bus that I hated him only had 24,000 hits. On the right side you could see LaVander Peeler's link, too. His only had 300,000 hits and it was called "Chitterlings are Chitlins." Right below that was a still picture of me from a distance throwing rocks toward Pot Belly's truck called "City, the Nigger, running."

Everything that had happened to me the past three days, except the whupping from Grandma and catching her making out, had made it onto the internet.

"City Be Busting Heads" had over 200,000 views and "City, the Nigger" had 90,000 in less than a day.

Uncle Relle showed me how someone had added the T-Pain voice coder to my voice when I was talking to the Mexicans from Arizona. Folks were selling T-shirts online with a picture of me brushing my waves and underneath, in deep black, was the word "niggardly" with a question mark.

I turned the volume down on the computer so only I could hear the sound and I pushed play on the video from the contest. I'd made YouTube videos before but they always had other people in them and really none of the videos I'd made were just about me. But this was so different. For example, when I was going off on that stage at the contest, on the computer, I looked like I wanted to kill that Mexican girl from Arizona when really I didn't even know her. I was just desperate to find something to make them feel pain and be sad and embarrassed like I'd been embarrassed on national TV. But when I saw the video, there were so many white kids around that I could have said mean things about and I didn't say hardly anything directly to them. Also, I never thought I was super cute but I didn't realize how much my thighs rubbed together and how the back of my head was bigger than every other head in all the videos. Even though I felt all of that strange stuff, I can't even lie: the thing I still felt the most was famous.

The first comment under the contest clip was, "dis my nigga right here. crackers mad city stay keeping it real. flav ain't got nothing on city. fuck white folks just like he said." It was posted by someone called "LockNess."

Beneath that, someone called "CawCuss" commented, "Note to Niggers: Niggardly is a word that has nothing to do with Niggers. Learn to read before complaining Niggers."

Uncle Relle said we had to go but after reading CawCuss's comment, I really had to look up "niggardly" and see what it actually meant.

"Uncle Relle, did you see a tape of the contest?" I asked him.

"Yeah, I watched your part 'bout a hundred times." He put his hand on my head and started laughing. "Why?"

"I'm saying, do you think 'niggardly' is, you know, about us?"

"City, you can't ever put anything past the white man. They knew that word had 'nigga' in it. That's all I'm—"

"But, you know, do you think maybe it just like, happen to have 'nigga' in it and anyone would have gotten that word?"

Uncle Relle actually paused and took his hand off my shoulder. He bent down and started twirling the threads that were coming out of his hem with his nubs, then looked back at me. "Look," he said, "they knew what they was doing. You shouldn't have had nothing to do with that word if you were on TV. That's all I know. Look how they did your friend. Let's get out of here."

"Naw," I told him. "Hold on."

Uncle Relle watched me open Microsoft Word on the computer and type "niggardly" in a new document. I highlighted it and dragged the mouse to Tools where the thesaurus was. Before clicking on Thesaurus, I just held my finger there and imagined what I'd see.

"If you gon' click it, click it," Uncle Relle said. "What you wasting drama for? You supposed to save all this drama for the show."

I looked right at Uncle Relle and begged him to shut the fuck up without even moving my lips.

"Ungenerous (adv.)" is what popped up under "meanings." Under "synonyms" were the words "stingy" and "meager" and "miserable" and "miserly" and "measly." Under "antonyms" was the word "generous."

The actual definitions confused me even more.

"Come on, City," Uncle Relle told me. "We gotta get it moving."

Uncle Relle was pissing me off. I looked at him in a way I'd never looked before. And he did something I'd only seen him do with Grandma. He looked down at his fingers, picked up a folded newspaper that was right between the computers, and said, "Okay, favorite nephew. Just hurry up."

In a huge color photo on the cover of the paper was a picture of Baize Shephard. The photo must have been one of those yearbook pictures, because Baize had a look on her face I'd never imagined her having in real life. The left side of her mouth was smiling and the right side had a little bit of her tongue sticking out. I figured the photographer probably told her not to make faces and she did the goofiest face she could get away with. Plus, she had this thick fake rope chain around her neck that she always wore.

The headline said, "Investigators Have New Lead in Disappearance of Honor Student, Baize Shephard."

I typed "niggardly" in the Google finder and clicked on the mouse.

Uncle Relle didn't say a word to me the first five minutes of the ride home.

"Look, City," he said as he pulled in the driveway of Alcee Mayes, his weed man, "just 'cause you the face of…"

"The face of what?" I asked him.

Uncle Relle looked down. "Sometimes the glass is way more than empty," he said. "That's all I'm saying. Sometimes the glass is way fuller than a motherfucker, even if you can't see it. You better drink."

Uncle Relle ran into Alcee Mayes's trailer and left me in his van. I knew he was thinking I should be happy that millions of people around the world were looking at me and typing my name on the internet, but seeing my picture pop up when I googled "niggardly" broke my heart. I just couldn't figure out how I had become the face of "niggardly" in less than three days. If I could have stayed at the library longer, I would have responded to every messed-up comment on YouTube and I would have typed my own response to the fake @MyNameIsCity Twitter feed someone made up.

Instead, I stayed in Uncle Relle's van and continued reading *Long Division*, a book that, according to the internet at the Melahatchie local library, didn't exist at all.

A few minutes after we walked in the house, Grandma pulled the screen door open and whispered something in Uncle Relle's ear. Next thing I knew, I was in the bedroom and was told not to come out until she or Uncle Relle came to get me.

I pulled out my book and wrote:

It was like she wasn't even Grandma anymore. I never heard my grandma say "ma'am" to someone who was younger than her. And I heard that my grandma brought the Jheri not "Gary" curl to Melahatchie from Milwaukee back in the early '80s. Now here she was acting like she couldn't even pronounce "Jheri" right.

Under the revving of box fans and the hum of crickets, I heard about 20 minutes of loud cuss words coming from mashed-up voices. Slowly though, the yelling and cussing slid from the trailer park to the back of Grandma's house, where the railroad tracks were.

And after a while, there were no voices at all.

When Grandma finally came in the house two hours later, she made me sit on the toilet in the bathroom while she took a bath. The suds in the tub were brownish and pink from the dirt and blood on Grandma's hands. I tried to only look at this little pinkish-brown moat of suds near the back of the tub the whole time she bathed, but I kept catching her long nipples out of the corner of my eye.

We didn't say one word to each other until I asked her, "What happened today, Grandma?"

"Nothing, City. That man, he gone far away from here."

"What man? Gone where?"

"Ain't nothing in that work shed for you, you hear me?"

"Did somebody mess with you? 'Cause I never seen you just ..."

"That man is gone home, I reckon," Grandma interrupted. "You got to be a special kind of evil to spend your whole life getting more than you deserve, then turn right around and hate on folks for getting half of what you was born into. Just evil."

"Who is a special kind of evil?" I asked her.

"Listen." She reached out of the bathtub and her hands touched my knee. "That man, that truck, this day, ain't none of it even real as you think. Treat it like it never happened, you hear me? You are a smart child, an educated young man. You try to act grown in front of them cameras? Well, grown black folks forget what they need to forget. That's what grown black folks do. Can you do that for Grandma?"

"Yeah, I can do that, Grandma, but you might want to ease up talking to me like this is fifth-grade special ed."

Grandma's eyes got to twitching. I looked at the ground, trying my hardest not to get whupped again. "Can you do what I asked you, City?"

"Yeah, Grandma." I had no choice. "I can do what you asked me."

"Okay," Grandma said, and got out of the bathtub. She dried off while I looked at the floor. While she was looking at herself in the mirror, she said,

"They always expecting us to forget. I'm tired of forgetting. You and that baby didn't do nothing to nobody."

I couldn't completely understand how Grandma could go from telling me that grown folks forget what they need, to saying she was tired of forgetting. I knew not to ask any more questions but, in a way, it was all starting to make a little more sense.

TENDER TESTICLES.

After all that weirdness with Grandma earlier, I just wanted to run down Old Morton Road and never stop until I was back in our garage in Jackson. Since I didn't have either the wind or the guts to do that, I called my friend Shay and asked her to come over.

Shay was the junior queen of Melahatchie and raiser of way more hell than a little bit. She walked in Grandma's yard wearing a pea-green muscle shirt and some Memphis Grizzlies shorts. Usually her Afro puffs were the same size but today the left one was way bigger than the right.

"I don't know what you was thinking," she said, with a voice that came directly from her nose. "Nasal" actually isn't the word for Shay's voice. Shay's nose was damn near wider than her lips, and it stayed clogged up so she only breathed through her mouth. Shay spoke fast, too, but it wasn't like she said certain words fast. It was more that she moved from word to word fast. "I knew you was crazy," she said, "but I ain't know you was that crazy."

"What you mean?"

"Wow!" she said. "On national TV, too? In front of all them dubs?" Shay called white folks "dubs," which was short for "W's."

"Listen," I tried to change subjects. "Have you ever heard of this book called *Long Division*? It's about Melahatchie."

"Quit changing subjects, boy," she said. "If there was a book about Melahatchie, don't you think I would have heard of it? Is it a book for dubs or a book for us?"

"Us mostly," I told her. "But it's complicated. It's a book for us and a few dubs, I guess. There's this one boy and he's in love with this girl named

Shalaya Crump, and they travel through time and find this girl who lives in Melahatchie. The girl's name is Baize." Shay looked up at me. "Baize Shephard. You heard of it?"

Shay rolled her eyes at me and told me to shut my lying ass up without even opening her mouth. Every time I saw Shay, it was like seeing someone you haven't seen in forever, and it was like seeing a star of a good show and it was like seeing someone you wanted to see every day. Shay never acted too excited to see me ever since I told her this secret when we were playing The Secret Game. The first time I had a wet dream, she was there—in the dream, I mean—and I told her that, and I also told her what we were doing with our hands and mouths.

We jumped the creek and went into this little path leading into the Magic Woods. After stomping through the woods and trying to dodge sticker bushes, we ended up in this dusty opening between pine trees and tree stumps. We were about 50 feet from the Melahatchie Community Center.

Shay walked deeper in the woods. "Keep talking," she said. "I'm listening." She wasn't really listening. I heard all kinds of sticks and leaves breaking before she came out with this huge stick. Right in the same spot where Shay found hers, I found the perfect stick. Not really perfect, but perfect if I was gonna be fighting her with the stick she had.

I was always scared to hit Shay's stick hard unless she hit my hand or my stomach with her stick. Sometimes you could hold your stick out and the person you were playing against would swing wildly at yours and theirs would get stuck in the dusty-ass ground, or the soft mud if it had been raining. It would be stuck just long enough so you had the perfect angle to smash that joker. If you did that technique to Shay, she got so mad that she'd quit or catch fade with her praying-mantis technique.

"I didn't know what else to do," I told her.

"When?"

"At that contest," I told her. "I swear I wanted to win it for all these people. Like you and Gunn and fat boys with waves like me, too." She started laughing. "You laughing, but I'm serious. I wanted to win it for all of us."

"You messed up before beginning, then," she said. "You should've been trying to win it for you. We wanted you to win, but if you ain't win, we would've been happy just 'cause you were in it. You didn't have to shout out Melahatchie like that either. You made us look like losers." She paused and looked like she was thinking of what to say. "I just feel as though you should've just sat down when you got it wrong. But whatever. That's you. Come on and play, City," she said. Shay hated if you held your stick away from hers. "Play, boy!"

"I am a playboy, ain't I?"

"More like a gay boy," she said and started laughing.

"Why you call me a gay boy? I ain't gay."

I swung my stick and tagged the mess out of hers, but it didn't break.

My hand bones were vibrating. "Dang, I hit that mug hard, too."

We were both happy as hell to see a stick that hard. It's hard to explain. The stick was a monument in itself and we just stood there smiling in the stick's direction for about fourteen seconds. Then, guess what I started thinking about? I started thinking about my mother. I wondered if she was in our garage missing me and if she had any clue what was happening in Melahatchie.

"Does this feel like *déjà vu* to you?"

Shay sucked on her teeth. "Boy," she said, "Quit trying to switch subjects, talking about *déjà vu*. Naw, this don't feel like *déjà vu*."

Shay started laughing and walked deeper behind some baby sticker bushes. "Come over here."

"For what?"

Time slowed down, I swear it did. When Shay walked her Afro-puffed self over in front of me, the sun coming through the woods hit her face perfectly. She had the color and the shine of a brand new genuine leather football. Shay rarely sweated so the Vaseline all over her face and shoulders never dripped. It just stuck to her and made whatever was surrounding her look pretty dull and blurry.

Shay took the pointing finger of her left hand, and joined it with her thumb, making the symbol that white folks on dumb television commercials used to say that everything is okay. Then she took her middle finger and her index finger of her right hand and pushed them in and out of the hole made by her left-hand fingers.

I wasn't as scared as you probably think I was. I just didn't know what to do. Shay walked over to me and grabbed my hips. "Stand right there and just put your back against the tree."

"I can't," I told her. "My grandma ain't in the mood for me to come back smelling like outside. I ain't lying." Shay just stood in front of me with her hands on her hips.

"Alright, City. Stop talking. Just put your arms behind your back and hold your body off from the tree. Okay?"

It was weird. My fatness wouldn't let me hold myself up like I wanted to. Plus, my lower back and arms started aching, too. All I was thinking about was if Shay was gonna think my belly button was deformed. I had a regular innie-style belly button that she'd never seen, but from what I'd seen, all the kids in Melahatchie had walnut-size belly buttons.

Shay told me to take my pants off but leave my underwear on. I did it and let my pants hang around my ankles.

"What's wrong?" I asked her as she was looking at my stuff.

"Nothing," she said. "Nothing at all. Close your eyes."

Sounded like a weird thing to say to someone, but I did it anyway.

"They closed?" she asked. "Don't be peeking, boy. You a virgin?"

"I ain't no virgin," I told her with my eyes closed and my penis getting harder and harder. "I did it once with this girl named Octavia. We recorded it on her stepdaddy's iPad. But look, I think we should probably get a condom from my Uncle Relle if we really trying to get nice. You feel me? You don't want to be pregnant in high school and I don't even know how child support works if I have a baby mama before I'm technically even allowed to work. Maybe we should think about this."

"I can pay my own bills," I heard Shay say before I heard the sound of a camera phone and...

Swinncrhuunch.

The pain in my testicles moved through my lower body and into my chest and head. I couldn't talk. I was on my hands and knees, just fiending for air. I looked up to see what happened. A blurry Shay had grabbed her broken-off piece of tree and recorded herself hitting me in my naked testicles.

I just crouched over the leaves damn near choking as Shay took pictures of me. She was dying laughing, too.

I got off my knees, grabbed Shay's shoulders, threw her to the pine-needled ground, and jumped on her. Her phone fell out of her hands. I felt crazy being on top of her like that. I mean, I thought about how no one had probably ever had the nerve or the skills to push Shay down like that.

"What the hell is wrong with you?" I asked her. "You can't just go around hitting people in the sack whenever you get ready." I was still all in her eyes. "You know how tender the testicles are? That stuff hurt." I felt goofy saying "testicles" and "tender" to her.

"It's called 'skin-sacks,'" Shay told me. "And it's all one word, with a hyphen."

"Wait." I started laughing. "What? That's the dumbest thing I have heard in a long time. 'Skin-sacks'? Who said it's called 'skin-sacks' with a hyphen?"

"My brother, Alcee. He said it's two sacks and it's covered in skin so it's skin-sacks."

"But the skin is the sack," I told her. "And there ain't two sacks. There's two nuts in one sack."

"My brother said it's called 'skin-sacks' so it's called 'skin-sacks.'"

"Well, first of all," I told her, "Alcee Mayes is my Uncle Relle's weed man and my uncle said he's steady overcharging him for an ounce, so I don't believe nothing Alcee Mayes says."

While I had her down on the ground and was yelling at her, that was the first time I noticed that people have hair under their eyes, you know? Plus, Shay had on that little pea-green muscle shirt, so I could see the little hairs under her arms. I had negative hair under my arms, not even minor hair bumps. I was looking in her big eyes and squeezing on her shoulders softly, and I'll be damned if my penis didn't start getting harder and harder. It made me too embarrassed, so I gave her one more good push in the shoulders and I got off of her.

"My bad, City."

"What?" I asked.

"My bad. I wasn't trying to hurt you. Me and Baize made a bet about who could make a boy do that first. I won't show the pictures to no one but her," she said. "I promise."

"Where you think she went? Baize, I'm talking about. The newspaper said they got a lead in the investigation."

Shay picked up some pine needles and walked toward the road. "The paper don't know shit," she yelled and came back towards me.

"Maybe something else happened to her."

"You met Baize before, City." Shay looked me right in the face. "Whoever took Baize either hurt her or killed her before they took her. Or maybe they knew."

"Knew what?"

"Never mind. You think that girl would let somebody just take her? We would've heard about it."

"Wait," I told her. The craziest thought in the world entered my head. "You think that white man knew whatever it is you're talking about? You think he took her?"

"You mean the one in your grandma's shed? Probably."

"Ain't no white man in my grandma's shed," I told her. She just looked at me with her arms folded.

"Folks say they saw her walk off in these woods one day a few weeks ago with a computer."

"A computer?"

"That laptop computer she always was messing with."

"Did anyone find the computer?"

"The white man in your shed," Shay changed the subject. "Didn't he kick you in your back yesterday, too?"

"Yeah, he did," I told her. "But can we talk more about Baize?"

I was expecting a little more quality heartfelt sharing between us, but Shay walked off toward the bushes again. "Where you going?" I asked.

"Gunn told me that your grandma's preacher, Reverend Cherry, got a carload of pictures of skanks from Waveland doing it."

"So?"

"So, that's where I'm going. He hid the pictures in his beat-up car, the one he always letting Deacon Big Shank drive," Shay said.

I thought for a second about what would be the point of stealing naked pictures that belonged to my grandma's preacher, especially with a girl who had just hit me in my skin-sacks with a stick.

Then it clicked.

If I stole the pictures and showed them to Grandma, there would be no way she'd let me get baptized by a preacher who kept that kind of nastiness in one of his cars.

"Can we take a picture of the pictures in the car with your phone?" I asked her.

"Yeah," she said, and came back from around the bushes. "Don't ask a whole lotta questions, though. You coming or not?"

Shay started texting someone as we walked toward Reverend Cherry's house.

Reverend Cherry lived about three minutes from Grandma's, on the other side of the woods. He lived right next to my friend Gunn.

"Hey, scown," Gunn said to me as we walked in the yard. "What you doing?" Gunn was fourteen, but his voice was a good four or five years deeper than mine. "Heard you went crazy yesterday."

"I did, kinda."

"They say it's on Worldstar and everything. Heard you had fools crying and calling you master."

"Yeah, I guess," I told him. "Sometimes you gotta let fools know, you feel me?"

Shay looked at me and shook her head. She was being strange and quiet but Gunn was steady nodding and chewing on a toothpick. The best thing about Gunn was that even if he heard you did something huge like embarrass yourself on national TV and the internet, he'd focus on the fighting you did instead. He loved saying the word "titties" and he loved anything that had to do with fighting. He'd been telling people he was going to be a professional UFC fighter ever since he was six. It was funny at first, but most folks in Melahatchie would be surprised if he didn't end up fighting for money. He'd beaten almost every boy's ass I knew in Melahatchie. Everybody he beat claimed that they lost 'cause they didn't want to "get close to no real-life faggot."

Gunn's grandma put him in a kung fu class downtown for his twelfth birthday present. Coach Stroud taught that kung fu class for a while until parents complained that he was too touchy. Soon as Coach Stroud quit, Gunn quit too. He said he quit because he wanted to chop people in the throat and throw ninja stars, but the new white teacher from Biloxi wanted folks to stretch their legs in yoga poses and work on soft punches to the solar plexus. Behind Gunn's back, everyone said he quit because his boyfriend, Coach Stroud, didn't want him learning from a new teacher.

Before he quit, though, Coach Stroud gave Gunn one of those white karate suits. And Gunn wore that suit with his own black leather belt at least three times a week during the summer.

"Y'all came to get them titties, scown?" Gunn asked, like he was ready for nakedness. "The car right over here."

We walked about 20 yards down the road and we were right next to the car. Gunn was looking funny, like he was laughing or something.

"What you laughing at, Gunn?" I asked him.

"You know I always be laughing, scown," Gunn said. "Go ahead and get them Waveland titties."

"Y'all ain't coming with me?" I asked them.

"Naw, that's your preacher car, scown," Gunn said. "Plus, it ain't no room for three people up in there."

I went up to the car and looked around to make sure that no one was coming down the road then. "Close the door behind you, scown," I heard Gunn say.

Soon as I got in, I saw a picture hanging out of the glove compartment. Shay didn't tell me that there were pictures in the glove compartment. I figured that if what was under the seat was anything like what I saw in the glove compartment, we were in for the freakiest naked pictures we'd ever seen.

Dangling there was a shiny slick picture with a creased breast down the middle of it. I unfolded it and saw this whole dark breast that was full and hanging. The picture cut the woman off at the neck and the waist but the breast hung just right, midway down her stomach, and the dark part around the nipple—I didn't really know what that part was called—was damn near bigger than my cheeks. It was the first time I'd seen just breasts cut off from a woman's face and even though the breasts were nice, it was wack to just see breasts and no face. But that was the first time I realized that seeing breasts of any kind was like eating pancakes. Even the nastiest pancake in the world was always better than the best stack of toast you could imagine.

Still, I hoped the woman who owned the breasts wanted her head cut off from the picture. If not, it was one of the meanest things I could imagine doing to someone.

"I see titties," I yelled. "Waveland titties ain't no joke."

"Go ahead and bring them Waveland titties out then, scown," Gunn yelled from way across the street. "Check the glove compartment and under all the seats too. Get all the titties you can."

I reached under the seat to see if there were any other pictures under there. There were about five issues of *King* magazine.

"Shay," I yelled and peeked over the dashboard. "Bring me your phone."

"Oh. Shay said she gon' be right back," Gunn yelled from way across the street. "She gone! Go ahead and get all them titties, scown."

"I told you I'm getting the titties, man. Damn," I yelled back. "I don't know why you faking like you love some titties anyway," I said under my breath.

I was about to raise up when I heard a weird noise coming from the glove compartment. I hadn't looked all the way in the compartment, but I hoped there would be at least ten more naked pictures up in there. I stretched out and pulled the compartment open with my right hand. All I saw was a map of Melahatchie. I pushed the map to the side to see what else was in there.

Wasps. Big wasps.

I jumped out the window of the passenger side of the car and the wasps stung me all upside the head.

Gunn was across the street just laughing his ass off, recording it on Shay's cell phone.

I did it for y'all, I thought as I ran home. *I did it all for y'all.*

THAT WORK SHED.

When I made it home, Grandma wasn't there. I was swelling from the stings, but I realized this was my chance to see if that white man was really in the work shed. Grandma kept the key to the shed on her key chain that was on the dresser under her old wigs. The key chain had a million keys on it. Plus, she had this heavy pocket blade connected to her keys. She never let me hold the blade, but you could tell from just looking at it that it could slice many necks if need be.

I took the knife and Grandma's keys and slowly made my way out to the work shed. The shed was covered in off-white vinyl siding and, like Grandma's house, it was raised off the ground by cinder blocks. There were two words written on the shed but they had been scratched out with a black marker. Every kid who ever saw the shed said it looked like the color of a second-grade writing tablet. You couldn't tell how much of the off-white-ness was bought and how much of it came from just being dirty. There were no windows, just four baseball-sized holes in the back, way up at the top. Every Tuesday, from sunup to sundown, my granddaddy used to sweat up a storm in that shed. Tuesdays and Sundays were my granddaddy's only off days. Tuesdays, he'd make tables, chairs, and cabinets out of wood. Sundays, he'd drink until he couldn't see straight enough to use anything he'd made. Grandma took all the saws out of the shed when my granddaddy drowned, but she left all the sawdust, wood chips, and cinder blocks on the floor. I liked to mess around in there, knowing I was walking on the same sawdust my granddaddy walked on.

After my granddaddy drowned, Grandma put a deep freezer in the shed filled with ice cream and animal parts. On the walls were these wooden shelves stocked with jars of pickles, preserves, pigs' feet, and just about anything else Grandma could think of to can. If you ever got hungry, there was always something in that shed to eat, and it was probably going to be something super country like pickled pigs' feet or raccoon. Or ice cream sandwiches.

Two little steps led up to the door of the shed. When I stepped on the second one, I heard some rattling and then four slow thumps. I stepped down from the steps and looked back at Grandma's house. The back door and all the windows were open.

The shed key turned and I was in.

On the floor of the shed, lying in fetal position, was Pot Belly, covered in dried blood, sweat, and sawdust. He smelled like rotten butt hole and piss, too. All he had on were white underwear and mismatching church socks. His legs were chained together from the knee to the ankle and his hands were handcuffed behind him. His hairy back had these softball-sized blue splotches on it.

"Aw, man," I said to myself and closed the door behind me. I could see his back and belly heaving in and out so I knew he wasn't dead. I touched his belly with my index finger and he started scooching away from me.

"Why are you in my granddaddy's shed?" I asked him. "And why is your belly so hard, man?"

He didn't respond, so I kicked him in the back really gently. "I said why is your belly so hard? I'll kick a hole in your kidneys if you don't turn around and answer me."

Quick as a match, the man turned as best he could. His mouth was stuffed with a grimy sky-blue-and-white rag. Pot Belly looked different in the fetal position, with chains wrapped around his legs. He looked a lot smaller, and I don't just mean smaller in size; I mean smaller in everything

I got on my knees and got closer to his face. Up close like that, I saw that his thin lips were long. They reached out further than Grandma's lips and connected with these frown lines that didn't really frown. And his eyebrows looked like some hyper five-year-old girl had gone HAM on him with one of those jumbo red crayons.

Without thinking, I grabbed a few hairs from his eyebrows and yanked as hard as I could. I figured he'd try to scream, but he just looked me right in the eye and started blinking slowly.

"What you do to my grandmother?" I asked him. "She wouldn't have done this to you if you didn't do something to her. You try to kick her in her back and call her a nigger, too?" I started flexing like I wanted to hit him in his mouth. "If I take that out of your mouth, what's gonna happen?" I asked him. "Will you yell?"

He shook his head side to side.

"I thought you were dead," I told him and touched the rag in his mouth. "And I hoped you were." I took my hand off the rag and looked at him. "My name ain't 'nigger,' you know, like you said it was. Nobody's name is 'nigger.' My name is City. Really, it's Citoyen. Folks down here call me City." He still didn't say anything. "But you probably knew that if you saw the contest, which I'm guessing you did since you made all those jokes and kicked me in my back. You know that if you had known my name is City in the first place, you wouldn't be bleeding and stinking up this shed." I took my pointy finger and pushed him right in the middle of his head.

It was so hard to look at his eyes 'cause neither one of them looked like it was looking at me.

He started using his eyes to direct me to his left side.

"What?" I asked. "What you want?"

He kept looking down toward his side. I pushed him over and looked beneath him. "What? Where'd this come from?"

There was a book beneath him with the cover facing down. I picked it up and turned it over. "Is this a joke?" I asked him. "How'd this get in here?" It was *Long Division*. "Is this my book? Or are there two copies?"

He looked at me and nodded his head up and down.

"Something about this ain't right," I said to him, and myself. I thumbed through the book to see if it was the same one I was reading in Grandma's house. "You know where Baize Shephard is?"

He shook his head side to side, then rested it back on the sawdust.

I sat a few feet from Pot Belly and decided I'd read a few chapters of *Long Division* before I left. It seemed like the right thing to do.

...

Quarter Black...

After Mama Lara disappeared down the road for her morning walk, I went back and brought my new computer and book out onto the porch. I knew Mama Lara would know I'd stolen the computer if she saw it, and she'd think *Long Division* was something kids shouldn't be reading since the word "nigga" was on the very first page. As cool as the book was, it still wasn't as cool as the computer, and I wanted everybody who walked or rode down Old Ryle Road to see that I had something they could never have.

I'd been typing on the computer and waiting on the porch for Shalaya Crump for 30 minutes when I saw a person out of the corner of my eye. I turned my head toward the Night Time Woods and saw the person jump back into the woods. I was never scared of those woods, or of the Shephard Witch, to tell you the truth. I kinda didn't believe in witches or magic. I figured it was just Shalaya Crump trying to play me for a fool.

When I got all the way into the woods, it felt like one of those dark dreams where you watch yourself get eaten by a bucktooth ghoul before waking up. I pulled my sweat rag out the small of my back, closed the laptop computer, threw the book on the ground, and got ready to pop a bucktooth ghoul in the forehead if one stepped to me.

Anyway, as soon as I took about three steps into the woods, I had to pee. One of the best things about coming down to Mela-hatchie for spring break was that I got to pee outside. I found a dusty area near the Shephard house where I could try to spell my name.

"Hey, boy," I heard a deep froggy voice say from behind me. "What you got in your hands?" The voice sounded like it was coming from behind a box fan. I didn't even plan on turning around, but I did just to see the face that was carrying a voice like that.

The only white boy I'd ever seen with a fro was this old dude on PBS who made you fall asleep and dream about floating while he painted the finest in bushes and clouds. But this white boy had the same kind of fro. He wore a puffy blood-red sweatshirt with bleach stains on it and "Fresh" across the front in green letters. The sweatshirt was way too big for him but he had it tucked in these nice sky-blue pants that were a mix of jeans and slacks.

I angled myself so he wouldn't see my privacy while I was crossing the T in my name.

"Ain't trying to see your johnson," the boy said. "Relax." I shot my eyes down to his feet and these glowing green fat laces in his All Stars. "What you looking at?" he asked me. "You some kind of queer? If you are, you are. Just like to know what kind of man I'm talking to."

"Naw, man," I told him. "Um, I like booties. I like girl booties."

"Boobies?"

"Naw. Booties," I told him. "I like booties. Big ol' girl booties, and boobies too, I guess. But mainly booties. You wouldn't know nothing about that."

"You like big ol' girl booties?" He knelt down, tried to stop himself from laughing and brushed his shoes off. "Where you from, buddy?"

"Chicago, man. I'm down here for spring break because folks stay shooting folks too much in Chicago. I'm in a gang, though." I was so nervous and being so raggedy with my lies and I had no idea why. "What about you, with that fro? White boys ain't supposed to have fros like that.

"Ain't white. From a little bit of everywhere, though," the boulderhead boy said. He started coughing and eyeing my laptop computer. "Where'd you get that contraption in your grip anyway?" He wiped his mouth.

The white boy's bottom teeth were so crooked that they zigzagged, and he had the chappiest top lip I'd ever seen in my life. It looked like frozen vanilla frosting was just sleeping on that thing. And his nose was closer to his top lip than it should have been, so it looked like he was constantly smelling his own chappy frosting. The skin on his face was so Saran Wrap tight, too, that the head and jaw bones damn near burst right through his skin. And I hate to gross you out, but there were a few scabbed-up scars on the top-right side of his face that jutted out like raisins. To tell you the truth, I kinda wished I had some scabs like that on my face so I could pick them off before I went to bed.

"This is a laptop computer," I told him. "What's your name?"

"Evan," he told me. "That's what they tell me."

"They? What's your last name?"

"Altshuler. What's the date?"

"Like aw shucks?" I asked him. "Man, your name, it don't make a lick of sense. It's 1985. March. You from the future? 2013?"

"Naw, I ain't from no future." He pointed past the Shephard house, toward Belhaven Street. "I'm Jewish."

Evan's eyes opened up big after he said that, like he expected me to say something mean. I was kinda surprised, because I never met a person who said they were Jewish before, and to tell you the truth, I didn't have a clue what it really meant. Since we moved to Chicago from Jackson last year, I heard the word a lot more, but people used the shorter version, "Jew," and sometimes it was a noun and sometimes it was a verb. In elementary school, I heard about Adolf Hitler torturing Jewish people and how some of them got hanged and drowned in Mississippi back in the 1960s trying to help black folks get the right to vote, read, and pee in the same bathroom as white folks, but that was it. I just didn't know what to do with this boy saying he was Jewish when he just looked like any slightly deformed white boy to me.

"Can I ask you a question?" I tried to change subjects and come back with a question that might make him stop looking at me so hard. "Is it okay if I ask you why you look so sick? And not even just sick. I'm saying you look crazy dusty. How old are you?"

He looked at the ground and mumbled, "Fifteen. Just told you that I ain't white."

"My name is Voltron," I told him. "Folks call me T-Ron."

"No it ain't," he said. "Citoyen is the name they give you. Folks call you City."

"What did you just say?" I asked him.

"I know who you are," he said and stepped closer to me. "Your name is Citoyen Coldson. You was born in Jackson and moved to Chicago two years ago. Your mama dropped you off at your Ma-Maw's house yesterday. And you lost your granddaddy, your Ma-

Maw's husband, in these woods. Right over yonder." He pointed toward the Shephard house.

"I gotta go, man," I told him. "Don't take it the wrong way. It's not that you're Jewish. It's just that I don't like the look in your eyes. You can understand that, right?"

"You need my help, City," the boy said. "Let me show you something."

"What?"

"The past."

"The past what?"

"I need to show you the past," he said. "Listen to me. We can change it."

I couldn't figure out how Jewish Evan Altshuler knew anything about my mama, my Mama Lara, or my granddaddy disappearing. It was something that only the truly craziest of white characters on a crazy show like *Fantasy Island* would say. Shalaya Crump always said that truly-crazy-white-folks talk always came before truly-crazy-white-folks action. And Mama, Mama Lara, and Shalaya Crump always told me that if you popped someone in head who was white and crazy, you could go to jail for life. So I had to be careful with this dusty white boy.

"Oh really," I said. "The past, huh? I hear that. That's nice to hear. So nice. And um, I want you to show me that past, but I'm finna go home first and eat me a bologna sandwich. You want me to bring you one?"

I started walking backwards toward Old Ryle Road, but Evan walked toward me. "I'm serious, City. You need to see this. We can stop it. Come back with me. That house," he pointed to the Shephard house. "It used to be a Freedom School. You know what a Freedom School is?"

"Yeah," I lied, "I know. It's a school where they teach freedom."

"They burned that school down to the ground with our families in it. Yours and mine. They took their bodies over to the—"

"So," I interrupted him, "you want some Sandwich Spread and mustard on your bologna sandwich, right?" And with that, I turned toward the road and sprinted like Carl Lewis until I was all the way out of the Night Time Woods, away from the craziest white boy I'd ever seen in my life, and back on the porch of my Mama Lara's house.

I wasn't on the porch longer than two minutes, wondering how much of what Jewish Evan Altshuler said was true, before Shalaya Crump opened the door to her trailer. She had an unwrapped package of saltines in one hand and a cold drank in the other.

Shalaya Crump walked to the middle of Old Ryle Road and stood across from my porch sipping on cold drank. I thought she'd come over to my porch immediately. Instead, she took a big gulp of cold drank, gobbled up three saltines at once, then walked down the road and hopped in the woods.

I figured Shalaya Crump was gonna go in the woods and wait five minutes for me to follow her. When she saw that I didn't come after her, she'd shamefully walk up to my porch and we'd talk about my new laptop computer, my new book, and how she was jealous of the girl with the greasy forehead. Or, I figured she'd come out screaming after seeing Jewish Evan Altshuler's ugly face.

I waited and waited and waited for her to come back to my porch. After 20 minutes, I don't know why, but I was sure that Shalaya Crump was never coming back out of those woods.

I stood up and got ready to go find Shalaya Crump when the worst thought in the history of thoughts just smacked me in the back of the head: *What if Jewish Evan Altshuler and Shalaya Crump travel through time together like superheroes and have lots of babies the color of cheap graham crackers?*

That thought stretched out for two minutes and some seconds until I remembered that I'd never ever heard Shalaya Crump say anything sexy about white boys in the seven years I knew her. Even when this one white boy named Parker Vincent who looked like a pudgy Michael J. Fox moved to Melahatchie from Memphis and all the other girls said they'd never mess with a white boy but if they did, they'd mess with Parker Vincent, Shalaya Crump told me, "I wouldn't mess with Parker Vincent or any white boy on earth, not even if I was white and white boys were the only boys left on earth. I'm serious. I'd start liking girls before I did that."

I walked back in the woods 20 minutes later with my computer and *Long Division* to find Shalaya Crump sitting on the ground with her legs crossed. She and Jewish Evan Altshuler were messing around with that calculator-looking thing I'd stolen from Baize.

"That's a phone," Shalaya Crump told me as she started pushing more buttons. "I figured it out last night but I can't get no reception." She put it up to her ear and kept saying "hello," but no one answered. "I know it's a phone," she said to both of us like we all knew each other.

"That ain't all that cool," I told her.

"Better than it is now," she said. "I'm tired of sneaking to use the phone all the time. You know how big of a deal it is if you have your own phone in your room? Imagine if you had your own phone that you could take with you everywhere you went. I wonder if you gotta pay for long distance with it?"

"Hell yeah! Why wouldn't you? And who you talking to on the phone long distance anyway, other than me?" I asked her. "I thought—"

Jewish Evan Altshuler interrupted my question and started talking to Shalaya Crump about something called a "bell boy" and "area-to-area calling." Shalaya Crump tried to explain to the white boy what the buttons were for on a phone, because he'd only used the slow-mo rotary kind. No matter how hard she tried, she couldn't make him understand how long distance, beepers, buttons, and answering machines worked.

"Show it to me one more time if you don't mind," he said. "Just the part about how you can tell someone you ain't home when you ain't home. They can leave a message that you can hear on your phone?"

I would've been laughing at Jewish Evan Altshuler's dumb ass, but I wasn't thinking about him being a country white moron from the 1960s. I was thinking of how I had never seen Shalaya Crump sit like she was sitting. She was leaning back on her hands and when she wasn't talking about phones, she was just listening to him. Kneeling right next to her on one knee was that sick-looking Evan. I couldn't figure out how they ended up in that position, with him kneeling and her sitting, in only 30 minutes.

"I reckon I need to see the answering machine working to understand it," he told Shalaya Crump. "But listen, we can save all three of the folks I told you about. Just gonna need your help for just one day. Y'all can make it back before the sun goes down." As I walked closer to them with my computer in my arms, Jewish Evan Altshuler looked up at me. "We need you too, City," Evan said.

"You know that hole we went in yesterday?" Shalaya Crump asked me. "It's not just a time tunnel to the future, City. He thinks—"

"My name's Evan," he interrupted.

"Evan thinks there's one in 1985, and that there's one we went to in 2013, and there's one that we ain't even seen to 1964." Shalaya Crump looked over at Jewish Evan Altshuler. "He said he's been there already. That's where he's from."

"This white boy is lying to you," I told her.

I was getting tired of Jewish Evan Altshuler. It messed with me that he knew my name and that my granddaddy disappeared in those woods, but that I didn't know nothing about his life. That's not even what messed with me most, though. When I looked in Evan's face and eyes, I couldn't see fifteen years old. His face was timeless in a terrible way. It looked like a face in a book that I would never read.

When I looked at Shalaya Crump's face and eyes, I could see how I thought she looked during every year of her life. I swear that I could look at Shalaya Crump and see her as a four-year-old girl straight running all the kids in Head Start. And thinking about it right there, and watching her, I understood that it was Shalaya Crump's eyes that showed me her age more than the face. Sometimes, Shalaya Crump's eyes stayed big as dirty silver dollars and they didn't blink for minutes. When they finally blinked, you would think you were in a tiny bathtub with a ton of hummingbirds 'cause they blinked so fast. Other times, Shalaya Crump's eyes looked right at me, blinked slow, and made me feel like I was jumping off of a space mountain onto a trampoline of clouds drawn by the baddest artist in the world. It's hard to explain, but I swear a lot of it had something to do with Shalaya Crump's eyes and how slow and fast they blinked at the same time.

If I could see all that in Shalaya Crump's eyes, you'd think it would be pretty easy to see something like that in Jewish Evan Altshuler's eyes, too. But this dude's eyes were so tired, so droopy, and so blue that it was hard for me to believe that he was fifteen *ever*. I mean, he looked thirteen or maybe even ten in the body, but his face looked like it had died a long, long time ago. Jewish Evan Altshuler looked like he had spent all of his years getting punched in the eyes by bucktooth ghouls with the boniest fists you'd ever seen in your life.

And I just couldn't figure out how a white boy who looked like that could get the attention of someone as magical as Shalaya Crump.

"Ain't lying," Jewish Evan Altshuler said. "And I ain't white. I told you, I'm Jewish. I'm a Jew. Born right here in Melahatchie in 1948. My Uncle Zachariah and his family live right next to us." He looked at me. "You from Chicago, you said. My cousins go to temple every now and again 'round over at Beth Israel on the West Side. You know where that is?"

"Can you hold on?" Shalaya Crump asked him. "That would make you 36 years old?"

"Fifteen years old. Be sixteen next month," he said.

Jewish Evan kept talking. He explained that in 1964, his family was one of a few Jewish families from the area who wanted black folks to have the right to vote and go to schools with decent books. He claimed that our granddaddies and his uncle and brother didn't just disappear. He said that all four of them were run up on in a Freedom School, and they were hanged and burned by "people acting like they were the Klan."

"Wait," I said. "What do you mean by 'acting like' they were in the Klan?"

"Folks who got them were dressed like they were in the Klan, but it wasn't really the Klan," he said.

"Why?" Shalaya Crump asked him.

"I don't mean no disrespect. It's just that in my life, I seen clear as day that there ain't really no 'why' when you dealing with the Ku Klux Klan," he said.

"Yeah, but you just said we ain't really dealing with the Klan," she said.

"Get your lies straight, man," I told him. "You said we were dealing with folks who dressed up like the Klan."

"What I know is—"

Shalaya Crump interrupted him again. "There's always a 'why,' Evan, and what you saying don't make no sense at all."

"Exactly. I know it sounds crazy as a four-eyed dog," he said. "It hasn't happened yet. But it's supposed to happen tomorrow."

I just stood there waiting and wondering if there was more to his crazy story. "Okay," I said, "but I still don't get why we should go back and risk our lives to save folks who we think are dead anyway." I looked over at Shalaya Crump. "What you thinking?"

"I'm thinking that I don't wanna wake up in the future and wish we would have done it."

"But do you want to do it?"

"I mean, City, we'd want someone to come save us today if we knew we were gonna be dead tomorrow. Shoot, that's a fact, right?"

"But would they?" I asked her. "Would your grandma even do that for you if some white boy who called her a 'Negro' was the one telling her to do it?" Shalaya Crump was looking all in my eyes and

I was so focused on what I saying that I couldn't even try to spit game front of her. "We don't know nothing about them old dudes, and nothing about no Freedom Schools and nothing about no Klan. All we know is the Klan ain't nothing to mess with. You told me that!"

"It's not the real Klan," Evan said.

"Does it matter if they kill black folks the same way the real Klan does?" Shalaya Crump asked him.

"The Klan killed Jews, too."

We waited for Evan to say more, but he just held his mouth open, kept both hands on his hips, and kept swallowing his own spit. I grabbed Shalaya Crump by the hand. "Shalaya Crump, we lived our whole life this far with no granddaddies. Think about it. I don't know if we somehow got stuck in a dumb book or movie. Right now, I feel like we supposed to say, 'Golly, let's go save the grandfathers we never knew.' But like you always say, life ain't no book. This is real life. In real life, do we really need our granddaddies?"

Shalaya Crump laughed and actually looked at me like she thought I had a point. Then she looked over at Evan and flicked her gum at his feet and started doing these weird toe-raises. "City's right," she said. "We don't know a thing about having granddaddies. Even if we did, I mean, what happens if we change our future by changing the past? It's impossible to not change the future if you change the past, right? More would change than just us having granddaddies."

Shalaya Crump was always taking the best thing you ever said and then adding something even better to it to make the best thing you ever said sound pretty lame. I understood what she was saying. Even if we saved our granddaddies and Evan's folks, what if it changed everything and we ended up not being born?

"Listen," Evan said, "you're both right, but I know the future."

"So what!" we both said. "We do too."

"Then you know that the future has to be changed? Look," he looked at Shalaya Crump. "I know what happens to both of you."

"You do?" Shalaya Crump jumped in.

"He's lying, 'Laya." It was the first time I had ever shortened her name to 'Laya. "How can this goofy white boy know what happens to us or even know the future if he can't even understand how an answering machine works?"

Jewish Evan Altshuler ignored my question and got right in her face. She kinda backed up. "I promise if you come back and help me, I'll tell you what happens to you in the future. Not only that, I can change what happens to you. I know what happens to your parents in the past, too."

"You lying?" Shalaya Crump asked him.

Jewish Evan Altshuler cut his eyes to me, before focusing on Shalaya Crump. "Ain't much to look at. I know that. Can you listen to me?" He actually grabbed Shalaya Crump's pinky. "I know so much more than you think I do. I give you my word, Shalayer Crump. Both of you."

"Oh God," Shalaya Crump said and took her pinky back, "Just promise. Don't say you 'give your word.' That's so Ronald Reagan."

"Hell yeah," I said and fake laughed. "And it's Shalaya, not Shalayer."

I wanted to fight Jewish Evan Altshuler so bad right there, but I could tell by the way Shalaya Crump's eyes didn't blink and by the way she was looking at his crusty lip and feeling sorry for it that we were headed to 1964. Shalaya Crump was gonna go back whether I went or not. That was a given as soon as the dude said he could help her find her parents in the past and find herself in the future. And if I didn't go, I was pretty much admitting that it was okay for her and Jewish Evan Altshuler to start loving each other til the end of time. You think I'm crazy, right? Well, I know that you can't travel through time with a girl and save folks from the Klan and not kiss them unless you're slightly deformed or unless you smell like death. And even then, there's still gonna be some serious grinding going on. *Serious* grinding.

Shalaya Crump got in the hole first. Jewish Evan Altshuler followed her. I followed him. Before I closed the door, I looked around at the woods and zeroed in on the Shephard house. "Wait." I said. "Who is that?"

I wanted to tell Shalaya Crump that there was a dark outline of someone watching us from the Shephard house window, but she wouldn't have believed me, since she knew I was the only one of us three that didn't want to go to 1964.

"Never mind," I said. "Don't worry about it." I lowered myself under the ground with the laptop computer in my left hand and *Long Division* in my right hand, and closed my eyes. Then I pulled the door down on all three of us.

When we pushed open the door to 1964, the air was thin and you couldn't even see Old Ryle Road because everything was so thick and green. Right in front of us, where the Shephard house used to be, was a building that was only half painted yellow. Evan told Shalaya Crump that we were looking at a Freedom School.

"Should we go over there?" Shalaya Crump asked him. "What's the plan?"

"I reckon our plan is to make sure the Klan in Melahatchie don't ever kill again," Jewish Evan Altshuler said. "I can get us some rifles."

I looked at Shalaya Crump. "I told you that this white boy is crazy and he gonna get us killed. Didn't I tell you? You see how he changed up his whole style now that he got us where he want us?"

"Wait," Shalaya Crump said. "Hold up. Why didn't you say something about killing white folks before you got us here?"

"I didn't think of it until now."

"White folks are the sneakiest people on earth," Shalaya Crump said in a whispery voice, but loud enough so Evan could hear.

"I'm not white."

"So you're sneaky because you're Jewish, then?"

Jewish Evan Altshuler just started huffing and puffing before finally saying, "Thought you were different, Shalayer Crump."

"Different than what? And don't say my name if you can't say it right."

"Different than anti-semitic," he said.

"Anti-septic?" I asked.

"Anti-semitic. Your li'l girlfriend right here hates her some Jews."

"I'm too big to be any boy's little girlfriend. That's the first thing," Shalaya Crump said. "I'm a black woman."

"Top to bottom," I said. "Top to bottom."

"You're a 15-year-old girl," Evan told her. "Ain't no woman. Trying to tell me that I'm white when I know I'm Jewish, ain't you? Reckon I can tell you you're a girl when you think you're a woman."

Jewish Evan Altshuler kinda had a point there, but I couldn't agree with him.

"All I did was ask you if you were sneaky because you're Jewish," Shalaya Crump told him. "Anyway, a question can't be wrong, especially if I ask it."

"Is your head on right?" Evan asked. "That's 'bout the dumbest thing I ever heard. Y'all don't know nothing about Jews, do you?"

I expected Shalaya Crump to give him an A+ speech about Jewish people, since she always seemed like she knew at least a little bit about everything. But she didn't say a word.

"Evan," I told him. "You ain't gotta get so sensitive, homeboy. There's more stuff to talk about than 'Jewish' stuff." I looked at Shalaya Crump to see if that's what she wanted me to say. "Right? It's shade tree to bring us here and expect us to take out white folks for you. It just is. You know what would happen to us if we killed white folks?"

"Exactly," she said.

Evan closed his eyes for damn near fifteen seconds and shook his head side to side. That was the first thing he'd done since we'd been together that really made him seem a lot older than us. "First of all, you got some colored Jews out there, too. Y'all know what these white folks do to Jews, no matter our color, if they find us out over 'cross Highway 49 after dark?" he asked.

Shalaya Crump and I were quiet.

"They slaughter us," he said. "Y'all don't know a gotdamn thing."

"Wait. What did y'all do to get slaughtered?" Shalaya Crump asked him. "And who slaughtered y'all? Ain't the word 'slaughtered' kinda so Chicken Plant?"

"Six million of us. And one million children. That's not so Chicken Plant. That's exactly what happened to my people, Shalaya."

"But what else?" she asked him. "Why would white people slaughter other white people for no reason if there was colored folks around for them to slaughter?"

"Why you saying 'colored' now like him?" I asked her. "You know we don't talk like that."

"Because I don't just mean black. I'm saying that if there was black people and Indian people and Chinese people and Mexican people around to slaughter, why would white people pick other white people?"

"Yeah, fool, obviously it's more than being Jewish," I told him. "You claim Jewish, right? And look at you. You ain't slaughtered."

"City, you're really 'bout the most ignorant bastard I ever met."

I stepped to him then, but Shalaya Crump grabbed me. "Step out that hole and let me show you how ignorant I can get," I told him. "I know Jews are white. How about that?"

"If we was just white, how come..."

"I don't know," I interrupted. "I don't know what you were gonna say and I don't know why white folks do half of what y'all do. All we know is that whether you Jewish or not, y'all get off for whatever y'all do to us." I looked at Shalaya Crump, who looked really proud of me. "That's all we know. Shit."

"I'm trying to tell y'all best I can that y'all are wrong," he said. "Once they know who we are, we never get off. They killed six million of us and they're killing us now over here if we don't act right."

"But that's the point," Shalaya Crump said. "We ain't white like you. You can be Jewish and white or you can just be Jewish or you can just be white. Either way, you said it yourself. You gotta not act right to get killed. What do we have to do?"

"I'm not acting right now," he said. "That's all I'm saying."

"No matter what, we can't be killing no white folks," I told him. "That's all *I'm* saying. This is the stupidest conversation I ever heard of. I don't even know why we talking to you."

"Y'all are sorry as hell," Evan said and looked at both of us. "I'm trying to help you."

"That's something else I don't understand," Shalaya Crump said to him. "If six million of your people got slaughtered and you know how time works, why not go back and help them?"

"If I could, I would, Shalaya." I really hated hearing him say her name. "I can go travel to three places, the same three as you can. Somebody out there can travel back and help my people, though. Just not me. Or maybe they already did. Maybe it woulda been worse."

I looked back and saw Shalaya Crump looking right in Evan's face again. I figured she was going to say something sweet to him after that heartfelt end of his speech. "You were so right, City," she said in the most calm, loving, and empty voice I'd ever heard her use. "This is a waste of time. Let's just go home."

After a while, as much as I wanted to hear Shalaya Crump slap the nasty taste out of Evan's mouth, I started to get lightweight bored. They kept going back and forth even though Shalaya Crump said it was time to go. You can only listen to people call each other sorry and anti-septic for so long before it makes you wanna cut your ears off.

I hopped all the way out of the hole and started walking toward Old Ryle Road with my laptop computer under my arm and *Long Division* in my hand. It was weird, because even before you really completely saw Old Ryle Road, you could tell that it wasn't a road. It was all dirt and rocks and it was a lot thinner than the road in 1985.

When I reached the edge of the woods, I peeked through at what should have been my grandmother's house. The house wasn't there. In its place was a little country-looking store with two cold drank machines and a gas pump. The store had these red letters taped on the door that spelled "The County Co-op."

"City," I heard Shalaya Crump say behind me, "don't say nothing to no one out there. This ain't how I wanted to change the future. When you come back, we're going back home."

I ignored Shalaya Crump and stepped all the way into the road. Down the road, all those clean and organized houses and yards made me think of how the future wasn't gonna do them too many favors. There were probably half the houses and trailers that were there in 1984. Mama Lara's house was gone but Shalaya Crump's trailer was still there.

I knew it wasn't the right thing to do, but I went across the street to the Co-op to ask people if they'd heard of the Coldsons. If our house wasn't there, I just wanted to know where we lived. Plus, I had my own plan.

Evan was stupid to think that we had to kill people. I know I wasn't supposed to talk to anyone, but my plan was basic. It was to convince my granddaddy to watch out for the Klan if I got a chance.

That's it.

It was that simple. Either my granddaddy would believe me or he wouldn't, but at least he'd know. All my time coming up with plans in my *GAME* book helped me know how to get from point A to point B with the least amout of stress.

While I was peeking in the dusty window of that Co-op, a sorry-sounding "meow" scared the mess outta me. I looked around and there was this skinny black cat with a fat head looking right at me. It had a thick collar around its neck with the words "Red Naval." You know what's crazy? I had never ever seen a cat in Melahatchie in my entire life. Never. And I never thought anything about it. There were more limping Dobermans than there were people, but you never saw a cat.

Anyway, the cat came closer to me and just kept meowing. "I ain't got no food for you. Is your name 'Red Naval' or is that like the name of your owner? What?"

Meowwww

The cat came closer and I backed up.

Meooowww

I put the computer down facing the cat. The cat just walked right around the computer and got even closer to me.

Meeooow

"Oh, you talking noise? Don't be mad because you don't understand how to use it." As I was talking, the cat walked off toward the side of the building. Before it turned the corner it meowed louder.

I looked toward the woods and into the Co-op, then walked toward the edge of the building, following the cat. I turned the corner of the Co-op and didn't see the cat anymore. But there were two doors on the side of the Co-op. The first door was closed and it said "WHITES ONLY—KEY IN FRONT." Scratched under the word "front" was the sentence "Nigger-loving Jews ain't wanted here." I tried to open it but it was locked. The second door, which was cracked opened, said "COLORED." I walked toward the door and was about to poke my head in when the cat came out and meowed again.

"I wish somebody would try and tell me I couldn't do number two in that white bathroom," I told the cat. "I don't play that."

Meoow

"I'm serious. If that white folks' bathroom was open, I swear to God I'd go in there and get to dookying right in that sink."

Meoow

"I don't care if it is a white folks' sink. I would be smearing dookie all on the mirror and everything! I ain't from here. I'm from 1985. I don't play that mess."

I stood there waiting for the cat to meow again, but it didn't. It just stood there looking at me. I realized when I stopped talking all big and bad that a heavy whiff of sad like I'd never felt before was getting closer and closer to my neck. Reading about my family and other black folks not being able to pee in a good bathroom was different than seeing a white folks' bathroom locked and a colored bathroom just open for anything that wanted to come in. It said "colored" on the door, but it might as well have said cats, spiders, possums, coons, and roaches, 'cause it was open to them just like it was open to us.

The cat took me all the way to back of the Co-op, where there was this rusty clothesline with white sheets hanging on it. Right there in the middle was this one scraggly Doberman doing the do to this other fatter Doberman. They weren't making no barks or no moans. They were just doing it like they were the last dogs on Earth.

The cat walked up about a foot from the Dobermans and sat on its hind legs. Then it started looking back and forth at the Dobermans and me. I can't really blame the cat. I'd seen dogs doing it before, but this was different. I would have bet my new computer and book that they wouldn't be doing it like that if they were doing it with any other dogs. You never think of dogs being in love, but those dogs were. They really were.

While I was watching those dogs, as crazy as it sounds, my body started to feel like I was watching *Porky's*. The Dobermans weren't even that cute as far as dogs go either.

I didn't like how the dogs were making me feel, so I started stomping and yelling, but they kept doing it like no one was screaming. All around the back of the Co-op were these little jagged gray rocks. They were too little to really throw far or hard, but they were good enough to hit a dog in the head if you threw a handful of them.

I cocked my arm back and dotted the heads of those Dobermans with gray rocks. The scraggly top Doberman got off the bottom Doberman real slow and they both just looked at me, along with the cat. And I swear the cat licked its paws and actually said in the most smooth voice I'd ever heard in my life, "Wow. You a real fat asshole for that right there. You don't know better than to throw rocks at love?"

"You talk?" I asked the cat. Right then, I wondered if everything I'd experienced in the last day and a half was a dream, or if somehow, some way, I'd gotten trapped in someone else's story.

"Don't even worry about what I do," the cat said. "You should probably get your fat ass to running, though."

I slowly turned the corner and headed back toward the woods to find Shalaya Crump and Jewish Evan Altshuler. When I looked over my shoulder, all three beasts were sprinting at me, led by the cat, whose head looked less fat when he was sprinting.

I took off.

They were getting closer, but I jumped the ditch and landed in the woods. Even though I scratched up my face, my legs, and the computer, I didn't even care. When I got closer to the hole, I wanted to tell Shalaya Crump about the Dobermans and the talking Red Naval cat and the colored bathroom. The closer I got, though, I didn't hear Shalaya Crump and Evan arguing at all. I figured I'd look in the hole and they'd be right there, wrestling or playing Mercy or Thump in a way that would make me wanna throw up.

I walked all the way up to the hole and peeked down in it. *Damn. Damn. Damn.*

I was in 1964 all by myself.

COMMON TO MAN.

On Sunday morning, Grandma and I got in the Bonneville and headed to Concord Baptist Church at a little past eleven in the morning.

Nothing made sense.

I had found out that there were actually two *Long Division* books, the one I kept in the house and the one I decided to leave in the work shed with Pot Belly. But the existence of at least two books was less confusing than the words in the books.

Maybe the book wasn't a book at all, I thought. Maybe the book was the truth. If it was the truth, I had to figure out what it had to do with me. And if Baize wasn't actually missing, but maybe just time traveling, that meant that Pot Belly hadn't really hurt her at all.

"City," Grandma interrupted my thoughts while turning down the radio, "when you get saved, act like you got some sense. You hear me? Whole lotta folks get saved and it take them an entire life before they start living by God's word. That's them ol' deathbed conversioners, them ol' heathens trying to get to heaven a lifetime too late."

I told Grandma that the car smelled like something died in the backseat and asked her who she was talking about. She ignored the comment about the smell and said that she wasn't talking about anyone in particular.

When we made it to the dirt parking lot of Concord Baptist Church, the Bonneville stopped and Grandma swiveled her neck toward me. With her eyes a-twitching and mouth a-moving, almost in slow motion, Grandma said, "Okay now, City. It's 11:45. We still got time to send you up for altar call. Don't act a fool up in here."

Grandma and I walked into this little heated waiting area before you walked all the way into the church. We held hands. "Your hand's wet as a wash rag, City," she said. "Don't be scared."

"I'm not scared," I told her.

Believe it or not, I wasn't lying. I stood there looking through the window at the congregation. Scared was in my mind, but it was way in the back closet. In the front of it was this excited feeling of walking into church and having all those folks treat me like the celebrity I was. Right beneath that feeling was another kind of wonder. I didn't wonder about what was going to happen as much as I wondered about what the white Jesus above the pulpit was thinking.

I wasn't sure if the white Jesus who my grandma had been praying to all this time was the same one above the pulpit, but even if he wasn't, I still wondered what he thought about Concord. I wondered if white Jesus felt jealous about the way the men marched in like penguins, sweaty thighs and armpits wrapped in these black suits shining like armor. Even better were the girls who had their dresses dipping and diving like new fluorescent kites.

Deacon Big Shank, the dude in charge of all the ushers, opened the door to the sanctuary. He always kept one arm behind his back. He one-arm hugged Grandma and shook my hand. Deacon Shank whispered, "We seen you on TV the other night, Little Citizen."

He couldn't pronounce my real name so he called me "Little Citizen." He had called me that ever since I was like seven years old. "Your grand-daddy smiling, son."

I stood in the back looking around the church feeling crazy lost. Uncle Relle was already in the church, filming it all on one of his cell phones. Part of me was still lost in thoughts of Pot Belly while another part of me was lost in the way Mama Troll was playing that organ when a little chirpy black bird flew right past my face.

It looked like there was a whole family of chirpy black birds in a nest up in the top of the church. They'd take turns swooping down during the service. It was cool because they never pecked or shitted on anyone's head or clothes. They just swooped and chirped throughout the whole service. The only time those birds would stop and chill was when Lily Mae did that Holy Spirit Shake or near the end of Cherry's sermon when Troll brought back that damp funk on the organ.

Reverend Cherry stood up and said, "Thank ya, choir." Reverend Cherry paused and looked at the congregation and said, "We are blessed." Then he breathed all heavy in the microphone, like he was about to stop breathing.

Reverend Cherry's whole style was thick cane syrup mixed with light-ning and lard. It really was. He had that sleepy, slow, dripping voice. Sounded like burning Bubble Wrap was up in his throat. His voice matched his sleepy left eye. You know how people with one sleepy eye look stupid, but smooth and in control at the same time, especially when they blink? That's how Cherry's left eye and voice were. Both looked and sounded real different and stupid at first, but you never felt sorry for him, and after hearing and seeing his face a lot of times, you wanted to have a voice and a sleepy eye like his.

His voice wasn't all slow so that you thought his bread wasn't done. It was slow on purpose, the slow where he was always in control of the next word that oozed out of his mouth. The thing that really made Cherry so special, and so damn strange, was that the old joker never said "uhhmm" or "uhh" or "I mean" or anything like that. Never. Not even when he was sweating and grabbing his sacks and spitting on folk and doing the death-breaths during his sermon.

I was sitting there fanning Grandma when Reverend Cherry made eye contact with me.

"Sister Coldson, could you send your grandbaby, City, up here to read the gospels for the church? Everybody in here already knows that City let them folks get him into a *niggardly* predicament a few days ago." The congregation clapped and amen'ed. "When you seen the video, didn't it remind you how we been missing him at Sunday school? Didn't it, church?"

Cherry tucked his chins into his neck, held the Bible under his arm like a football, and inched toward me. He didn't blink one time and he didn't look at anyone in the whole church but me. I tried looking down but Grandma elbowed me in my rib cage.

I damn sure didn't want to, but I stepped to the cone-looking microphone and read anyway.

The congregation wasn't smiling like I wished they would've, so I kept reading. "*No temptation has overtaken you except such as is common to man;* —" I never really knew how you were supposed to pause at those semicolons. I always thought I read through them too fast, but Mama wasn't there to correct me so it was okay. "— *but God is faithful, who will not allow you to be tempted beyond what you are able, but with the temptation will also make the way of escape, that you may be able to hear it.*"

Cherry took the Bible from me and closed it. Then, even though he was talking to me, he walked over by the microphone, looked at the congregation again, and said all slow, "Thank you, City."

I hated when people said thank you just so people other than the person being thanked could hear it. I stood there beside Cherry. He had his paw on my shoulder. I looked at Grandma. She was looking so proud.

"Awright. Amen. Little City'll be entering God's army soon, ain't you?" I just looked at him. Didn't nod or nothing. "Thank you, City. Go ahead and sit your smart self down." He pushed me in my back.

"I hope y'all listen to what City just read," Cherry said. "The Lord say that you ain't run up on no temptation no different from nobody else. Listen to what he sayeth. He sayeth it's a million different folks in this world. Black. White. Oriental. Indian. Jews. Womens. Mexican. Whatever. Mens. Gay Fruities. Whatever you is, you got the same temptations as the next man and as all men that done come before you. But ain't but one way to escape them temptation, is it?"

Everybody started saying "Yeah" and "Only one way, chile."

Cherry kept going. I was into it, I think, because I had read it. "And the same voice, that Lord's voice, makes the escape possible if you, what?"

Silence. Pews started squeaking and wrists were popping from all the fanning.

When folk didn't know what to say, they said, "W'hell." When he asked questions—I'm not even lying—Grandma was the only one in the church who could answer his dumb questions right every time.

"Hear it, Cherry," Grandma said. "Lord say you got to hear it."

"That's right, Sista Coldson. Y'all hear what Sista Coldson said? You got to hear it, church. You ready? I don't thank y'all ready to hear it. Y'all ready to listen? Y'all ready to hear it, not just for yourself but for our baby, Baize Shephard? We gotta hear it for the babies who ain't here to hear it for themselves. Y'all ready?"

The church roared "Yeah" and "We ready, Rev."

"Church, somebody in here, if it wasn't today, maybe it was last Sunday or the Sunday 'fore last or maybe even a Sunday last year sometime, but whenever it was, you woke up and said to yourself, 'Self, I sho' do want to do the right thing.'

"Naw, lemme tell y'all another way," he said. "You woke up and say to yourself, 'Self, I need to go to church.' Then you thought about that comfortable bed, that box fan blowing that good air on your face. You wanted to come to church. You say you wanted to come to church. Then, that voice crept up in that right ear and said, 'You need to go to church. It will help you. It will help the community of God. Go ahead and get your wretched tail on up.' But temptation was already up in that left ear and it made that head get real heavy, didn't it?"

People were laughing their ass off now. I wanted to elbow myself in the head for laughing, too.

"All that temptation made that head so heavy," he said, "like a watermelon, or a sack of sweet potatoes. Then it fell back on that pillow. Bam! And you said, 'I'm tired' or 'I'm sick. Uhh. I'mo come next week. Next week.' Only thing is…" Reverend Cherry slowed down a bit "…next week wasn't promised. Next week ain't never promised. All we got is the moment and yesterday. Tomorrow ain't guaranteed. We know that better than any of these folks."

Reverend Cherry sped up again. "But you wanted to come to church, you claim. You knew what was right and you wanted to do that. Church, Lord don't deal in no wants. Lord coulda carried you to church that day, but that ain't his way. Lord give us the power to make sense of all this noise around us. Lord give us a way to slow down the noise and see everything that's in it. Lord give us a way to recollect this chaos. And the Lord deal in what is. Lord give you the ability to do the right thing. Lord tell you what to do when you standing in front of a sea of white folks and they want you to act a fool. Ain't that right, Li'l City?"

He looked right at me and started yelling.

"Open up your ears! 'Lot of us got our arms open and stretched out to the Father, Son, and the Holy Spirit because that's the pose we thank He want to see, but our *ears* ain't open. We are steady posing, but who we thank we faking out? You can't fake out Jesus. He unfakable, City! Them folks got you joking and jiving, acting like you ain't got good sense, but the Lord ain't going nowhere.

"Jesus speaketh in many tongues, but he always speaketh so you can understand. Always find you, no matter where you at. I say *always*! You might hear it in a deep voice. Somebody else might hear it in a little light voice. He might sang to you. He might throw it at you in sign language or maybe even one of them ol' rap songs."

The church was loud as hell, half laughs, half amens. Lots of claps. Then silence, no squeaks in the benches, no wrist-popping, just Cherry's voice and Troll's wet quilt.

"Or his voice might sound like mines do right here, right now." Cherry slowed down. "Whatever it is, open up your ears. It's there. He tried to tell us where our baby, Baize Shephard, was. But we ain't listen. We ain't wanna seem crazy!"

"I ain't crazy," a voice shouted.

"Who out there ready to open they ears to the right voice? Who out there ain't crazy? Who ready to save our babies so that Baize and the rest of our children won't be lost in vain?"

"Right here, Rev. I hear it," another voice shouted. "Right here, praise Jesus!"

"Come on up here, if you ready to open your ears," Rev said. "Can't open them ears, without opening them heavy heads and hearts. This ain't no sometimes thang. Sho ain't. This a life thang. This here is a Lord thang! Come on up here if you ready to be part of this Lord thang. Come up here if you tired of faking out the Lord."

"I'm ready for this Lord thing," my voice shouted. I was standing up, clapping like a seal. I swear I didn't remember telling my voice, my hands, or my legs to move. "I love your sentence style, Rev," my voice yelled again. "I knew better."

"Come up here then, City," Reverend told me. "If you really ready to give that life and soul to Jesus, come on up here. This ain't no sometimes thang, City."

Grandma pushed me up there, but she didn't have to. I hoped that four or five folks who Grandma called heathens would come up to the front of the church with me.

"Wait, Reverend Cherry." I didn't know if Cherry could hear me but I spoke to him anyway. "I just said you had smoove sentence styles. I'm really not trying to be all about that Lord life, though."

No one could hear me on top of all that mess. Finally, Ren and Raygord, the two grandsons of Deacon Harper known for having good hair, came up there with me.

Reverend Cherry looked at the deacons on the right and the ushers in the back and said, "Raise your right hand, sons. Tomorrow, at our First Monday Baptism, do you give yourself to the Lord? Are you ready to be saved by right? Tomorrow in the holy waters of heaven, do you..."

I looked at Grandma before glaring up at white Jesus again. I wondered if any folks in the church knew about the cross-eyed white man in Grandma's work shed. I wondered what they would think about my grandma's relationship with the Lord and with right if they really knew. If they ever found out, maybe two of them would talk smack about my grandma, but I figured that everyone in the church had been treated like a visitor on their own road, in their own town, in their own state, in their own country. It wasn't really complicated at all, but I'd never understood it until right then in that church. When you and everyone you like and everyone who really likes you is treated like a pitiful nigger, or like a disposable nigger, or like some terrorizing nigger, over and over again, in your own home, in your own state, in your own country, and the folks who treat you like a nigger are pretty much left alone, of course you start having fantasies about doing whatever you can—not just to get back at white folks, and not just to stop the pain, but to do something that I didn't understand yet, something a million times worse than acting a fool in front of millions at a contest.

One sentence.

That one sentence had the potential to be the greatest sentence I'd ever thought of, and I wished LaVander Peeler was there to hear it and help me figure out what the last part actually meant.

"Ahhhhhhhhhhmen!"

Everyone dropped hands and we made our way out of the church. I walked out feeling that my First Monday Baptism might be the last thing I ever experienced. Whether it was because I was going to die during the baptism or because I was going to be some wack holy dude I never imagined being, I didn't know how I could live another day as myself after that baptism. Either way, I figured I needed to go home and write a will on the blank pages in *Long Division*. If I did die, I wanted to give something to all the folks I was leaving behind.

A WILL.

1. I leave my Pine wave brush to LaVander Peeler.

2. I leave my XL mesh shorts to Shay.

3. I leave my grown-folks books to Shay and Gunn and a few of my illiterate kids' books to MyMy.

4. I leave my cell phone to my grandma because she needs one even though they don't ever get decent reception down here.

5. I leave my essays to Mama.

6. I leave my vintage Walter Payton jerseys to LaVander Peeler.

7. I leave my notebook to Grandma because she taught me how to read.

8. I leave my Obama Loves the South T-shirt to Shay.

9. I want to leave my spot on that TV show to Grandma too. She'd be better than I ever would be. And if Grandma won't do it, I leave it to that Mexican girl from Arizona, the one who I should not have dissed.

10. I leave my password to my email, Twitter, and Facebook to my Uncle Relle. It's W-H-O-S-T-A-N-K.

In the middle of my will in *Long Division*, I smelled Pot Belly and got that feeling that someone was looking at me. I turned around and there was Uncle Relle filming me with one of his cell phones.

"Oh hey, Uncle Relle. You smell funny."

"Funny how," he said, and he put one of his hands in his pockets. "Don't worry about how I smell, City. Keep doing you, like I ain't even here."

"It's hard to do me when I know you're trying to tape me doing me," I told him.

"Well, you better get good at acting like you're doing you in the future. The reality TV shit, it's about acting like the camera ain't there. You can't be looking all in the camera and making faces." Uncle Relle turned his phone camera off and put it in some leather case he kept on his belt. "It's a few basics that I think you haven't really ingratiated yourself to."

"You mean gravitated to?"

"Just listen, City. Close that gotdamn book."

I closed my book and braced myself for another one of Uncle Relle's speeches.

"This writing thing, it ain't like that hip hop shit, City. For li'l niggas like you," he told me, "this writing thing is like a gotdamn porta potty. It's one li'l nigga at a time, shitting in the toilet, funking up the little space he get. And you shit a regular shit or a classic shit. Either way," he said. "City, you gotta shit classic, then get your black ass on off the pot." He actually grabbed my hand. "You probably think I'm hyping you just for the money. It ain't just about the money. It's really not. It's about doing whatever it takes for you to have your voice heard. So I don't know what you're writing in that book you always carrying around, but it better be classic because you ain't gonna get no two times to get it right, you hear me?"

"I hear you."

Uncle Relle put Grandma's keys on the stove next to all this German chocolate cake she'd made. He told me he had some phone calls to make so he was about to walk down the road and try to find a signal. That was his way of saying he was going to buy some more weed from Alcee Mayes.

When Uncle Relle walked down the road, I decided to go look in the work shed again. Before I went out to the work shed, I found this little battery-operated CD player that Grandma took outside with her whenever she hung up the clothes out on the clothesline. The only song Grandma listened to while she was hanging up clothes was this Halona King song called "Monsters in the Night." I had no idea what other songs were on that CD because "Monsters in the Night" was the only song Grandma ever listened to or liked that wasn't gospel. She'd play it on repeat over and over and over. Pot Belly didn't seem like the kind of white dude who would like Halona King, but I figured he might want to hear something other than squeaky mice and bullfrogs since he was chained up in that work shed all by himself.

Pot Belly was lying face down in the sawdust of the work shed. He had these bloody welts up and down the top of his butt cheeks. Lying next to him was a half-empty bottle of pepper sauce.

"My uncle came in here and beat you down?" I asked him and turned on the CD player. "I thought maybe you'd wanna to listen to something. You like Halona King?"

Pot Belly's chest was heaving in and out. "You okay? Look, I might decide to save you tomorrow. For real. I mean, if I don't die at my baptism. I'm serious. You want anything?"

He started trying to turn over. To the left of his hips, on the floor of the work shed, were the words "So sad..." written in the sawdust on the floor. It looked like he'd used his finger to write those two words and three dots.

"Damn man, you wrote that? Why did you add the dot-dot-dot? They use that a lot in that book. I can't even lie to you, that's one of the saddest things I ever seen in my life. I guess I'm sorry my uncle beat you, but you shouldn't have called me names and kicked me. At last not in the back."

He started trying to talk but you couldn't hear anything thing but muffle since his mouth was filled with that rag. "Shut up and listen," I told him. "If it helps, I've seen him be mean to folks who wasn't even white. For real. Well, don't think I'm gay, but I'ma pull your pants up and leave. It's too sad up in here."

I turned my head so I wouldn't smell him too much. "Kindly pause," I said and pulled his underwear up all the way on his butt with the tips of my fingers.

"Look, man." I picked up the copy of *Long Division* that was still right where I'd left it on the floor. "I know you gotta be bored as shit up in here. I'd be bored and sad, too, if all I had to look forward to everyday was sweating and breathing in sawdust and having someone like my uncle beating my ass."

I thought about those two words: "So sad."

"You know that I never told anyone on earth that I'm so sad?" I told him. "I'm serious. Even after all that stuff happened on TV the other day, I never thought to tell someone that it all made me feel so sad. But that's the truth. That's what I felt." For the first time since I'd been in the work shed, I thought about Baize Shephard and whether she was chained up in someone else's work shed. I didn't think she was, but you just never could tell. "I wonder how sad Baize Shephard is right now."

He actually turned his eyes toward me when I said that.

"This book is crazy," I told him. "You want me to read you a little of it? It might help you feel less sad. Is it wack for me to read to you while that music is playing?"

Pot Belly didn't move.

"Beggars can't be choosers," I told him. "Remember that. Sometimes the glass is full as hell, white boy. You better drink. I'm trying to help you out."

It might sound weird to you, but even though I hoped that I would never do anything that could lead to my being chained up in a work shed, if I was chained up in a work shed, feeling so sad, I would have wanted someone to read a chapter of a book like *Long Division* to me with Halona King playing in the background.

So that's what I did.

...

Eyes Have It...

In the movies or a dumb book, I knew that I could look down at the ground and follow footprints to see where Shalaya Crump and Jewish Evan Altshuler had gone to, but the problem was that I'd never even seen a real footprint. There wasn't much sand or even dirt in Chicago or Jackson, and when there was, I can't say that I spent even a second looking for somebody's footprints.

I walked over to what Evan called the Freedom School. To the left of the door was a tilted black cardboard sign with white letters, a dot-dot-dot, and an exclamation point.

Be a FIRST CLASS Citizen

REGISTER...VOTE!

I peeked in the window at three people covered in sheets. They were walking around the inside of what looked like an old-fashioned classroom. There were three desks in the middle of the room. The ceiling was super high and you could see bird's nests all at the top. The floor was part carpet, part wood, part tile and all around the corners of the room were wooden sculptures and saws and pictures. The men in sheets weren't wrecking the room or trying to set anything on fire. They were just walking around, looking at the walls, talking to each other. I was zoning out when all of a sudden, I felt a shot to the back of my knees.

I turned around and another man in a white sheet was poking me in the kidney with a T-ball bat. I still didn't drop the laptop computer or the book. I'd seen plenty of movies about people in the Klan. In the movies, they always talked in those rough country voices that are only ever used by Northern white men actors playing Southern white men. But in real life, the men weren't saying a word. They didn't even grunt. They didn't even breathe loud. I never really understood before that Klan sheets didn't have mouth-holes. You would think that they had to breathe heavy unless they wanted to suffocate under those sheets.

When they pulled me into the school, they sat me in an old-fashioned desk I could barely fit in. The men walked around and circled me. One of them reached down for the computer, but I didn't let it go.

"I ain't letting this go," I told him. "I'll give you this book, but I can't give you this computer, man." He pulled his sheet up and showed me the barrel of his rifle. "Oh, but you know what? I'ma show you how to turn it on," I told him. "Did any of y'all see this pretty black girl and this other white boy with a fro who looked... he looked...um, not good. His name was Evan. He was your color and..."

Before I could finish, one of the men slapped me right across my mouth and looked me right in the eyes. I couldn't see his eyes because he had on glasses. I looked at all the men's eyes for the first time and realized that they all had on glasses under their sheets.

"Just so you know," I told them, "that's the first time I ever let someone hit me in my mouth. I'm serious. And if you didn't have that gun, I'd probably pop that old ass right in the jaw. I'm serious."

Another man slapped me right across the mouth after I said my piece. My problem was that I'd seen so many pictures of Klansmen. The pictures made you know that the men under the sheets were real men with real stinky breath, real rotten teeth, real pot bellies. I figured it was like football. As soon as you put on your helmet and shoulder pads and your jersey, you were like everyone else on your team, especially to people watching. Our football coach, Coach Foots, wouldn't even let us have our names on the back of our jerseys because he said the team is more important than the player.

But even dressed in the same uniform and with no name on the back of your jersey, the *GAME* was filled with seconds where it was up to you to make a play. Not your teammate.

You.

I knew that each of the Klansmen was feeling fear and trying to figure out a way to seem less afraid than he was to the other teammates on his Klan squad. But when you're getting the taste slapped out of your mouth for no reason, it doesn't matter if the person doing the taste-slapping is probably just as scared as you. And it makes you feel weird that no matter what, the taste-slappers never talk...they just breathe like new asthmatics and watch you. It made it easier to believe they lived their whole lives behind those white sheets, slapping black kids up and never breathing right.

"I wanna be honest with you," I told them.

One of the men was looking at the laptop computer and playing with the keys. He tapped the shoulder of the one who was standing over me and he bent down and started looking at the laptop computer, too.

"Look, I wanna be honest. You know what that is? That's a computer."

They didn't say a word. "A laptop. I can get you three of them, but first, you gotta let me go and you gotta let me take that one with me."

One of the men stood up after I said my speech and stood over me. "I'm serious. I can get you whatever you want. I'm good at stealing. Computers, telephones, color televisions, tape players, penny loafers, Bibles, tickets to Fresh Fest. I know y'all lackin' in 1964. Just tell me what you need."

I held my hand out. "Look, let's go ahead and shake on it. I'm serious. This book...how about I give you this book, and you let me go?"

The Klansman who slapped me in mouth a second earlier looked at the book and actually reached for it. I pulled it away from him and, without lingering at all, he reared back and hit me in my head so hard that the blood in my mouth tasted like canned spinach. "Nigger," one of the them said, "you talk too damn much..." I couldn't hear anything except the crunch of his work boots stomping my legs to mush and the echo of *nigger*.

Everybody I knew, at one point or another, had called someone "nigger," but I never heard the "er" when we said it to each other. It was just something that all of us said. We didn't mean it to hurt each other and we didn't mean it to make someone feel lucky. It was like the only word that meant lucky, cool, and cursed at the same time. But when that white man behind that sheet called me "nigger," I heard all the "er" and I knew when he said it, he thought I was not just less than him, but less than a human. Or at least, he was trying to really convince himself.

Either way, it made sense to me in that second, while that white man was stomping my legs into rubber bands, why Mama Lara would whup me so hard when I acted up in front of white folks. In 1985, every little thing we did in front of white folks had to be perfect, according to Mama Lara. And if I acted like I wasn't perfect around them, Mama Lara would tell me to go get her switch and she'd give me twelve licks. I didn't know if Mama Lara had ever been beaten by a white man in a sheet. I did know she had walked by the locked white folks' bathroom, though. She had seen and felt what I was feeling in that Freedom School, whether she'd had her legs stomped to rubber bands or not. I wondered if Jewish Evan Altshuler's people knew the same feeling.

I was trying so hard not to scream when the door to the school busted open and Jewish Evan Altshuler and Shalaya Crump rushed in. One of the men who had been looking at the computer ran toward Evan. And you know what that boy did? Evan pulled out this long wooden BB gun and just started shooting at the chests of the whole Klan. I figured that the Klansman with the real rifle was gonna shoot us all in the head, but he didn't reach for it at all.

Shalaya Crump came over near me and helped drag me out of the school. She let me rest a lot of weight on her, but I didn't wanna put too much weight on her because she'd know how heavy I really was.

"I'm okay," I told her. "But they got Baize's computer."

"We'll get it later. We gotta get outta here."

Shalaya Crump didn't say a word until we got to the hole. I tried to let her get in first but she didn't want to. "City," she said, "let me help you."

I got in the hole and she looked back toward the school. I peeked my head out of the hole and all three of the men had their hoods off, and one of the men was whupping Jewish Evan Altshuler like he was his grandma or something.

"That's his uncle," Shalaya Crump said.

"What?"

"It's hard to explain. They had to do it. He took me to his house and he told me the truth. He showed me."

I backed away from the mouth of the hole to give her room to get in. "Just come in the hole and tell it to me more when we get home."

"We can't leave him, City."

"Listen to me. I saw a talking cat, Shalaya. For real! And I saw this colored bathroom. We don't belong in a place like this. We ain't built for this." Shalaya Crump looked back toward the school. "Please let's just go home. Please! I went to 2013 for you just like you asked me. Please."

I couldn't see what was happening but I heard Evan screaming and I heard what sounded like wet open palms slamming down on someone's back. "You're right," Shalaya Crump said. "Scoot back and give me room to get in."

I crouched and made more room for Shalaya Crump. It was the first time I'd been in the hole by myself and I'm not sure why but it seemed bigger and colder than before. I was crouched for a good ten seconds, but Shalaya Crump didn't get in so I stood up. "Come on, Shalaya. Let's go."

She looked me right in the face. "I'm sorry, City," she said. "It's for the best."

Shalaya Crump slammed the door to the hole shut.

I pushed open the door of the hole slowly. Before my eyes could adjust to the light, a pine cone bounced right off my forehead. "I knew you'd be back. Gimme my damn computer, and my book!"

It was Baize.

"Where am I?"

"You know where you are." She snatched *Long Division* from my hands. "I want my computer, too! And my damn phone."

"Oh, I didn't take a phone. I only borrowed your computer." Baize was wearing the same outfit she'd had on when I saw her before, but with different shoes. She had on these red, black, green, and yellow hightop Nikes.

"Where they at, Voltron? I'm serious."

"Umm." I was trying to decide whether to lie or not. "One of my friends has the phone and someone else has the computer." I looked at her face and, more than anything, I just wanted her to hug me. Sounds crazy, but after getting your legs stomped to dust by white dudes in sheets, you kinda want someone black to touch you in a way that's soft. "Okay, look, I'm gonna tell you everything."

Baize picked up another pine cone and threw it right at my head. "I don't want to know everything," she told me. "I don't even want to know *anything* from you. I just want my computer back." She picked up another pine cone and stared at it. "When was the last time knowing everything about something ended up good for you?"

I didn't know how to answer her question, so I got out of the hole and told Baize how my friend had showed me the hole a few days earlier and took me from 1985 to 2013. I told her about meeting a white boy who said he could take us back to 1964. And I told her that I needed to go back and help my friend get back home alive.

You know what she said after I explained it to her?

"I believe you. I still really need my computer back, though. All my rhymes are in there. And I need it for the Spell-Off."

"You do?" I stood up and tried stretching out my knees. "Why?"

"Why what?"

"Why are all your rhymes in there?"

"Because it's my computer."

"Oh. I'm saying why do you need a computer for a Spell-Off?"

"Because I wanna look at some Spell-Off clips on YouTube. I got this perfect introduction and I wanna make sure they let us introduce ourselves. It's so dope."

"Oh. I don't really know what you talking about. One more question? Well...uh, why do you believe me?"

"Because I know people can disappear."

"Wait. What?"

"Never mind. Let's go."

Baize said that I could come stay at her house until the morning, when her great-grandmother got off work. I told her that I didn't need to stay that long. Before I limped into her house, she told me to sit down on her porch. My legs were killing me. I just wanted to eat something and come up with a plan to save Shalaya Crump.

"Just tell me," she said. "Is it us or is it the hole that sends us back in time?"

"You know about the hole?"

"I saw you jump in that hole after you stole my computer," she told me. "And I got in the hole myself the next day."

Part of me thought it was just Evan and Shalaya Crump who could time travel. But if Shalaya Crump could time travel and Evan could time travel and I could time travel, and now Baize could time travel, I figured it must be the hole.

"I ain't gonna lie to you," I told her. "I think it's the hole. Can we go inside? I'm hungry."

Baize's house and porch were so raggedy that I didn't really wanna walk in. Super nasty houses always made me itch even if nothing was crawling on me. The TV in their living room looked like it belonged in Richie Rich's house, though. It was nearly as tall as me.

"Why your TV so big and nice but your house is kinda, you know..."

"To' up from the flo' up?" she said, and started grinning.

"Yeah, how do you..." I paused to try to get my words right. "How much is a TV like that? Like $2,000?"

"More like $35 a month."

Baize sat in the one chair in the living room and I sat on the floor. She turned on the TV with one of the three remotes.

Before the TV came on, all these lights went from red to green. When it finally came on, a new version of *Soul Train* was on, and it was the sound as much as the screen that I couldn't understand. *Soul Train* on that TV sounded like life. You know how in life, there's hardly ever just that one sound you're listening for? Like even when I imagined Shalaya Crump telling me she loved me, I imagined hearing the wind whistling and a few different car horns behind us and maybe a freight train miles away and definitely some barking dogs. That's how the sound was on that TV. You could hear people moving their feet and snapping their fingers and it sounded like the *Soul Train* line was happening in your room. If everything you saw in real life had the best light behind it, and was polished super shiny, that's how *Soul Train* looked on that TV.

Baize gave me the remote and told me that she was gonna make something to eat. "Even if we had a lot of money, we wouldn't waste it on the outside of our house. That could be gone in a second if another storm came. You want oriental ramen or chicken ramen with your french fries and butter beans?"

"What's ramen?"

"Noodles, boy. Y'all don't even have ramen in the '80s?"

Baize walked through the other room into the kitchen.

The first thing I did with the remote was check how many channels the TV had. When I pushed below 1, the TV went to channel 1,975. Back in my time, we'd watch TV and say "Ain't nothing on." I didn't know how anyone could ever say "Ain't nothing on" in 2013. *The Flintstones* was on. Basketball was on. Soap operas were on. Andy Griffith was on. *The Cosby Show* and *Good Times* were on. And PBS shows that looked exactly the same as they looked in 1985 were on.

And on more channels than you could imagine, there were black women with real *JET*-centerfold booties yelling and fighting each other.

Baize came back in the room and just sat on the floor next to me.

"What?" I asked her.

"What, what?" she asked me. "Don't 'what' me in my house."

"Why you sitting next to me so close?" She didn't answer, but her hip was touching my left hand. So I moved it and asked, "Is the ramen ready?"

"Almost. I warmed up the biscuits to go with the butter beans and french fries."

"Okay." I kept changing the channels. "What happened to real actors and comedians? On all these stations, you see people you would see at the mall fighting. And when did McDonald's start using black folks on their commercials?"

"I don't even know, Voltron," she said. "That's a good question." I could tell she wasn't really listening to me. "Um, do you wanna smoke?"

"Smoke what? Aren't you like twelve?" I asked her. "I'm good. You ain't never heard of 'Just Say No?'"

"Wow," she said. "I'm thirteen. You should have your own reality show. Keep doing you, Voltron. I'm smoking before I eat."

Baize walked back toward the kitchen and I just sat there in front of that TV. I hated Baize for smoking without me even though I didn't want to smoke. After a few minutes I got really curious, though. I had seen plenty of folks smoke weed and cigarettes, but I'd never seen a girl younger than me smoke.

I walked toward the kitchen and saw that there was a screen door. Sitting on the step on the other side of the screen was Baize. And she had a square in her mouth. Right in front of her was the area where I had seen those two Dobermans doing it. And next to that was a huge, grimy work shed.

"You ever wonder what happened before you in the same place you're standing now?" I asked her. "Like, I saw this talking cat right around the corner."

I looked at her and waited for her to ask me to explain myself. "Look," she said, "let's talk, but don't be coming out here messing up my high. Don't say nothing to me about how I shouldn't smoke, either. I'm thick and I'm extra and I smoke. Leave me alone."

"You're extra what?"

"Just extra." She took a puff and exhaled it.

"If you ask any girl in Melahatchie about me, they'll be like, 'Baize, that bitch is extra,' especially after my song blew up on YouTube. It's a compliment. I know myself."

"That's nice," I said. "You don't mind people calling you that name, though?"

"What name? 'Bitch?' Yeah," she said. "I mind hating-ass bitches calling me 'bitch.' But my girls, they could call me 'bitch' and I could call them 'bitch' and it wouldn't be a big deal."

I just looked at her.

"If you called me 'bitch,' I'd get you," she told me. "I'm just keeping it one hundred. Somehow, some way, I'd have to get you, 'cause it's hard for boys to really love girls anyway, so I can't really see letting a boy get away with calling nobody a bitch. Mama taught me that a long time ago. And if a boy did love me, knowing how much it hurt..." she started trailing off. "I don't know what to say. A nigga who loved me wouldn't call nobody a bitch. But I don't even like boys like that anyway."

"Oh," I said. All I could think about was how Shalaya Crump whupped this boy, Damon Frazier, to his knees for calling *me* a "yap-mouth bitch" the summer before last. The whole time she was whupping him, she kept saying, "You gonna respect me." I thought it was weird she would say that after I was the one that Damon was calling a "yap-mouth bitch," but it was all making a little more sense now.

"Seem like you thought a lot about that word," I told Baize. "Can I switch subjects? You ever wonder why people smoke with their hands so close to their lips? Like if your fingers were more off your lips, smoking wouldn't even look right."

"Then you'd burn your fingers," she said. "Look Voltron, no offense, you messing up my smoke, though, for real."

"Oh. My bad. People still say 'for real' around here? You know, you talk like you're way older than thirteen. Sometimes you call me 'mayne' and sometimes you call me 'boy' and sometimes you call me 'Voltron.'" Baize inhaled more but actually took her fingers away from her lips a bit. "You know why I think you sound so old to me? Because your TV has every age on it. Every age! Like my TV back home, we get four channels including PBS, and you gotta watch all the commercials because you can't be flipping a lot or your mama and them claim that'll break the TV."

Baize looked like she was listening, but she wasn't. "Whatever," she said. "You know what was weird when I went back to the past? I was on this same road in my same hood, but no one cared."

"Why do you just switch subjects like that? I bet when you watch TV, every time a commercial come on, you get to flipping, don't you?"

"Shut up. I was tired of talking about music."

"Wait. You walked around back then?"

"Hell yeah, I walked around."

"Girl, that was dumb. Why would anyone back there care? You ain't even born where I'm from."

"That's what I'm saying." She lit another cigarette. "It's hard to go back because you see that there was a time when people in the same space where you are ain't even care or think nothing about you. But somehow, I'm still related to those folks. When I went back, I wanted to see what the music was like and to see if I could find my parents."

"Did you find them?"

"I was scared to look."

"Where they at now?"

"Dead," she said. "I mean, I think."

"Both of them?"

"Dead."

I had never had someone tell me that both of their parents were dead, and I wasn't sure what to say. I didn't want to say something to ruin her high, but since I'd never ruined someone's high before, I wasn't sure what kind of stuff could ruin your high.

"Man, having dead parents must be like, um, like having to eat dessert first for the rest of your life and having that dessert be something like, um, pears when everyone around you is eating greasy fried catfish platters and hot peach cobbler, huh?"

That's all I could come up with.

Baize didn't say anything. She just kept smoking. "Naw," she finally said. "Having dead parents ain't nothing like eating pears." She blew smoke right in my face. "I only half knew them. They had me when they were young and they died when they were young. But they loved me."

"You're still young," I told her. She just looked at me and didn't say a word. "They died together?"

"Yep. We had come back from the swings over there at Gaddis Park. And everyone knew that the storm was coming. So me and my little brother was gonna go stay with my cousins and my grandma up in Jackson. So they dropped me off, and went back because...

shit, I don't know why they went back. Never made much sense to me."

"Then what?"

"Then nothing." She blew smoke like a professional smoke-blower. "I never saw them again."

Baize threw what was left of the cigarette on the grass and mashed it with her Nikes. "They got swallowed up by the water, I think. Or the wind."

"Why don't you know?"

"I know."

"How do you know?"

"Because they wouldn't have left us." Baize got up, looked down at me, and walked inside the screen door. I followed her. "If I had my computer, I could play one of the songs I made for them."

I figured I'd read the words to Baize's song, but I didn't want to hear her rap it. It would have embarrassed me too much if she couldn't rap a lick. I knew I should have been thinking more about her dead parents and what kind of storm could just make people disappear, but I wasn't. I was thinking of that talking cat and those two Dobermans who just earlier in the day were right where I was looking now, and I was thinking about what Shalaya Crump and Evan were doing. I didn't think they were kissing any more. I knew that they were trying to stay alive or fighting to not disappear together, which was even worse.

"Baize?"

"What?"

"What happened to your brother?"

"He disappeared, too."

"Oh. Wait. Can I ask you one more question?"

"What?"

"That wasn't a real cigarette, was it?"

Baize liked to control the remote, and she never left it on one channel for longer than five minutes. "I usually don't watch this much TV, but since you stole my computer and my phone, I don't have a choice."

"You could read that book. What's it called?"

"*Long Division.*"

"Yeah, you could read *Long Division* since you were so pressed about getting it back," I told her. "Have you read that book? All of it?"

"I read some of it and it made me feel weird."

"Me too. I like that part where they all got together and listened to that boy talk about that kid LaVander Peeler's fade. Who wrote it?"

"I don't know. I told you that I just found it in the woods."

"Don't you think it's weird that there's no author's name on it? Is that how they do books in 2013?"

She just looked at me. "That's what I'm saying, Voltron. There's something painful in that book. Real painful. And I just don't feel like reading to the end and finding out what it is."

"Then why'd you want it back so bad if you weren't gonna read it?"

"Because it's mine," she said. "Whatever is wrong with that book, I wanna be the one to find out before anyone else does."

"Do kids read a lot in 2013?" I asked her. "Like, in my time, I read a lot because if I don't, I get my ass whupped. I usually hate whatever I have to read, but when I finish something, I feel so happy. I can't even lie, though. I probably only finished two books in my whole life."

Baize was laughing at me. "Nobody around here really reads unless it's something on a computer, but nobody writes to folks around here either. But that's the thing about that book. If I gave it to the most illiterate fool in my grade, I bet he'd at least get through the first chapter, you know?"

"Yeah, I do know," I told her. "I got through the first chapter."

"No comment."

"Why no comment?" I asked her. "I would have read even more of it if I didn't have your computer to mess with. It's hard for us in 1985 to finish books, and we don't even have a thousand channels or phones that look like calculators or laptop computers." I waited for her to ask me something, but she didn't. "You know what else? I never typed on a typewriter before. But when I typed on your computer, I felt like what I was typing was famous. It just looked so famous on the screen, like I could have written that *Long Division* book."

"Voltron, you dumb. I bet you only wrote a few sentences. That's a big-ass book. I ain't trying to hate, but you couldn't write something like that. You have to really have gone through a lot and then have a lot of time on your hands to do something like that."

"I'm not that dumb," I told her. "Look. We could turn the TV off and you could just write in a tablet, or we could watch a movie," I said. When I started talking about watching a movie, Baize muted the TV. I don't know why, but her turning down the TV to listen to me took my like for Baize from 20 MPH to around 50 MPH. I tried to keep talking and not look as thankful as I was.

"Are you one of those people?" she asked me. "My father used to be like that. I remember he was always telling my mother to turn the TV off so he could watch a movie or tell some ol' silly story."

"Were they good stories?"

She started smiling. "Yeah, they were. You would have liked them." I knew I was supposed to ask why, but I didn't really want to. Didn't matter, though, because she kept talking anyway. "He said a lot in his stories, kinda like you do."

Right after she said that, there was this picture of this white woman with stringy black hair and big eyes and a nose that reminded me of a tiny paper boat.

"Who is that lady? Turn it up."

"That's Michael Jackson."

I got closer to the TV and watched different scenes with this person dancing and sounding like Michael Jackson. But nothing about the person looked like the Michael Jackson I knew.

"Wait."

"Yeah," she said. "He died four or five years ago." She started scratching her head. "Sorry."

I slumped on the ground away from the TV and just watched the first part of the show about the life and sound and death of Michael Jackson with my head resting on my shoulder. I thought about Shalaya Crump telling me to just be myself. What did that even mean if years in the future, you could look like a totally different person and be dead? There was no way to be yourself and be the same way you were. And even if you did manage to be yourself, one day you were going to die and regret it all anyway. That's what I realized watching the show about Michael Jackson.

"This is real, Baize. This shit is real." I stood there not caring what I looked like. I understood that if Michael Jackson was really dead, it meant that people I knew were dead too. "I gotta find my ma and my Mama Lara. What if they disappeared in some flood just like your parents?"

"Tomorrow, okay? Look," she stood up and took the remote controls from me. "You gotta rest so your legs feel better. Then tomorrow, well..." She paused.

"What?"

"You gotta decide if you go back and help your friend or if you stay and look for your family. I don't care what you do. When the morning comes, I'm jumping back in that hole and getting my computer and my phone back."

"But what if all my family is dead?"

"What if they are?"

"Well," I said, and thought about her question. "I guess if they're dead, I'd want to know and maybe when I go back to my time I can do what I can to stop them from dying."

"But what if *you're* dead?"

"What do you mean?"

"What if you go looking for your people and you find out that they're alive, but you ain't?"

"Then, well, I guess..." I just didn't know what to say. "Where am I sleeping tonight?"

"On the floor in my room, I guess."

I followed her in the bedroom and then I stopped. "Baize?"

"What?" she turned around and looked me right in the eye.

"Is all of New Edition dead too?"

"New who?"

Baize made a nice little area to sleep on the floor next to her bed. I should have asked to take a shower, but I'd seen when I went in their bathroom earlier that there wasn't a shower. Couldn't understand how they had all the technology to get over 200 channels and make the TV sound like life, but they didn't have technology to make their tub go from the brown of a double-yolk egg to a somewhat regular white.

I sat there on the floor of Baize's room and pulled up the sheet to look under her bed. There were maybe 20 green notebooks piled there, and all kinds of raggedy keyboards, drumsticks, and broken turntables. Surrounding all that stuff were these tiny fingernails.

I grabbed one of the green notebooks and opened it. There were all these sketches of connected circles, and surrounding the circles were these long winding lines of numbers that looked like they were coming out of the circles. I opened another notebook and it was the same thing. Different-shaped circles and long lines of winding numbers.

While I was trying to figure out if Baize was doing some kind of long division in the notebooks, Baize leaned her head over toward me. "If things start to crawl on you, you can just get in the bed with me, long as you stay on your side."

"Wait, what's gonna crawl on me? Fingernails?"

"No, asshole. Roaches."

"Can I ask you something?"

"What?"

"Why are these notebooks filled with circles and numbers?"

"They're not circles," she told me and took the notebook from my hand. "They're holes."

"Holes to where?"

"I don't know. Never mind, Voltron," she said. "Just watch out for the roaches down there."

"Well then, can I just...you know...get up there with you?"

"Don't get it twisted, okay?" she said and moved over. "I'm really not about that acting ho-ish life."

"Whatever that means." I told her and got in the bed. "I been wanting to tell you that the slang y'all use is kinda stale in the future."

Baize put four of her green tablets between us. She told me that I couldn't cross over the tablets without getting punched in the gizzard, and I told her not to worry. It's not hard to explain what I felt about Baize. She had the perfect mix of funk and perfume. And even though she had a Mr. T-style haircut, she was cuter than a cute girl. And she was finer than a fine girl. And she was way smarter than a smart girl. And she was even weirder than the weirdest girls. But she wasn't as good-smelling, as cute, as smart, or as weird as the girl I loved. And even if she was, which she wasn't, I really told myself that if I didn't touch Baize, then maybe, just maybe, Evan and Shalaya Crump weren't touching either.

I wanted to stay up and ask Baize more questions about life in 2013, but the day had beaten me down. A few minutes after my head hit that crappy pillow, I turned away from Baize and was cold knocked out.

Some time during the night, I had one of those dreams where you know you're dreaming. Everything in the woods was a different shade of maroon. Shalaya Crump had my hand in hers and she was pulling me through the woods toward the Freedom School. When we got to the door, everything turned black and white.

"Why you talking weird," I asked her, "like this is a stupid book?"

We walked all the way to the center of the room, into the smell of burning hair and pancakes. When we stood in the room, the sound of one of those TV shows I watched on Baize's TV was surrounding us.

"He's different than you think he is, City."

"Who?"

"This guy." Shalaya Crump pulled out a picture of a white boy I'd seen before on TV. He looked like Ricky's friend on *Silver Spoons*. "Evan."

"That's not Evan. That boy is way cuter than Evan. Why you using words like 'guy' too? You kissed him, didn't you?"

"No, I didn't, but I want to."

"Wait. This is a dream. I know it's a dream, but you can't really think Evan looks like that? For real. 'Laya, he don't look like that at all. Why couldn't you pull a picture out that looked all sick and gangly and like he's smelling something? You know he's raggedy as a roach, right?"

Shalaya Crump put the picture in her front pocket and put her hands on my shoulder. I'd practiced kissing her enough to know that I was supposed to put my hands on her hips and come in with my eyes closed and my nostrils kinda flared.

"Open your eyes," she said, and kissed me on the left side of my lips, then on my cheek, then on my neck. Everywhere she kissed felt like a trail of rubbing alcohol and smelled like butterscotch.

Shalaya Crump was coming back toward my lips. "Do I keep my eyes open?" I asked her. "I ate a banana Laffy Taffy before we got in here. You smell it?"

"Shush," she told me. "Let's just do what we want."

"What if Evan finds out?" I asked her.

"I'm gonna tell my guy," she said.

"Me too," I said.

Shalaya Crump pulled me even closer and took my bottom lip between her lips. Every feeling in my body sprinted between my wide hips. And for just about ten seconds, all those feelings screamed and tried to blow out these candles I didn't even know were lit. After ten seconds of blowing hard as they could, the feelings ran from my hips back to my feet, my toes, my knees, my eyeballs, and wherever else they came...

When I woke up, Baize was standing up looking at me like I was straight crazy.

"What?" I asked her.

"Nothing, Voltron," she said. "I just read more of that book while you were sleeping this morning."

"So."

"So nothing," she said. "Let's just go."

We had to get up early enough that Baize's great-grandma wouldn't see that I was in the house. She said her great-grandma got off work at eight and went to her second job from nine to two. The plan was to head back to 1964, get Baize's stuff, save Shalaya Crump, and never ever jump back in the hole again.

Baize was running around the house getting everything ready, so she really didn't have time to talk to me about what had happened the night before. I waited out on the porch. When she finally came through the door, she had on a backpack and had a little carry case and a brush in her hand.

"What you doing with all the mess? This ain't no vacation. We gotta go!"

"It's a diva thing, Voltron. You wouldn't understand."

"What does that even mean?"

"Means that you should mind your stanky business, and let this brush touch your beady beads." She handed me the wave brush. "If I wanna go outta town looking fresh, that's on me. If you wanna go outta town looking like the number-one driver on the nappy-head truck, that's on you. Niggas from the '80s gotta do what niggas from the '80s do."

"It's just that we ain't going out of town," I told her. "I bet you brought money, too, didn't you?"

"Like I said, you wouldn't understand. If I had some money, I would've brought all of it." I stood there shaking my head. "Wanna be useful and carry my book for me?" She handed me *Long Division*.

We walked across the road into the woods and headed toward what used to be the Shephard house—what Evan had called the Freedom School. It now had a sign that read "Melahatchie Community Center." Baize introduced me to a Mexican-looking man named Oscar who had a mullet and a yellow short-sleeve shirt. Oscar held out his hands and gave me some dap. Baize said he worked security at her school, and that he was deaf.

I whispered in her ear, "You know deaf Mexicans?"

Baize ignored me and started throwing sign language with the dude.

After a while, we walked down the hall. "What did you just say to that Mexican dude?" I asked her.

"Don't call him 'that Mexican dude.' His name is Oscar. Please don't tell me that you're one of those niggas who stay hating on Mexicans."

"I don't know any Mexicans," I told her. "They seem like they work hard."

She shook her head. "Dude, just be quiet for a few minutes, okay? I didn't ask you if they worked hard. Hell, some of them don't work hard, just like some of us don't work hard. Don't you get tired of being such a hater?"

I ignored her question and looked around the center. "So is anyone you know gonna be in the contest with you? This reminds me of that first chapter in *Long Division,* where the main character..."

"Say his name."

"I think his name was City."

"If you read the first chapter, you know his name was City."

"Yeah, well I only read the first chapter, so I don't know what happens, but City and that other dude compete in some kind of contest, right?"

"Right. But that was a crazy contest. This is just a basic real-life county spelling bee. I hope you know how to act around white folks."

"Girl, I lived in Jackson my whole life until we moved last year."

"So what," she said. "Jackson is way blacker than Melahatchie, dummy. You stay catching L's, don't you?"

"L's?"

"Losses!"

"I feel like I've done all this before," I told Baize. I wasn't lying. Something about the words, the temperature, and the sound of what I thought was about to happen felt like it had all happened before.

"You haven't done this before," she told me. "You just read something like it before, or maybe you had a dream about it."

While we walked down the hall, we had to shake hands with people. Well, Baize did. I had her dictionary in one hand and brushed my hair with the other. Soon as someone put their hand out for a shake, woman or man, girl or boy, I'd make a fist while gripping my book. I'd never seen that many white people on Old Ryle Road before, and I was surprised that all the white folks we passed knew to give me a pound. I knew it was the future, but white folks in 2013 acted way more familiar with you than white folks in 1985.

"We've been waiting for you, Baize," said this white lady named Cynthia. "Who is your friend?" She took both of our dictionaries and said that there were no aids allowed beyond this point. Baize said hold on, looked up two more words, and gave it to her.

"This is my friend, Voltron."

"Voltron what?" the lady asked. "Did you compete in the pre-lims? I don't remember seeing your name."

"Voltron Bailey," I told the lady. "I was out of town during prelims."

"He's from Jackson," Baize told the lady. "West side."

"Well, bless your heart."

"Yes ma'am. Well, he was born and raised in Melahatchie, but he went up to Jackson after the storm. He's just back here visiting for the week because of all that gang violence up there. You know how it is."

"Why'd he say he was outta town, then?" she asked Baize. "Is his mind right, Baize?"

"Yes, ma'am. His mind is fine. He's one of the best spellers in Jackson. He won eighth place in the Jackson Spell-Off last year, didn't you, Voltron?"

"Yeah, I umm, I made that Spell-Off tap out."

Baize put her hand on my shoulder and whispered in my ear, "Go 'head and chill with the ad-libs, Voltron. I'm working something here."

The lady took off down the hall. She kept looking back, though, saying, "Don't leave. I'll be right back."

"Why you lie to that lady?" I asked Baize while we walked into the room.

"Because now I know she'll let you spell."

"Why? I don't even want to spell."

"Because these folks think Jackson is a shark tank and you're a black boy and they want to save you before you turn into a shark."

"Wait," I said. "Who is a shark?"

"Wow! I'm so glad I didn't grow up in the '80s," she said.

The room we walked into was only thing I'd been in since I'd been in 2013 that felt like home. Everything else from the shiny hubcaps to the six-foot TVs to the music to how folks wanted me to compete in a Spell-Off seemed different. I guess I should describe the room or something since it felt like home, but there ain't really nothing to say about it except it felt like home. Looking back on a room, you can make up all kinds of flowery stuff about it if you want to, but this room had four dirty walls, a high ceiling, and a dusty floor, and it was empty just like most of the rooms in 1985.

"Let's do this," Baize said, and we walked toward the stage.

Even though Baize and I were there together, I felt embarrassed. Embarrassed, I understood on that stage, was just another way of saying I felt alone. It was the first time I'd felt alone since I'd been in 2013 and that was mostly because of Baize.

Right there, though, I remembered that I'd forgotten about Shalaya Crump. Even though I'd dreamed about her, I'd forgotten how I needed her. If Shalaya Crump would have been there, we could have dealt with the cameras and the crowd together. I didn't know what I was supposed to do on that stage in front of those people. And even more than that, I couldn't believe I was on some raggedy stage in 2013 when the girl I loved was 50 years away from me, probably doing something fun and nasty with the ugliest boy I'd ever seen in my life.

I couldn't see anybody in the crowd because the lights were shining so bright. I sat on the left side, third seat from aisle, and Baize was in the same seat on the other side.

The judge made us stand up for the Pledge of Allegiance. While everyone stood, I walked over to Baize, who stayed sitting. "Look," I whispered in her ear. "I'm gonna go, okay? Shalaya Crump needs me. Thanks for everything. If I find your computer, I'll bring it back to you, okay?"

"You can't leave yet," she said.

I started walking away from Baize when I heard, "Baize Shephard is our first contestant. I'm sure most of you know that Baize tied for fifth place in last year's Spell-Off. Baize lost her parents and brother in Katrina eight years ago and she actually lives right down the road. In addition to doing her homework, Baize is an aspiring hip hop performer and entrepreneur. Sounds fantastic. She writes in her bio, 'If you get it twisted, please tighten it back up, Boo Boo. My name is Baize Shephard, a.k.a. the Baddest Baize in Mississippi. I do not need to win the Spell-Off to know I'm special. This is Baize Against the World, not that *Akeelah and the Bee* life. Hashtag Baize killed swag hashtag my hood to your hood.'"

I looked over at Baize and she was frowning.

"Baize, your first word is 'abnegations.'"

Baize stepped to the microphone with her fist clenched, looking down at her red, black, green, and yellow hightop Nikes.

"Um, I don't know how to spell it," she said. "I thought we were supposed to introduce ourselves." Baize walked right back to her seat, still frowning. The crowd and the spellers started clapping in spurts. I was clapping loud and hard as hell for her until they called my name.

"Voltron Bailey, from Jackson, Mississippi, we'd like to welcome you. Voltron has been added as an alternate. He is a special wild-card competitor in our Spell-Off. Voltron was born in Melahatchie but moved to Jackson after the storm hit. As a result of all that gang violence, he is back in Melahatchie, where people know how to act. We expect great things from him. Since you didn't provide us with a bio, Voltron, would you like to say something about yourself?"

"Oh, okay," I said. "Back home, we...uh, we say that reading, it's...umm...it's fun-da-mental. You know, like it's fun and mental, duh. There's a lot of violence in Jackson but it ain't a shark tank. I'm serious. If kids had more programs and our parents had more money, I don't think it would be that violent at all." Everyone was quiet. I guess they expected more, but I was done playing a role in this dumb Spell-Off. I needed to go find Shalaya Crump. "I'm sorry, but, um, I have to go home. My stomach hurts. I feel like I'm about to lose my manners, to tell you the truth. Listen though," I said into the mic. "Be nice to Baize, okay? Let her do her bio like you let me do mine."

No one said a word, so I looked down at my feet as they slid off that stage, and tried not to imagine the looks on folks' faces as I headed out the door of what used to be a Freedom School.

I wanted it all to be a dream.

I wasn't out the door more than 20 seconds before Baize came run-ning after me. When she caught me, we didn't say a word. We just walked toward the hole. During the first minute of our walk, Baize was quiet and I watched my feet miss most of the thin branches that had fallen in the woods. Every time I stepped an inch from a branch, I thought about how I couldn't wait to tell Shalaya Crump that I had been on a stage in 2013 talking about stuff I knew nothing about.

During the second minute of our walk, every time we passed an ant bed, I thought of all the folks in 1985 who would have been shamed if they had seen how I represented them. I had looked like a complete fool in front of folks I didn't even know. I could feel Baize looking at my face too hard while I was thinking. "Don't worry about it, Voltron," she said. "How you feel?"

"Why you even asking me that?" I asked her. "I'm fine."

"I mean, you caught an L," she said. "No doubt about that. That was a fail and a half back there, but you had your heart in the right place." She put her hand on my shoulder as we walked. "We should have never come anyway. It was more important that we went back and saved your friend."

"You didn't have to come, though. You should have stayed."

"Naw, I'm good. I just really wanted to say that 'This is Baize Against the World, not *Akeelah and the Bee*' line on stage. I thought they were gonna let me say it in my own voice. I think it could have gone viral."

It was weird, because up until that point, I hated any folks who were skinnier than me and taller than me and smarter than me and funnier than me and sweated less than me. And I hated folks from different states and folks who had shinier penny loafers and folks who had rounder heads than me, and folks who didn't like as much tartar sauce and hot sauce on their catfish as me. But right then, I didn't even hate those folks. I did, however, hate this future—I mean, Klan-hate. After I saved Shalaya Crump, I wanted to do everything I could to come back to the future and make it suffer for helping me embarrass myself.

With all my hate bubbling, we walked to the hole. Out of nowhere, Baize fell to her knees right outside the hole and told me to hold on a second.

"What are you doing?" I asked her.

"What's it look like?"

"Looks like you praying. But why?"

"The question is, why ain't you praying," she said. "My parents and great-grandma told me that every knee must bend, especially when you have no idea what's gonna happen next. You should probably pray with me."

I looked down at her. "I pray before I go to bed like two times a week."

"That's on you," she said. "Just give me a minute."

And with that, Baize brought her hands together, closed her eyes, and actually started praying right outside the hole. After a minute or so, I started breathing heavy wondering how much longer this prayer was going to take. Near the end, she touched my calf and said, "Amen."

Baize got in the hole first and I followed her. While we were in the hole, deep in the dark, Baize grabbed both of my wrists and made her way down to the palms of my hands.

"Baize." It was the first time I'd called her by her name. "You were scared to stay back here by yourself, weren't you?" I asked her. "Your eyes open?"

"Yeah, Voltron. They're open, and yeah, I was scared to be there alone. Are you scared right now?"

That was the new best question anyone had ever asked me. The thing is, I was never scared of what I should have been scared of. For example, I wasn't scared of people finding out I stole those Bibles for Shalaya Crump. I wasn't really even scared of the Klan. I was only scared of knowing that Shalaya Crump could love someone else. Nothing else scared me. And if nothing really scared me, I wondered if anything else really even mattered. Everything else just made me mad or made me embarrassed or made me nervous. But all of those feelings had to do with Shalaya Crump in some way or another.

"Ain't no reason to be scared," I told her and took my hands back. "What can people do to you, really?"

"They can make you disappear," she said.

"Yeah, but then you're gone. I ain't afraid of disappearing. I bet disappearing doesn't even hurt, to tell you the truth."

"People can mash your heart in your chest, Voltron, while you're still alive. They can take people from you. That's something to be afraid of. Stop fronting like you're 'bout that life, boy."

I said okay, but I knew people could hurt people way more than Baize would ever know. Shalaya Crump and I had this friend named Rozier. I liked to think about big ol' *JET*-centerfold booties for as long as Rozier knew me, and Rozier liked to think about big ol' boy booties for as long as I knew him. That's just how he was. The thing about Rozier was that he was the kind of guy who you met and 29 minutes later, you knew he would be better than Eddie Murphy when he grew up. Rozier invented farting out loud in homeroom. He also invented calling people "ol' blank-blank-blank-ass nigga." Like if you ate an apple too fast, Rozier would call you an "ol' eating-apples-like-they-plums-ass nigga," or if you failed a test, he'd call you an "ol' watching-*Three's Company*-when-you-shoulda-been-studying-ass nigga."

If you called Rozier a name he didn't like, Rozier could slap you in the face better than any kid in Melahatchie, except for maybe Shalaya Crump. The summer of '84, Rozier got jumped by some dudes from Waveland. Rozier had embarrassed one of the dudes in front of his family earlier at the arcade. After the boy called Rozier a faggot, Rozier said he'd never met a boy who smelled like sack and dookie through his church clothes. He called him an "ol' wiping-your-ass-forward-instead-of-backward-so-the-dookie-get-caked-up-under-your-sack-ass nigga." He said the boy needed Mr. Miyagi to teach him to correctly "wipe on, wipe off." Even his friends started laughing, and when the dude got in Rozier's face, Rozier slapped the boy across his mouth twice with both hands. That's four slaps right in front of his family. Then he ran.

The boy who got slapped four times got three of his older cock-strong friends to help find Rozier when he was by himself in the Night Time Woods the next day. Rozier slapped the best he could, but they ended up calling him a faggot and beating him down with T-ball bats. They didn't ever hit him directly in the head, but they crushed his larynx. He was in the woods by himself for a whole day before we found him. Rozier ended up in a coma, and one week later, he was dead. Shalaya Crump and I didn't speak a word about revenge until the night after the funeral.

That night we planned how we were going to kill the boys, and we planned for the whole rest of the summer. I came up with a good plan, too. But that's the strange thing about planning to kill boys from Waveland with someone like Shalaya Crump. She had the worst temper of anyone I knew, but she was also the smartest person I knew. At some point, Shalaya Crump realized that we didn't really want to kill the boys from Waveland.

"We just want them to hurt like we hurt," she said. Shalaya Crump claimed that in order to hurt the boys, we'd have to "kill some little boy they loved, but not kill them." And neither of us really had it in us to kill some little Waveland boy we didn't know. By the end of the summer, all four of the boys involved got sent to juvenile detention centers for five years.

Anyway, I didn't feel like explaining to Baize how I'd seen Rozier disappear, too, so I just said, "I hear you. You're right. I should be afraid."

I opened the door to the hole slowly so we wouldn't be slapped across the face by the 1964 Klan. I sniffed as I opened the door to the hole and knew we were where we needed to be.

"It's so dark," Baize said. She was bent over coughing under a magnolia tree. "Everything is so green here, too. You know why?" I didn't answer her. I was busy looking around for the Klan. She kept coughing.

"Look," I told her, "we can't play in this place the way we could in 2013. We gotta be quiet and we gotta always keep our head up, you hear me?" I was trying to make my nostrils flare and make lines form in my forehead. "You got folks around here who will slap the taste out of your little mouth if they think you did something small, like farted in a way that don't smell right."

"You got people like that back in 2013," she said and kept coughing. "I'm talking about straight goons." Baize's nose was bleeding. She wiped it on her shirt. "You okay?" I asked her.

"Yeah, I just feel a little weird."

I was starting to feel a little weird too, but not in my body. It was more in my head. I guess there were all kinds of ways to say it, but the easiest way was that I liked Baize more and more the longer we were together. And she liked me, too. It didn't hit me until we got out of the hole that instead of just wanting to get her computer back, maybe she really just wanted to come back with me. I didn't want to like her too much, though, because of Shalaya Crump. I could never like her as much as I liked Shalaya Crump, but still, if I liked Baize too much, I knew Shalaya Crump would be able to tell, and then everything would be ruined.

"Get all that sickness out of you," I told her. "They got these Red Naval cats around here. And those things will come after you and start talking if you don't watch it. And these folks here, they don't even dress like real people." I picked up a few acorns and tossed them at the base of tree. "All you can see is their eyes, and if you joke with them, they love to make you suffer."

"That's better than it is back home, where them goons look just like you. I'm serious. Female goons get to hating on you, too. The most basic of bitches wanna fight you for being glamorous and focused."

"Did you really just say that?" I asked her. "Hard head makes a soft glamorous ass. You gonna be begging to get stomped out by a female goon after the Klan get ahold of you and throw you up in that colored bathroom with one of them Red Naval cats." I threw an acorn at her forehead. "You laughing now, but when they start choking you out, don't say I didn't tell you."

"Damn, Voltron," she said, "can you not hate for like the next five minutes? Damn!"

We walked toward the Freedom School and peeked in the window. There was this slim, light-skinned lady talking to a tired, greasy-looking black man. The lady was walking around pointing and yelling and holding some paper with her back to us. The man was facing her, sitting at a desk and laughing.

"Who are those people?" Baize asked me.

"I don't know. Be quiet." I looked harder. "Is something wrong with that lady's face?...I can't tell. Just stay behind me."

We decided to go in the Freedom School, since the people looked nice enough. They didn't look rich at all, but the hair on both of their heads was so shaped up and neat that I started brushing my own hair.

"Whose babies y'all is?" the lady turned around and asked when we opened the door. I'm not sure how to describe her face, but the skin beneath her eyes and all over her forehead looked like it had been burned really bad and it was maybe just starting to heal. The craziest thing was that her eyes looked normal and they were huge and shiny.

"We ain't babies," I told her. I looked at Baize and she looked back at me.

"I'm City and Shalaya's baby," Baize said, stepping forward. "But I stay with my great-grandmama."

I dropped *Long Division*.

And a Way.

After reading the craziest chapters yet of *Long Division* and sitting there with Pot Belly, I started to understand the sad that he was feeling. There were some red, green, yellow, white, or orange sprinkles in the sad I felt, but mostly, the sad was all just layers and layers of the thickest blue you'd ever seen in your life. Whenever I'd come close to feeling that blue before, I'd pick scabs, or I'd turn off the light and get nice with myself, or I'd come up with a plan about how to get some shine in homeroom at Hamer, or I'd troll the internet with the screen name Megatroneezy, or I'd post something inspirational or something extremely ratchet on Facebook, or I'd eat bowls of off-brand Lucky Charms until I got severe bubble guts. For some reason, I didn't want to do any of that since I had lost at the contest.

I started thinking about Grandma, Uncle Relle, LaVander Peeler, Baize Shephard, and Mama. And when I really thought about all of them, I just felt so much bluer than ever. Yeah, all those folks tried to mask their different blues, but after the praying, smoking, rapping, thinking, drinking, and running, there just seemed to be nothing else left but blue rooms with people who were really even lonelier and bluer than Octavia Whittington, the bluest girl I ever knew.

Octavia Whittington was the light-skinned girl at Hamer with ashy elbows and the bad self-esteem. Octavia almost transferred from Hamer after her adopted parents said, "Fannie Lou Hamer doesn't provide an environment conducive to Octavia's depressive condition." At one of those parent-teacher-student meetings, I remember LaVander Peeler Sr. saying that he was offended that another parent would try to bring that "doggone language of depression" into our school. He didn't say it as plain as he wanted, because a decent number of students were at the meeting, but I do remember him saying loud and clear, "Those other folks might do it that way, but how are we any better than them if we start drugging the doggone feelings out of our kids."

I remember the standing ovation he got, even from Mama, who was usually too busy to come to those meetings. I don't know why, but I always felt sorry for Octavia after that. Yeah, she always stayed alone, and her eyes looked crazy as hell because she only blinked once every minute, but if there was any kind of pill or drank that could make Octavia love living, I really think she should have been allowed to take it at school, especially if other folks at school were chasing the blue away by getting nice with themselves in the bathroom and dissing the hell out of each other with long sentences.

I pulled out a pen from my pocket and finished writing my will on the last page I'd read in *Long Division*.

11. *I leave my favorite pen to this white man in the shed because he needs to write an apology to Grandma and maybe even to Baize. That would make him not feel so sad.*

12. *I leave this copy of* <u>Long Division</u> *to LaVander Peeler.*

13. *I leave the other copy to share between Grandma, Shay, Baize, and this white man in the shed if he decides to apologize.*

14. *I don't want to die yet but I don't want to feel this kind of blue ever again. So sad ain't no joke.*

WEARING BLOUSES NOW.

I was two hours and twenty minutes from my baptism and Grandma was already at work on Monday morning. She planned on meeting Uncle Relle and me at the church on her lunch break. To tell you the truth, Grandma left the house heated. First, she hated that she had agreed to make me wear this dashiki that my mama had left in her closet. I hated it, too. It was bright yellow with brown half moons and full red sun splotches all over it. She said that Mama had always wanted me baptized in the thing, but she was pissed when Mama called her and told her she wouldn't be able to make it to Melahatchie. I could tell the dashiki was too big when Grandma handed it to me. When I put it on, the damn thing came all the way down past my navel, all the way past my thighs, and damn near touched my kneecaps. Plus, the neck part was too wide, so you could see the suit coat, vest, and tie underneath. I needed a shape-up, too, and there wasn't one wave in my head since that white dude had taken my brush.

Uncle Relle came out on the porch while I was stewing in shame. He had a crazy smile on his face. "Anything you want to say to people before your big day?" he asked with one of his little phones in my face.

"Naw, not really. I'm good. I just hate my outfit."

He laughed and said, "That shit looks real fucked up, but you good! Anyone you wish could be here to see you go through this day?"

I just looked at him. Couldn't believe Uncle Relle was using the word "wish." Wasn't his style. "Naw, Uncle Relle. I'm good."

"I'll be right back in like ten minutes."

I asked him where he was going, but he ignored me and jumped in his van.

Ten minutes later, Uncle Relle was pulling back into the driveway and someone else was in the passenger seat with him. Uncle Relle got out, walked around the passenger side, and opened the door. In what felt like slow motion, a patent leather blue-black Adidas hit the gravel.

I knew those Adidas.

Uncle Relle focused his camera phone on LaVander Peeler's face as he got out of the van. As soon as I saw him, I thought about how stupid I looked in that damn dashiki. The LaVander Peeler I knew before the contest would have ethered me in one epic sentence for that outfit, but I wasn't sure how much of that LaVander Peeler was left since he'd gone through that hell at the Coliseum. Plus, I hated that MyMy and Shay couldn't meet him.

"What up, LaVander?" I tried to be real cool when he walked up on the porch. "What you doing here?"

He looked at my hands. "Where's your brush?"

"Oh." I used my left hand to go over my hair. "Long story."

"You straight up wearing blouses now?" he asked me.

"Oh," I tried to get my lie straight. "This is the new thing they wearing down here. But it's not a blouse."

"What is it then?" he asked, and just stood there reminding me of the old LaVander Peeler. I was deep into thinking of all the ways I could blame LaVander Peeler when one of those crazy things happened where we both looked up at Uncle Relle hoping he would turn that camera off so we could say what we really needed to say.

Surprisingly, he told us we'd be leaving soon and walked in the house.

"Why are you at my grandma's house?" I asked him again.

"My father told me I had to come."

"But why?"

"You doing that show your uncle told me about?" he asked me. "That seems like something you would wanna do. They say we could make over a million dollars each if we do it. All things considered, only a fool could turn down that money."

"Yeah, I guess that's true," I said. "But I feel different after being here for a few days. That contest or that show ain't nothing compared to what I been through this weekend."

He just looked at my feet, shook his head, and said, "…"

"What?" I asked him.

"Nothing, City. It's just, you always think you've been through something harder than somebody else."

"Follow me," I told him and walked behind the house. I pointed to the work shed. "Be quiet, okay? Just listen."

We were still as could be. Then there was thump from the shed. Then another one.

"What's that noise?" LaVander Peeler asked.

"A white man and this book. You heard of a book called *Long Division*?"

"No. Should I?"

"It's the realest book I've ever read in my life, man."

"The most real?"

"It's the most real book ever, man. For real, it's about tomorrow and yesterday and the magic of love. I'm serious. A version of me is in the book and Baize Shephard is in there, too. You might be in there, too. I haven't finished it so I don't know."

"All things considered," he said. "I believe you."

We started walking back to the porch. I was leading the way. I realized it was the first time that LaVander Peeler had ever followed me anywhere. When we were under Grandma's cottonwood tree, LaVander Peeler tapped me on the shoulder. I turned around with my fists balled up.

"City, why'd they do that to us?" he asked me. "My father just told me that the difference between me and President Obama is that President Obama never took his eyes off the prize. President Obama was clutch when they did things to him they'd never done to another president. He didn't cry or cause a scene. He was always perfect when it was most important."

"But you were perfect," I told him. "You know what I mean? You were better than them. You were better than me. You coulda won that whole thing. For real." He just looked at me. "I mean, if they gave you a real chance, you coulda won. You know that." He started tearing up again so I put my hand on the top of his back. "You know I hate you, right?"

"I know that," he said.

"But I can't even lie to you, man. You're the smartest person I ever met in my life, other than my grandma."

"But I didn't win, City." He was grimacing and gritting his teeth like someone was giving him a shot in his neck. "All things considered, the point was to win, to beat them."

"You weren't running for president," I told him. "Look, I'ma show you this white man after church, okay? It'll make you feel better about yourself when we free him. Say something."

LaVander Peeler wouldn't say a word.

"You gotta promise that you won't let me drown at this baptism, though. I have a weird feeling about it. Wait. Can I ask you a question?"

"If you want to."

"What did you see before the contest that made your eyes water up? It's like you knew what was gonna happen before it happened."

LaVander started scratching his chin and looking at my chappy lips. "I don't want to say."

"Why not? It's over now. Just tell me."

He looked up and over at Grandma's chinaberry tree. "I heard the woman who ran everything tell someone on her headset…" He started trailing off.

"Tell someone what?"

"She told someone to change the final order and let the tall one beat the Mexican girl because the fat one was going to be difficult."

"Wait." I thought about what LaVander Peeler said. "So does that mean that they were—"

"City, all things considered," he interrupted me and wiped his nose. "If you don't know what that mean, you really are dumbest, fattest homosexual on earth. "

CANCELLATION.

Uncle Relle, LaVander Peeler, and I met Grandma two blocks from the church. The sun was beaming and the grills of Cadillacs, Impalas, and Bonnevilles made the usually dusty Ryle Boulevard look like a conveyor belt of cubic zirconia. Grandma commenced to rubbing gobs of Vaseline all over my forehead. She said I didn't need to look tired and ashy on the most important Monday of my life. Then she kept saying not to be scared, that Jesus would make sure everything would be okay if I just believed.

When we got to the church, Grandma took me to a special room and told me to change. Hanging on the back of the door were three plush maroon robes. I'm talking about long fluffy towel-type robes, with the plushest belts imaginable. One had a piece of masking tape on the chest part with "City" written on it in black marker. The other two had pieces of tape that said "Ren" and "Reygord." I figured those roguish jokers had found some way to skip out on this whole baptism thing.

My dashiki, shirt, and slacks were off when all of a sudden the door opened. In walked the rogues, Ren and Reygord, eating thick slices of cucumbers.

I was glad that I was out of my dashiki before seeing them. Not only because I looked straight crazy in the outfit Mama made me wear, but also because those jokers were wearing dirty camouflage shorts and yellow V-necks that had their names airbrushed on them.

"Y'all ready?" I asked them, and covered my thighs and skin-sacks with my robe.

They just kept eating on those thick slices of cucumber.

"Y'all ready for this dunking?"

They both looked at each other and started taking off their clothes. It was like they were having a contest to see who could take his clothes off the fastest.

"Y'all know about the white man behind my house?"

They both laughed. I liked that they were laughing, but it pissed me off that they wouldn't talk to me.

"Hey, y'all. Hey." Still no answer. "Hey. You know how we can get out of this, don't you?" They looked at me and kept taking their clothes off. Both of them were down to their drawers. A heavy dose of Mama Troll's organ slid under the door. The twins looked at me, looked at each other, and took off out of the room and out of the church.

I was all by myself.

Deacon Big Shank knocked on our door. When I opened it, he said that when Reverend Cherry said, "Let us have our young candidates for baptism," I would walk out with my head down and my fists couldn't be balled up.

While Big Shank was talking, I faded out, still thinking about *Long Division* and all that had happened over the past few days. I tried to think about it all as if it had unfolded like slow-motion scenes in a movie or soap opera, but it didn't work. Then, I tried to think of another kind of movie music that would cover the slow-motion scenes, something like grainy guitar strums or light toe-taps.

That didn't work either.

The only music that fit the scene was Big K.R.I.T.'s single, "Something," or the whiny stuff being spat out by Troll's organ.

Then something else happened in that hallway. Deacon Big Shank kept talking, telling me how much he liked watching *Family Feud* with Steve Harvey on his new flat-screen TV. Deacon Big Shank was always talking about TV. That was one of the best things about him.

"Your granddaddy would've been some kind of proud of you, Citizen. I'm telling you what I know. He would have. Don't believe what no one else tells you. Your granddaddy knew some thangs that no one else ever knew.

It's like he grew out and everybody else grew up…" Big Shank kept talking and my head kept nodding, but my mind was zoning out of his speech.

For the first time since all this mess started, I thought about what it really meant to die and what my granddaddy might have felt before and after he drowned.

I realized, standing there in that hall watching Big Shank's mouth move in slow motion, that stories—sentences, really—were all I had of my granddaddy. He died when I was two and I couldn't remember one thing about him. I heard that he took me everywhere, dressed me up in little suits. Made me a pimped-out leather brim when I was thirteen months. He never went to church a day in his life, but somehow took the church with him. He was the best bootlegger in Melahatchie and the second best in Scott County since it went dry. He loved all the old black sitcoms like *Sanford and Son* and *Good Times*. He wasn't scared of hardly anything and when anybody touched him or his family the wrong way, even if it was white folks, he damn near beat the walk out of them. I heard that after he beat the walk out of someone he'd apologize and say, "I'm sho' sorry about that. I reckon I reacts like a demon when anybody touch me or mines." I heard he had a son named Ralph with a jump-off named Ms. Kyla Pace, and that Ralph had a number of children that my granddaddy never claimed. I heard that he hated to bathe and loved to eat and fight, like me, and that he loved thick, curvy women with big ankles and bigger mouths who liked Newports.

Deacon Big Shank was still in front of me, going on and on, and all of a sudden the truth kicked off its shoes and started clipping its toenails, just lounging in my fat head. The stupid truth was that even though Uncle Relle had killed some people in Afghanistan and LaVander Peeler's brother had killed a man, no one I'd ever really known had died yet, except for maybe Baize Shephard, and *Long Division* was convincing me that she might not really be dead at all.

If Baize wasn't dead, the closest anyone I'd known had come to dying was the white man in the work shed. And the scariest thing about it was that even if I had really known someone that died, at that moment, in that hall, death felt like the only thing in the world that you could do *once*. As scary as the contest had been, I knew something like that could happen again. Death, I understood, was the only thing promised, the only thing that could happen once after you were born. And no one could come back and tell you how it felt.

Or could they?

I figured that must have been the real reason everybody was swinging from Jesus's sack. I'd paid enough attention to Grandma and Sunday school to know the story of Jesus's resurrection. I figured that after he arose, with the help of his almighty powerful father, the Lawd, he knew what it was like to die, and probably started spreading his sentences about beating death to the whole town. Folks started following and loving and believing, not just to be saved or whatever, but to hear sentences about what it was like.

I made the decision right there in that hall that I was definitely going to die during my baptism. I just knew it. And after or while I was dying, I'd find some way to come back and save Pot Belly like I said I would, and then I'd tell Grandma and Mama how to beat death so they could be equipped and not be all surprised when it happened to them. And I'd bring special gifts for Shay, MyMy, Gunn, and maybe even LaVander Peeler, who at that point was probably going to have his own TV show on VH1 called "All Thangs Considered," where his eyes watered up a lot and he said "All things considered" fourteen times an episode.

SAVED SAFE.

I felt a push in the back and heard more of Troll's damp organ. "I *said*, let us have our candidates for baptism."

The back yard of the church was packed with heads everywhere. Some folks had on church clothes, but most had on work clothes. Just Reverend Cherry, Uncle Relle, and me had robes on.

The people parted and we had to walk through the middle. Gradually, they formed this humongous semicircle. All those eyes were tearing my insides up. Grandma was right there near the front. She was crying and trying to hold in tears when I looked at her. I tried to fake-smile, but I couldn't. My damn cheek started quivering all fast. Then I saw the water hole in the ground. Reverend Cherry and Uncle Relle were in the water hole, below everybody else and dressed in the same robes I had, except theirs were plush white instead of plush maroon. Folks stood on both sides just watching and humming the refrain to "Precious Lord." I walked all the way to the front and saw that Uncle Relle and Reverend Cherry were sitting on the steps of the water hole.

"Brother Relle, is you ready?"

Uncle Relle shook his big head up and down. I wanted to beat him through the ground for agreeing to help with this. I swear I did.

"Wait, y'all." Everyone looked at me like I was crazy, but I didn't care. I swear I didn't. "I want my Grandma to help," I said. "Doesn't that make more sense?"

Grandma just stood there smiling and lightweight crying. I loved the smile and all, but it really wasn't helping me out of my situation. Cherry put his hand on my shoulder.

"Little City," he got right up on my ear and acted like he was whispering, but he was saying it loud enough, with his drippy deep voice, for everyone to hear. Troll's playing got even lower and damper.

"Everything need order," he said. "And order, in this here real communified world, order come from tradition, and it's always been two men that do the dunking and take you to that other side. Now, it's the men's fault in this community that every time we goes to dunk a head, 'tain't no hair of the birth daddy. And that's something we gon' have to take care of, but right now, one of them gots to be me and one gon' have to be Brother Relle."

I looked at LaVander Peeler while Cherry was talking and thought about what he said back in Jackson about my mama not being able to keep a man.

"My mama and grandma been doing what daddies supposed to do," I told him. "Plus, you were there when my granddaddy drowned. Who you trying to fool?"

Uncle Relle was recording it all on his camera phone and smiling big as he could.

"Little City," Reverend Cherry said. "That's where your little smart self is wrong. I wasn't there. My shell was there. Inside that shell was a coward, Little City. Sure was. That shell done filled up with something I ain't ever knowed was possible." He kept talking right up on my ear, but he was still looking at the crowd.

"And when you refill a shell with a substance altogether different, the whole thang changes. It was that shell that watched Tom Henry go in and try to save that white boy. That shell knowed Tom Henry was a drunk skunk and didn't have no faith that Jesus would make a way for him. You see what I mean, Little City?"

I shook my head side to side, but he ignored it. "But now, that shell done become a man with a warm right soul. Big soul. See, look here," he said. "Real man let his core shine from the inside out and he ain't got no fear." He started looking out to the crowd and pointed at his chest. "Real man, Little City, is the Lawd's no-fear vehicle."

Everyone started clapping and 'w'hell'ing and 'amen'ing.

"And the only thing I can do about what that shell of me already done did when it watched Tom Henry do what he knowed to be right...is save part of Tom Henry right now."

"What do those sentences even mean, Reverend Cherry?" I asked. Then I whispered, "I'm serious. That sentence doesn't even make sense."

Reverend Cherry ignored me and raised both his hands toward the clouds. Folks started clapping. Grandma set it off. Not disjointed claps on top of one another, but really organized claps, with a second between claps. Like this:

Clap.

Clap.

Clap.

What y'all doing? Everybody else joined in and the claps sped up a little bit. *Clap. Clap. Clap.* It got faster and faster. *ClapClapClapClapClap.* After a while, it started sounding like burning trash, twigs, plastic, and skin, but way louder. Uncle Relle and Reverend Cherry grabbed me on both sides and pulled me to the middle of the pool.

Save me, Grandma, I said, I think. *Please save me. LaVander Peeler!*

They just stared and clapped. The claps were all on top of one another and I couldn't hear Troll or anything. All I heard were claps and Reverend Cherry.

Ouch. I told them. *Quit.* I looked down at the Lord's rusted tears around my shoulders. I should have been cold, but I wasn't. I knew what was next.

Reverend Cherry and Uncle Relle crossed my arms across my chest, in the shape of an X. "In the name of the father," Reverend Cherry boomed, "we shall deliver this vivacious child to a land of the Lord's tears, majesty, and freedom! He will be one of your greatest soldiers, Lord."

My head flew back. One dunk.

"And in the name of the son, we invite him home. Free him from his anger!"

My head flew back again. Two dunks.

"And with the Holy Ghost, we anoint this hyper baby in your tears, the Lord's tears, and let them tears rid him of all the physical worries of his life. He need nothing anymore, for his soul is now and forever with You, Lord. We sacrifice his shell and pray for blessings of his soul. Keep him safe from Your children!"

My head flew back again. Three dunks.

The third dunk felt way longer than the other two. I opened my eyes and saw all these blurred squiggles floating around. I wasn't drowning yet, but water was making its way into my mouth and it tasted like rusty rocks. I couldn't believe how nasty Jesus's tears tasted. I started choking and my heart began beating the hell out of my chest, so I reached both of my hands between Reverend Cherry's and Uncle Relle's legs and pulled hard as I could on their soggy skin-sacks like they were cow titties.

As soon as they let go, I came up moaning, fiending for breath. My heart didn't slow down. It sped up, got ignited by that hot energy, and started screaming to the rest of my insides. It really did. Then my body followed my heart. It ran toward the semicircle of people. They got closer together and kept clapping. I ran back toward the water. I didn't know what I was doing.

I just wanted to be free.

Uncle Relle grabbed the hood of my robe. I slid out of the robe and kept running, swinging, and screaming.

I saw formless shades of liquid brown that looked like a bowl of mashed oatmeal, peanut butter, chocolate chips, burnt butter, and cane syrup. And after a while, I could see regular stuff again. I saw Uncle Relle wobble to his cell phone.

I ain't going. I said. *I ain't going.*

Reverend Cherry was after me, too. I ran back by the pool and grabbed Uncle Relle by the nubs and pushed him in the way. I think I was still yelling and screaming. I looked over at Grandma and LaVander Peeler and they were both smiling, but Grandma was crying, too.

Good tears.

Troll was steady playing that organ, bringing the dampness like it was going outta style. *Grandma, I ain't going,* I think I said. *I ain't going, Grandma.*

The semicircle of clapping folks started getting closer to me. There was nowhere for me to go. The sweat was steady gushing out, sloshing around my inner thighs, dripping off my forehead.

I ran over where Troll was and got under the bottom part of her organ. She was pumping the hell out of her feet, and I was right there next to them, breathing hard as a fat asthma victim, trying to ball myself up and go through the bottom of the organ. Troll's wet music was smacking the hell out of my ears and chest, and she was literally kicking me in the hip, she was pumping it so hard. She had these dry, sand-colored, knee-high stockings that tried to cover the lightened blotches on her old legs.

A hand reached down. It was Grandma. I could tell by the stained silver ring on her pinkie. But part of me figured she was a demon with a hand that looked like Grandma's and when I looked at her whole body, it would be all splotched up like Troll's legs.

"That your hand, Grandma?"

She started fanning me, like she would do to her friends after they caught the Holy Ghost. All this chalked-up foundation was dripping off Grandma's chin like gobs of Tootsie Roll spit.

She was smiling just as big as she could.

"I ain't dead, Grandma." I looked at Grandma eyes. "I ain't dead, am I? Tell the truth."

"Naw, baby," she told me. "You was just free for a little while." She reached for my hand and helped me get up.

I asked Grandma why she let them hold me under for so long. She claimed that as soon as they dunked my head the third time, I started going into a fit.

I put the plush robe on and stood there thinking and looking at the folks in the semicircle for the first time. Gunn, Shay, MyMy, Coach Stroud, and LaVander Peeler were all there and they were all looking at me like they knew something I didn't.

This funny-looking oldhead in a robe similar to mine, but a little more old school, was there too. He was in the back of the crowd, pumping his fist, rubbing the sweat off his old bald head, licking his lips, nodding his head side to side, looking at everyone else.

You know what everybody did after about fifteen seconds? Led by that older joker I'd never seen before, they all started cheering. Not clapping or robotically saying amen, but cheering with their whole bodies, with all that loose energy that fourth graders have during recess.

I wondered if what I'd caught was the same Holy Ghost that Lily Mae and them caught every Sunday. I wasn't trying to catch nothing. I just wanted to live and breathe and keep my heart beating and be free, but maybe that's what they were doing when they went crazy too.

I doubted it, but I figured everything was possible.

Out in the parking lot of Concord, all the kids crowded around LaVander Peeler and asked him questions about what he did at the contest. The grown folks did something different. They ignored LaVander Peeler and got in a line to shake my hand like I was the newest member of their gang. Finally, I wasn't worried about waves or sweating or niggardly or stretch marks or Baize Shephard or dashikis or representing my people or feeling *so sad*.

I'd beaten death, and unlike Jesus, I'd beaten that joker on video. I felt free.

EVERYTHING.

As soon as we pulled into Grandma's driveway, I jumped out of the Bonneville. "City, where you think you going in such a hurry?" Grandma asked.

"I gotta go get ready to show LaVander Peeler something."

"Oh, no you don't. You better take your behind in there and get outta those clean clothes. We leaving in an hour."

After mashing all my stuff in my backpack, I ran back out to tell Grandma one more thing before I left. "Grandma, if you weren't my grandma, I'd still want to be down with you," I told her. "I'm serious. Ufa D is the luckiest oldhead in the Mid-South. The second time I got nice with myself, I imagined getting nice with a younger version of you. I just did. I been wanting to tell you that for a minute. Now that I'm saved, I feel like I can be honest."

Grandma's crooked frown broke into a half moon. She brought her bushy brow together, tilted her head to the side, and looked me right in the eyes. "What, Grandma? I'm serious. I'm just saying I love you. Like I for real love you. I don't just love how you make me feel. I really love you. And until today, you were the only person I knew on earth who really loved me, too."

"Who else you know loves you today, baby?"

"Jesus," I told her. "Right now, I feel like Jesus likes me whole lot, too, Grandma."

Grandma blinked finally, and said, "Problem was that you was always wanting to taste why. You too young and that little bread you got is too soft to understand there ain't no why but Jesus. Them atheists can say what they want, but Jesus, he the only thang done kept us from killing them folks." She fixed the strap on my backpack. "Don't waste another second trying to taste why by yourself, though. Jesus is already in love with you. He been in love with you. That's what you was feeling at the church just now. I know you ain't felt nothing like it, have you?"

"Um, naw, Grandma," I told her. "I never felt something like that before."

"I know. But now, see, you gotta fall in love with him by your actions. Show him you love him by acting as you know he would act. Jesus has seen parts of you that you ain't even know was alive. And even if you was the biggest, baddest nigga in the world, he done seen the wonder and goodness you capable of. I'm just telling you what I know, baby. Jesus is in love with you, City. Let yourself fall all the way in love with him and everything'll be awright."

I stood there wondering about what Jesus told Grandma about that white man in the shed. I felt closer to Jesus after baptism, but I didn't really know how he or anyone else could be in love with me. I thought about how I looked, how I'd felt the past few days, how I'd acted. I really didn't know what I'd done to make Jesus fall in love with me, but I was damn sure ready to start reaping the benefits of that love.

Grandma interrupted my thought. She told me she was going to run down to Troll's for a little while to handle some business. She handed me the keys and told me to put my stuff in the car when I came back.

This was too good to be true.

I wouldn't have to come up with some crazy plan to steal the keys if I wanted to get to Pot Belly.

"Hurry up, City. We gotta get you and that Peeler child on that bus before two o'clock."

LaVander Peeler walked in the bedroom while I was writing in my book. He told me Uncle Relle had dropped him off and claimed he had to run some errands. "Your uncle should stop doing so many drugs."

"You're right about that," I told him. "He should."

"Those two straggly-looking girls, the black one and the white one, and that homosexual boy in the karate suit told me to tell you bye."

"Okay," I said. "You ready to see what's in that work shed?

LaVander Peeler and I could smell what was left of Pot Belly's funk from outside the shed. Couldn't decide if breathing in through my mouth or nose was better, so I alternated.

I opened the door and there he was. Unlike the other times I'd been in the shed, this time Pot Belly was facing me when I opened the door. Immediately, he started squirming, making loud muffled sounds, begging me with his crossed eyes to let him go.

"I told you I was coming back to save you today, didn't I? But first, you gotta do something, okay?" He nodded up and down. "This is my friend, LaVander Peeler. You said you saw me at the contest so you probably saw him too, right?"

Pot Belly nodded his head.

LaVander Peeler wasn't blinking at all. He couldn't believe what he was seeing. "I told you, LaVander Peeler. You can't tell nobody at school about him, though, okay?" LaVander Peeler's eyes were big as I'd ever seen them. "You see where it says 'So sad ...' on the floor? He wrote that with his finger."

I plopped my knees down on the sawdust of the shed and looked at the chains on Pot Belly's legs. "I think both of y'all should read this whole book when you get a chance. It's really short and it's more of a young-adult book for adults, so even if you aren't the best reader in the world, you can still get a lot out of it. I know this is corny but I wanna read these last chapters out loud with y'all, okay?"

It was one of the corniest sentences I'd ever said, but with LaVander Peeler standing above me and Pot Belly chained on the floor of the work shed, I read the end of *Long Division*.

...

Yes Indeedy...

The lady came closer and looked right in our eyes. "Ma'am, we're not from around here," Baize said. "We were just looking for one of our friends. What exactly is supposed to happen in this school?"

The lady looked at both of us for almost a minute without saying anything.

"Both of y'all look familiar to me," she finally said. "Sound like both of y'all been educated somewhere, too, with all them questions. Charlie Cobb and them just mailed this down here to us who fixing to help with the teaching. Cobb say children ain't educated if they ain't been taught to question." The lady handed Baize and me two stapled sheets of paper with some typing on them.

"What's this?" Baized asked her.

"Read it," she told her. "You tell me."

SNCC'S NOTES ON TEACHING IN MISSISSIPPI

Dear Teacher,

This is the situation. You will be teaching young people who have lived in Mississippi all their lives. That means that they have been deprived of a decent education from first grade through high school. It means that they have been denied the right to question. The purpose of the Freedom School is to help them begin to question. They will be different, but they will have in common the scars of the system. Some will be cynical. Some will be distrustful. All of them will have a serious lack of preparation, but all of them will have knowledge far beyond their years. This knowledge is the knowledge of how to survive in a society that is out to destroy you. They will demand that you be honest...

Baize flipped the page and kept reading, but I stopped. I just watched as Baize's round red eyes moved over the page. Just like Shalaya Crump, you could see her read sentences over if they were too short or too long.

The lady in front of us started explaining what was happening in that school while Baize was still reading. "These SNCC folks think our children ain't got no more sense than God give a light-head possum. I reckon they got they heart in the right place. My thang is what's the use in having a school if we ain't giving the students no tests? Everybody need a test, don't you think? We gotta work on that. Yes indeedy."

The lady went on, saying words like "organization" and "compassion" and "justice" and "education" and "future," but I was zoned out. The last thing I heard her say at the end of her long speech was, "Last year this time, y'all probably already know this, but our house got fire-bombed. My daughter was hit in the head with some pillars off the fan, and I got my face a bit burnt up trying to see about her."

"Why'd they bomb your house?" Baize asked. "I mean, I know why they bombed people, but why you?"

"They been shooting in folks' houses, burning down they' churches, anything they can to scare us away from working with them college kids," she said. "That's enough questions. What y'all doing up in here? We told all the children to stay in they' house this week. Didn't nobody tell y'all?"

If I had wanted to hear the words coming out of that woman's mouth, I could've stayed in 1985 and watched PBS. I just kept looking at Baize wondering how what she said about her parents being City and Shalaya could even be true. I hadn't seen any pictures of us in her house, but then again, maybe we looked completely different 20 years older. Or maybe I was too focused on other things to look for pieces of myself in her place. Or maybe she took down all the pictures because it made her sad.

"Wait," I said to Baize. "Were your parents really married?"

"Yeah. Why?"

"Just wondered."

The woman walked over to the man, who now had his head on the desk. She looked at us and didn't say a word, so I just started looking up at the bird's nest at the top of the room. Thin pieces of nest kept falling to the ground.

"Before y'all came in, I was trying to tell this one right here to put that bottle down. This one here is in serious need of a test."

"Why?" Baize asked her.

The woman told us that the man sitting in front of us cut trees for a man named Gaddis. That was the same name as the park Baize had talked about back in 2013. Gaddis had a sixteen-year-old daughter named Brianna. Brianna came out to watch the man cut down some trees a week before that Freedom Summer was announced. Brianna and the man had known each other for years, so they talked and laughed for a while. When Brianna got ready to leave, the man patted her on the bottom of her back and said, "Good luck with everythang, baby. Fine as you is, you sho' ain't gon' need it."

Baize said, "You can't put your hand on a Becky or go around calling them 'baby' and expect good to come from it."

"Who is Becky?" I asked her.

She ignored me.

Neither of us knew what to say after that. Baize was really into what was happening, but I was just looking at her, trying to see if I could find a part of me in any part of her face. People always said I looked like all these people who I never thought I looked like. That made me think I really didn't know how I looked at all. Baize definitely had my hips and maybe she had my forehead, but other than that, I couldn't see or hear a drop of me in her. If she was my daughter, I hoped to God that she had my tiny belly button and not one of those big ol' country ones like Shalaya Crump that made you look like you had a brown Vienna sausage growing out of your stomach.

"Is your mind or mouth broke?" the woman said to me. "You gonna let your baby do all the talking for you?"

"Umm. Oh, naw," I said. "I talk. She ain't my baby, though. We're from a land far away." Baize just looked at me and started shaking her head. "Um, have you ever heard of a man named Lerthon?"

Baize cut her eyes to me. "Lerthon Coldson?" she whispered to me. "You never said we were looking for Lerthon Coldson. You said we were coming to save your friend."

The old man with his head down on the desk started giggling. "Yeah, we know who he is," he said. "We know that lowdown son of a bitch good and well, don't we, baby?"

"Where can we find him?" I asked and got closer. "I got some information Lerthon might need."

"Found!" the man said. "I'm 'Thon. Why you asking?"

Mama Lara never married my granddaddy, and now I understood why. You could tell that one day, maybe a long time ago, maybe even a month earlier, Lerthon Coldson was one of those beautiful men that people, including other men, loved to watch smile. Even now, he had the kind of smile that made you think that all people, no matter how old, were beautiful eight-year-olds who drank with their whole mouth covering the water fountain. That didn't mean he wasn't also completely drunk out of his mind, though. *Shame, shame, shame*, I thought to myself. "Oh, okay. Mr. Thon, I have a message for you?"

"Is it a message in a bottle?" he asked me. "If it is, just gon' and give me the bottle. You can keep that message, though, big boy."

Lerthon wouldn't stop laughing and then he started slowly crying and apologizing while he was laughing. "Gotdamnit," he said, "folks do whatever they can to stay alive. I just be hating that mirror. That's 'bout it. That little white girl was going off to school. She was making them eyes at me so I told her what was on my mind."

"But you said she was 16," I said.

"Don't tell me," he said. "I know how old she is. I got me a 13-year-old daughter myself. Shit, if her daddy woulda called my daughter 'baby,' wouldn't nobody be after him. Wouldn't nobody get to shooting and carrying on, would they?"

"But that don't make it right," the woman said and started walking out of the door, shaking her head from side to side. "You got a wife, Thon. Even though my face burnt up don't mean you can fill my chest up with salt." From nearly out of the doorway, she said, "Y'all need to get out this building and go 'head home. Thon don't listen to reason. Never did until it's too late."

"Oh, okay," I said and looked at my wrist like I had on a watch. "Well, Mr. Thon, we need to get on out of here. I have a message for you. You might need to watch out for the Klan," I told him and put my hand on his back. "Somebody told us that they were coming to get you. We were supposed to tell you so, yeah, I guess we're telling you. Watch out for that Klan. So..."

I looked at Baize and she was looking right in my mouth like it was covered in purple Kool-Aid. "What you looking at?" I asked her. "That's true. Well, we're gonna go now. You should probably leave here soon. Thank you. We'll holler."

Baize and I walked out of the school and she headed across the road toward the Co-op. She didn't say a word, and I had no clue what she was thinking. I just kept looking at how she waddled like me, and had a perfectly shaped head like Shalaya Crump. *Was I really a father?* I kept thinking about how crazy time was even if you weren't hopping from present to future to past. In just like five minutes, I had discovered the daughter I never knew I had, met the shady granddaddy I never knew, and found out that the girl I would have given up my eyeballs to kiss was actually my wife. In that five minutes, I met the human being I would become without actually remembering becoming that human being.

People always say change takes time. It's true, but really it's people who change people, and then those people have to decide if they really want to stay the new people that they're changed into. I wasn't sure if I wanted to be this new person. But I was sure that my daughter didn't need to be fighting Klansmen.

Baize stopped in front of the Co-op and rested with her hands on her knees. She was straining to keep her breath.

"You okay?" I asked her.

"I'm fine. Allergies, I think," she said. "I just wanna see if the water is still back here."

As we passed the Co-op, I tried to shield Baize's eyes from the "COLORED" door. The cat and the Dobermans were just chilling in front of the sink in the bathroom. Baize looked at the door, then looked at the animals, then just shook her head.

"That cat, that's the one that talks," I told her. "I swear to God."

"I believe you," she told me. "You ain't gotta swear to God."

The work shed was right next to the clothesline, but I hadn't even noticed it before. Behind the Co-op and the work shed were these train tracks and on the other side of the train tracks was the Gulf of Mexico. In 1985, there was this rickety little pier where we'd go and sometimes throw rocks or watch people fish. The pier's wood was this splintery deep brown and maroon. Baize kept her book bag on and just walked right up on the pier. At the end of the pier, she just stood up on her tippy toes.

"You hear that, Voltron?"

I listened. I heard birds singing and sea creatures dipping in and out of water, but mostly I heard wind. When you're listening for something special and you don't hear it, you start to sniff for something different. "I don't hear nothing but wind, Baize. Can we go?"

"Back home," she said, "there ain't no pier. When you come out here, the water, it's still crazy black in some places from all that oil."

"Oil?"

"Yep. You can light a match and throw it in one of the oil spots and sometimes the flame can stay lit for a whole minute. You know what's really ill? When you come out here and look at the water, you can see the lightning bugs getting their wink on, you know, lighting up against all that black."

"Is it pretty?"

I waited for her to say something but she didn't. She just cut her eyes at me and blinked in slow motion the same way Shalaya Crump would when she thought something I'd said was ignorant as hell.

"It's blue," she finally said. "All of it."

"Blue? You said it was black?"

"It is, but it's all so blue, too, because of the black. Don't you see it?"

"Look Baize, we gotta go."

"Man, I come out here all the time and imagine this is a beach with palm trees and mountains in the background," she said, "but no matter how nice I see it, the sky ain't never quite right."

"Why?"

"I don't know," she said with her back to me. "I hate it. Folks act like they hate the oil now more than the wind, but me, I'd kill the wind, the sky, and water if I could. I ain't lying. I always imagine that my first video is gonna be me rhyming against a computer-generated dude who looks like he's made of black water, like *Terminator 2*, except he's gonna be called Swaginator and I'm killing that fool in the first minute of the video."

"Why, though?"

"Why what?"

"Why kill the sky?"

"Because it took my family. Shit. I told you that."

"No, you didn't. What do you mean, the sky took them?"

"I mean, I never got a chance to see them again because the sky took them away from me."

"They didn't drown?"

"If they really drowned, their bodies would have come up sooner or later." Baize turned around and headed back across the pier and over the railroad tracks.

I grabbed Baize's hand as we walked by the bathroom again. The cat and the Dobermans weren't in there any more. We looked across the road and headed toward the hole. "Look, I hear what you're saying about your parents disappearing and all that, but I'm taking you home."

"Home as in 2013?"

"That's the only home you got, right?"

"I ain't going back home without you," she said, and kept trying to look me in the face. "Voltron? Voltron! Yo! You said you wanted my help."

"I changed my mind, Baize. You're too young for this. You sound sick, too. I bet it's that time of the month. Things are about to get crazy. And you know what else? Folks can tell just from how you dressed that you ain't from the '60s."

"They can tell the same thing about you, Voltron," she told me. "Don't worry about my time of the month. I came prepared. I just gotta get right with the air here."

"Look, don't make it harder than it has to be," I told her. "2013 is farther away from 1985. So I'm closer to these folks just based off of time. Plus, look at you. You got that ugly haircut for a girl and that dumb backpack on and folks in the 1960s, they be knowing things?"

"Okay, for real." Baize got right in my face even though I was running from her eyes. She grabbed my chin. "No, you did not just say 'Folks in the '60s be knowing things?' Really? It's like that? You should feel so lucky that someone thinks you're kinda cute," she said, "because..."

"Don't say that!" I grabbed her by her shoulder blades and shook her. "Don't ever say I'm cute. You don't even know cute. My line is crookeder than a Smurf house and I fart in my sleep all night long, and when I smile one of my eyes...see it?" I pointed to my left eye. "It's a little bit crusty and bloodshot all the time. I think I got permanent pink eye. For real! It's contagious, too. Don't—"

Baize tried to knee me in the privacy but I turned and she got me in the left thigh. In the middle of our tussle we heard twigs breaking and leaves crunching. "Shhh," I whispered to her. "You hear that?"

"Don't tell me to shush," Baize whispered back. "I only said someone thinks you're cute. Not me, dummy. Don't act like I'm trying to get with you. I don't even roll like that."

We were both still, but it was too hard to see if someone was coming because everything was so green and full.

"Voltron," she whispered.

"What?"

"I think that lady back there was my great-grandma."

I started to ask her how she knew when from about ten feet away, we saw someone on the ground crawling toward us. It was

Shalaya Crump. I ran over and helped her to her feet. She hugged my neck and held me tight as I'd ever been held for a whole minute without saying a word.

I let go of the hug, but Shalaya Crump kept squeezing tight. I whispered in her ear not to say my name in front of Baize, but Shalaya Crump was actually crying right there in my arms while looking directly at Baize. It was one of the top two things I never thought would happen. I pulled away from her hug and asked, "What happened to your Jewish friend, Evan?"

Shalaya Crump tried to talk, but something terrible must have happened. Every time she started to talk, her teeth got to chattering. Baize walked up and started rubbing her back, too. Finally, she got something out. "It's worse than we think. They..."

"Who? I don't understand."

"I didn't know how to turn it on. The mayor...his uncle...if they didn't stop this Freedom School from being used, the Klan was gonna go after them. They wanted to run them out of Melahatchie."

"Why?"

"I didn't know..."

"Know what?"

"The Klan was going to kill Evan's family if they didn't put on sheets. They Jewish and they were gonna help with the schools. They gave Evan a gun. It was Gaddis's plan."

"Who gave Evan a gun?"

"His brother gave Evan a gun and they told him to shoot me in the shoulder."

"I know you scared," I told her, "but you doing your own long division right now. Just get in and get out like you tell me. Please! I don't get nothing you're saying."

Baize jumped in. "Wait, who is Evan?"

"Girl, don't you see grown folks talking?" I told her. "There's a guy named Jewish Evan. Go ahead and finish. Damn."

"Evan took the gun and he pointed it at me, then he aimed it at his brother's leg and pulled the trigger but he missed. Then they beat him even harder."

"Wait," I said. "So his family was planning on killing our granddaddies and burning the church? Where's your granddaddy at?"

"They made them do it. They ain't never meant to kill him," she said. "They only wanted to kill your granddaddy. That's what they were planning to do when they caught you."

"Me?"

"Yeah."

"But they got thrown off with that computer. That's when Evan came in with that BB gun."

"He didn't really save me," I said. "You know that, right?" Shalaya Crump didn't say anything. "You think Evan saved me, don't you?"

She ignored me and kept talking. "They got the computer and they said that if I didn't bring back something to turn it back on in the next hour, they were gonna beat him even harder. If they give the power cord to the Klan, they think the Klan will leave them alone or they could sell it for enough money to start over in another place."

"What? That's the dumbest mess I ever heard in my life. Are you serious? What's wrong with these folks? This is the stupidest place I've ever heard of in my life. I hate this ol' backwards-ass place. Don't you feel like this is someone else's story?"

"What do you mean?" she asked.

"I don't know what I mean. It's just that this ain't our story. It wasn't supposed to happen like this."

Baize walked up between us. "The computer ran out of juice. That's all." She went in her backpack and pulled out this weird-looking long cord with a big square head. "This cord right here is what they need."

I kept asking Shalaya Crump questions when Baize interrupted again. "Wait. Do you have my phone, the little thing Voltron stole?"

"Why do you call him Voltron?" Shalaya Crump asked.

Shalaya Crump and Baize stood there looking at each other. I said, "What y'all looking at? Why y'all staring at each other like that? Damn. Talk."

They moved their eyes back to each other. While Baize was looking at Shalaya Crump's feet, Shalaya Crump was looking at Baize's forehead. Then they locked into each other's face. And you know what Baize said? "You're hotter than I thought you'd be, up close." She really said it. "Seriously, you must work out."

"Just pushups and crunches," Shalaya Crump said, and went in her pocket and pulled out Baize's phone. She handed it to her and Baize flipped it open and pushed a few buttons.

"You think that school thing has some electric outlets in it?" Baize asked. "If you can get those people to bring my computer back, I got an idea. Y'all are killing me with all this drama."

While we were walking, I thought about how I wanted to tell Shalaya Crump about all that Baize and I had experienced. I wanted to tell her about watching a huge TV and eating dinner and shaming myself at that Spell-Off. But after she said all that about fighting off the Klan and almost getting shot in the shoulder and meeting Jewish folks who were forced to act like they were in the

Klan, my time together with Baize in 2013 looked super lame. It really did. You really never know what other folks are doing when you think you're having the craziest experience of your life. Plus, I thought that if I would have just gotten back in the hole earlier, I would have experienced that crazy time with Shalaya Crump and Evan, instead of making a fool of myself in 2013.

I was thinking of something to say when we heard *Pow! Pow! Pow!*

The smell of gasoline was everywhere when we walked into the Freedom School. Lerthon Coldson was slumped face down on the desk.

Baize didn't scream, but she kept gasping and coughing. Shalaya Crump held Baize's hand and I don't even know why but I went toward Lerthon.

"Don't touch him!" Baize said. "It's a crime scene." I looked at Baize like her bread wasn't all the way done. "I'm serious. If you get your DNA in it, or compromise the crime scene, the police could blame you."

I had no idea what she was talking about, but I wasn't about to walk up and touch Lerthon at all. I had never been one of those people who loved blood. A lot of my friends in Chicago and Melahatchie would split open baby birds or throw puppies into cracked ceilings. I always fought them after they did it because it seemed like the meanest thing to do, especially to something that would never really hurt you that much. This was different, though. Right in front of us was a man who wasn't alive any more. And the fact that this dead man was related to me didn't even matter. What mattered is that he was alive and smiling and lying through his teeth ten minutes earlier, and now he'd never be alive or smiling or lying again.

Baize was actually sitting down in the corner coughing into her shirt. And Shalaya Crump was watching me watch the body.

"We never should have done this," I said really low to Shalaya Crump. "I wish someone would've told me not to follow you. We never should have done this. I wish I woulda stayed my fat ass at home. Now everything is messed up. I did this for you. I stole Bibles for you. Went to the future for you. Followed some white boy for you. Made a fool of myself in 2013 for you. You know that, right?"

Shalaya Crump and Baize had their eyes closed. "Open y'all damn eyes. Look!" The voice that was coming out of my body was mine, but it was a voice I'd never heard.

I walked over and saw the blood dripping from the desk to the floor. I let some of it drip on my Weapons, because that's what I knew they would do in a dumb book.

"You came back so Evan could tell you what happens to you in the future, right? Did he tell you?" Shalaya Crump just looked at me. "Did he? Because I know." Shalaya Crump stepped toward me. "I know what happens, what really happens. What all did he tell you in between getting his ass kicked? Did he tell you that we get married? Me and you."

"Please don't start mess now, City," she said. "Why you gotta be so two days before yesterday?"

"I ain't so two days before nothing! You always telling me not to start something, Shalaya Crump. Always talking about I'm so 'yesterday' or I'm so 'long division' or I'm so *Young and Restless.'* You ain't never said I'm so foolish, though." I stopped to think about what I'd just said to Shalaya Crump. It was the best five sentences I'd ever said to her and I hadn't even practiced them in the mirror. This wasn't even *GAME*. "That's what I am, though. I'm so gotdamn foolish for wanting you to love me like I love you."

"Don't say that."

"I can say what I want. I love you. I do. That's why I ask you everything under the sun except if you ever had a boyfriend. Because if you'd ever had one, even if it was way before me, it woulda broke my heart."

"You never told me that," Shalaya Crump said.

"So what. I shouldn't have to. You shut that door on me. If you had come back with me, none of this would have happened," I told her. "None of it."

"I was trying to protect you," she said. "You were hurt and I knew you needed to go home. And I...I think I need to be here."

"Why? Just say it."

"I believed Evan when he told me he knew where I was in the future. I believed him when he told me he could tell me who my parents are. I wanted to know what happens to them and me on the other end. I know you hate me for this, City, but I really want to change the future." Shalaya Crump got closer to me in a way that would have made me so happy in 1985. "I just wanted to change it so bad that I didn't care. And to change it I just had to know what happened."

"Oh. Okay," I said. I kept finding the body of my granddaddy out of the corner of my eye, no matter which way I tried to look. It made me sadder and madder. "You just wanted to know? Well, I want you to know, too. Baize, tell her who your parents are."

Baize sounded like she was whimpering, but I figured it was just that her nose was stuffed. "Why? Don't yell at me."

"Just tell her."

"Tell me what?" Shalaya asked.

"City Coldson is...was my father's name...my mother's name... was...Shalaya Crump-Coldson."

"Who?" I said. "Say it louder."

"Shalaya Crump-Coldson was her name."

"Was?" Shalaya Crump said.

"Tell her what happens to your parents, Baize. And stop crying."

Baize wiped her eyes and opened her phone. She pushed a few buttons and looked at something in the phone that made her close her eyes super tight. "These are my parents," she said. "These were...umm..." I couldn't tell if she was having a hard time talking because she was sick or because she was sad.

Shalaya Crump and I looked at the picture. She had long shiny braids in the picture and dark patches under her eyes, but she was even more beautiful as a grown woman than she was as a kid. Her cheeks looked like they were about to burst open and knock her glasses off her face she was smiling so hard. A gold locket with an "SC" charm hung around the middle of her neck and I was behind her smiling ear to ear, kissing her cheek. All my hair was gone and I had a strange kind of goatee that made my face look less fat than it was. Both of our eyes were so shiny, too.

"That's us," I told her. "We disappear, Shalaya Crump. You couldn't find you in 2013 because there *is* no you. You're dead in 2013. And so am I. We disappear in 2005."

I wanted to just slump to the floor and cry, but what I said sounded so crazy, I didn't even know how to slump to the floor right after saying it. Not when directly in front of us was a dead relative with a hole the size of a Coke can in his back. I just wanted to go home to 1985 and slump by myself in the year that I knew the most about.

Maybe we all did.

While we were looking at each other's eyes and trying to avoid looking at Lerthon Coldson's dead body, two Klansmen appeared and slowly made their way into the room. These two weren't as big as the ones who beat me down. They didn't have glasses on either. The taller Klansman had a rifle that was as tall as me in one hand and Baize's computer in the other hand. The smaller one had a can of gasoline that you could tell was nearly empty by the sloshing sound it made.

"Look," Baize jumped in front of them and said in the direction of the bigger one, "we know how to work the computer. Can we show you?"

The Klansmen just stood there not saying a word, moving their heads side to side. "Did one of you shoot him?" I asked. "That's my granddaddy. He shouldn't have done what he did, but did you have to shoot him?" They just stood there looking at me. "What if someone shot your granddaddy? Look here, man. We in the middle of some family drama, you know what I mean? I ain't even lying. Can't y'all just let us go? We won't tell nobody."

Baize walked slowly toward the men with her bag. She looked at us, then tried to take a deep breath and couldn't so she bent at the waist and coughed into her shirt. I grabbed for her but she walked off and looked at me in a way she hadn't looked before.

"Hold up. You want the cord, right?" she said to the Klansmen. "What's the use in having the cord if you can't use the thing? Look."

Baize plugged the computer up and typed a few things on the screen. "Okay, come here." Music came from the computer. "Walk right in front of the screen and see what happens." Baize did something that made the computer screen turn into a TV screen, and whatever was in front of the computer ended up on the screen. The bigger Klansman looked down at the screen and saw himself. "I can show you how to work it," she said.

Just like before when all the words I typed on the screen were famous, whoever walked in front of the computer looked famous on the screen, too.

The bigger Klansman handed the gun to the smaller one. He walked in front of the computer and started moving his arms like he was an Egyptian. If the past day hadn't been filled with more craziness than a little bit, this would have been the craziest thing I'd ever seen in my life. Baize knelt down and pushed a button that made these twinkle sounds come from the computer. A voice from the computer whispered, "…1, 2, 3, uh."

It wasn't loud overall, but the specific sounds in it were louder than anything I'd ever heard. It really sounded like something from the future. Not the 2000s, either—more like the 3000s. Baize actually stood up and started dancing in front of the computer screen as best she could. You could tell it took a lot for her to actually move because she was getting so weak. She started dancing near me and said, "When I give you the sign, clothesline the big one."

I said okay and kept watching her dance. I couldn't believe I was watching her dance on a TV screen with Klansmen in the background and a dead man slumped over a desk with a bloody hole in his back in 1964.

After a while, though, Baize had all of us, including the two Klansmen, dancing in front of the screen and trying to move in front of each other to see who could look the most famous. Baize made us form a version of a really tight *Soul Train* line. Two of us danced on the side and one person jammed in the middle going toward the camera.

I started it off by doing a robot into the Pee-wee Herman, and then I mixed it with a Prince move, where I looked at the camera and licked in between my fingers right in front of the computer.

Then Baize came through trying to do some dance where she acted like she was hammering really fast with her whole body. She was so sick and so weak, though, that it looked like she was doing it in slow motion. Her nose was bleeding a little bit the whole time, too. She broke the hammering thing off into some hard locking, too. Boom! Bam! Lock! Lock! Then she acted like she was riding a bike side to side, and she ended it doing this dance I saw Doug E. Fresh do.

Next came Shalaya Crump, who tried to do a back glide into a moonwalk and a Michael Jackson spin, and then she got right up on the camera and started prepping. She put both hands in the air and worked them back and forth in sync with her long neck. Those other years didn't have nothing on 1985.

Finally, the bigger Klansman stood in the middle. He asked for the rifle back from the smaller one and just stood there posing, with his hands folded up like he was on top of a mountain. At this point, the voice in the song started chanting something about a Polaroid picture: "Shake it…" The bigger Klansman didn't move at all until he handed the rifle back off to the smaller Klansman and broke down into this mean twist, super close to the ground. When he was right up on the computer checking himself out, the dude copied Baize and did the Doug E. Fresh dance, too.

I kept looking at Baize for the sign, but I didn't know what the sign looked like. Then she looked at me and raised her eyebrows a little bit.

Out of nowhere the smaller Klansman swung the butt of the rifle like a baseball bat and hit the bigger Klansman right upside of the head.

He went down, and a small box of matches fell out from under his sheet as he knocked over the computer as he fell. I picked up the box of matches, jumped on the man, and grabbed him by his neck. While I held him down, Baize was kicking him as hard as she could in the privacy while the song was still playing. His eyes kept blinking as the white of his sheet turned liquid maroon right below the left eye hole.

It looked like magic.

Standing above us were Shalaya Crump and the smaller Klansman. He dropped the rifle and both of them looked at it.

"Take the rifle, Shalaya. What you doing? Pick it up."

She finally took it.

"Shoot him."

She looked down at me. "Just shoot that asshole somewhere!" It was the first time I'd used "asshole" around a girl.

Shalaya Crump tossed the rifle back down and took the sheet off of the smaller Klansman.

"Oh. My. God," I said to Baize. The smaller Klansman under the sheet wasn't a man at all. "Jewish Evan Altshuler?"

The room was silent, except for more music that came from Baize's computer and her constant coughing. Evan and Shalaya Crump stood in the middle of the room touching fingertips while Baize and I managed to tie the hands of the bigger Klansman with this cheap-looking black belt that she had in her backpack.

Shalaya Crump saw me watching her so she pulled her hand away from Evan's. I didn't know where to throw my eyes, so I threw them at the tied hands of the Klansman. His hands were so small for his size. They couldn't have been much bigger than Baize's hands. And you know how grown white men have a lot of hair on the outside of their hands? This Klansman's hands were bare as mine.

Baize pulled out her phone and started taking pictures of the man. "Should we take his sheet off, too?" she asked me.

"Nah. It'll be harder to hurt him if we take it off. He looks like a monster now, right?"

"Not really," she said. "More like a white boy in a white sheet."

"Good point."

Baize and I started busting more jokes about monsters, goons, and Klansmen when Shalaya Crump hugged Evan with her back to me. I looked up and his eyes were closed. When they opened, he came near me.

"City, I ain't mean no harm with all this," he said. "You think you can save someone's life, you do it. I reckon it can get messier than you think. You know what I'm trying to say?"

"Not really," I said.

"That's my brother," he said and pointed to the Klansman. "Never thought in a million years I'd have to let loose on my own brother with a rifle."

"I never thought in million years I'd follow a white boy who calls himself Jewish into a hole in the ground in 1964," I told him. "Thangs happen, I guess."

"Ev, come on, man," the Klansman said through the sheet. "These folks ain't none of your friends. Tell 'em why we did it. I never did nothing disrespectful to a Negro in my life. You know that."

"You shot my granddaddy," I told him, "just because you could. That ain't disrespectful enough?"

"No I didn't," he said through that sheet. "I didn't. We were just coming to burn the school down."

"With him inside?"

"Yeah, but they said he'd already be dead."

"Who shot him?" The taller Klansman didn't answer so I looked to Evan. "Who shot him, Evan? You?"

"City, you know he didn't shoot no one," Shalaya Crump said. "Quit being so Perry Mason."

"How do I know? Just because y'all went through something, I'm supposed to trust him. His plan got all us in trouble in the first place. How come you can't see that?"

Baize went in her bag and started blowing her nose and hocking up mucus. She spit it in these blue napkins she'd brought with her.

"Mr. Gaddis probably did it," Evan said.

"Wait. It's real convenient that folks can blame everything on Gaddis, ain't it?" Baize asked, but she didn't wait for an answer. "And how come you ain't the real Klan? Y'all were gonna burn up this building with a black man's dead body in it, right? And y'all wearing white sheets with holes for eyes, right? That's real Klan-ish of someone who ain't in the Klan, don't you think? Maybe all white folks in the Klan are just Klan-ish, you feel me?"

I looked at Baize and loved her smart mouth so much in that second. I didn't love it because I was somehow responsible for it. I just loved that there was someone alive who could say the things I thought but didn't know how to fully say. It would take me a week of planning to come up with the clever stuff she could come up with in seconds.

"Yeah," I said to Evan. "Y'all might not be all the way Klan, but y'all both are mighty Klan-ish to burn down a building with my granddaddy in it."

"But they didn't burn down the building," Shalaya Crump said. "Nothing got burnt down."

"We was just trying to save our family," his brother said. "That what y'all were fixing to do, too. If it's right for y'all, it's right for us, ain't it?" It was so odd to hear a teenager's voice coming from under a Klan sheet. "Some of these folks hate anyone who ain't them. If you ain't the right kind of white or you ain't Christian or you ain't Southern or you ain't whatever they want you to be, you might as well be a Negro, especially with that Freedom Summer coming."

"But y'all can hide," Shalaya Crump finally said to the brother. "Don't you see what we're saying? We can't ever hide." She looked hard at Evan. "That's all I was trying to say earlier."

"We been trying to hide long as I remember," Evan told us. "And hiding, it's damn near worse than the getting caught. Because you only hiding from yourself. How you supposed to like yourself or anyone else if you done convinced yourself that you deserve to be hunted by yourself?"

"First, that's too many 'yourselfs' in one speech," Baize told him. "And whatever you talking about, y'all decided to fix that by walking around in sheets, acting like the Klan?" She looked up at me. "Can I cuss?"

"Go ahead."

"Fuck that, Mr. Klan man," she said. "This ain't Halloween, yucka."

"Yeah," I said. "This ain't Halloween, yucka. What's a yucka?"

Baize laughed at me and shook her head.

"Say what you want," his brother broke in. "They was coming for us just like they came for y'all and we was just trying to survive. What would you do if y'all were in our position?"

"But that's the point, dummy," Baize said. "We can't be in your position. They came to *you* to get *us*. Would they ever come to *us* to get y'all? Ever?"

"But if they did come to you to get us," Evan asked, and looked up toward the trees, "what would y'all do?"

I looked at Baize, who looked at Shalaya Crump, who looked at me. Then I looked at Evan and wanted to want to say something so much that my throat muscles started cramping, but nothing came out.

Nothing could.

"Yeah," he said. "Exactly."

"What y'all think we should do with him?" Shalaya Crump asked me and ignored his comment. "Can we just let him go?"

I looked up at her and the strangest thing happened. Jewish Evan Altshuler, Shalaya Crump, Baize, and the teenage Klansman were staring right at me. Somehow, some way, I was supposed to have a plan.

"Um," I said and snuck a look at Baize's face. I kept my eyes focused on the wooden desk and thought about how much I hated eyes. I had this dream one time where I was backstroking in a bowl full of pound cake batter. In between strokes, something exploded. The explosion made the bowl turn upside down and all around the outside of the bowl was this slow-dripping pound cake batter. The batter started forming these eyes that stared and blinked slower than human eyes. I knew the eyes couldn't touch me, so you'd think I would feel safe, but being surrounded by blinking pound cake eyes was the scariest thing I ever felt. At least, that's what I thought before I was sitting in a desk in the middle of that Freedom School in 1964. Three sets of eyes in that room belonged to people I wanted to love me, and those three sets of eyes were burning my insides out.

"I got an idea," I told them. "Let's put him in the hole and send him to another time."

"But how do we know that'll work if we're not sure if it's the hole that's special or if it's us that's special?" Baize asked.

"You're special, Baize. You are, whether you were born a time traveler or not," I told her.

"Just because we're blood doesn't mean you have to say even wacker stuff than usual," she said. "I'm for real."

"Good point," I said. "Look, we got a fifty-fifty chance of getting it right. Let's go."

We kept the hood on Evan's brother and walked toward the hole. He talked the whole way, mainly to Evan. "Evan, come on, man. Take off the gotdamn hood. What was I supposed to do?"

Evan never said a word back. He just walked with us, but I could tell he was nervous about what was about to happen to his brother.

"You sure you want us to do this?" Shalaya Crump asked him. "You might never see him again. You don't have to do it to make me happy."

"Where you think he'll end up?" Evan asked her.

"You know what's messed up?" I said. "If your brother ends up in 1985, I don't think nothing bad would even happen to him. Without the sheet, he's just a regular white boy. No one would know he was Jewish unless he told them, right?"

"I don't know about that. He wouldn't be safe in 2013," Baize said. Her voice was cracking at this point.

"Why? Because the goons'll get him?" I laughed.

"Yep," she said. "They would! They wouldn't even care if he was Jewish or Italian or none of that. You show up wearing a white sheet like that and it's a wrap for you."

"Girl, are you a secret goon? You act like Melahatchie goons are worse than the Vice Lords or something. Only thing is when I was there I didn't see no Melahatchie goons." I waited for Baize to say something back but she just smiled at me, shrugged her shoulders, and tried to catch her breath.

"Wait," Shalaya Crump said and stopped walking. We all stopped too, even though we were just a few feet from the hole. "My question is, why send him to another time if he'll be fine no matter where he goes? Ain't that so lip sync?"

We all looked at Shalaya Crump, including Evan's brother. I tried hard to think about what it meant to be so "lip sync" but I couldn't get it. "Lip sync?" I asked.

"Yeah, like *Puttin' on the Hits*. Why go through the motions if it's just a motion?"

"E-motion?"

"Naw, City, a motion."

That was a good question, but if I said I didn't know, it would have made my plan look half-baked. "We want him to experience what we went through, right? All the e-motions."

"Does that mean he has to suffer?" Shalaya Crump asked.

"We suffered," Baize told her, and walked right up to the hole.

"Right, but we're gonna remember suffering whether he suffers or not," Shalaya Crump said.

We opened the hole and after tons of punching, scratching, screaming, and kicking, Baize and I got Evan's brother in the hole while Evan and Shalaya Crump watched. Evan grabbed the hood off his brother's head while he was in. His brother had a young face but half the hairs on his head were actually gray.

"Why'd you take that off?" I asked him.

"I don't know," he said. "Just didn't seem right to send him to another time with that thing on his head. We gotta be fair."

"Who put 'that thing' on his head?" I asked him. "Ain't nobody make him wear it, did they?"

"You're right," Evan said. "But we can't put it back on him now."

"Gimme the hood," Baize said. She was sitting at the base of a magnolia tree. The color in Baize's face was fading. Part of me thought she was gonna put the sheet on her head just for fun. That's kinda what I wanted to do.

Evan handed it to her and she put the hood on her little left hand like a huge glove. "Don't you think it's crazy how all the Klan members are always boys?" Baize asked. "I mean, what would a Klansgirl even say? If I was white and messed up in the head, I'd be the first Klansgirl in Mississippi. Then I'd change the whole Klan style, too. I wouldn't be messin' with no fire or lynching nobody. My Klan would go town to town with coloring books asking folks who didn't get along to color together. If they didn't color right, they'd have to spit a sixteen-bar freestyle about sheets. I'm for real."

Baize took out her phone and snapped a few pictures of the hood like it was a puppet. After she was done, she threw the hood in the hole and started coughing. With Evan's brother begging and pleading, all four of us pushed the door to the past, present, and future shut. Well, two of us did. Evan and Shalaya Crump acted like they were pushing but I saw them both keep their eyes closed, gritting their teeth, just going through a motion.

After a minute of silence, I opened the hole and looked in. We couldn't see anyone, but none of us knelt down and really looked all the way in. "I wonder where he went?" I said. "You think y'all would've sent him away if you were by yourself?"

"I know I wouldn't," Shalaya Crump said.

"Me either," Evan said and looked at Baize. "Is she okay?"

Baize, who was already on her knees, put her head in the hole to make sure he was gone. "I'm telling you," she said. "I would've done it by myself. Ride or die. You think that dude can just come back tomorrow, though? Or like, do you think he's gonna just fuck up whatever time he lands in?"

"I don't know," I told her. "Anyone who says they really know anything about yesterday or tomorrow is a liar. Look, we need to get you some help."

Baize turned her head to me, forced a smile, and said, "You're too worried. Don't worry. I'ma be fine."

We were all lying on the ground outside the hole. I was on the end next to Baize; Shalaya Crump was next to her; Evan was on the other end. The whole time I'd been in those woods, I'd never stopped and looked up. The tops of the pine trees swayed in tiny circles like long green index fingers. Behind those fingers, the sky was changing from faded-blue-jean blue to new-Levi's blue, and drunk-looking lightning bugs were starting to, as Baize said, get their wink on. "Baize?"

"Yeah?"

"So you knew all the time, didn't you?"

"Yeah, I knew."

"When did you know?"

"After you stole my computer, I kept wondering why your eyes seemed so familiar."

"Why didn't you tell me?"

"I wasn't all the way sure, and I didn't want you to disappear again. I figured if I played along, we would all be friends. All of us. That's the most I was hoping for. We ain't got to be family again, but I at least wanted us to be friends."

Shalaya Crump turned her head toward Evan, then looked back at Baize, who was still looking up at the sky. Then Shalaya Crump slowly turned back toward Evan. "Do you even care about how the time travel works?" she asked him. "I mean really care."

"I care," he said, "but, like I said, I think I know."

I grabbed Baize's hand. "Forget them," I said under my breath because I didn't know what else to do. "You think the sky changes when people jump from time to time?"

"No," Baize said. "Do you?"

"If it don't change, can you imagine what the sky sees? Like the sky, it probably knows how the time tunnel really works." I looked at Evan. "The sky probably knows what's gonna happen next. It probably knows what's happening in the Freedom School and the Shephard house and that community center right now. I bet no one else knows how truth can change except the sky."

"Yeah, but what's the point in knowing if you can't change it?" Shalaya Crump said. "I'd rather be able to change it than to know it."

"I guess you're right, huh? That's kinda worse than even watching a bad television show you've already seen. Then at least you can change the channel when you know exactly what's gonna happen next. The sky, it's gotta just watch everything and sit there changing from dark to day to dark to day no matter what."

"That's what I'm saying," Baize said.

"But I still wonder."

"Wonder what?" Baize asked me.

"Well, if you could ask the sky anything about change and time, what would you ask it?"

We were all quiet, listening to the wind, blowing at the lightning bugs, and squeezing the hand in our hand whenever we heard a car or footsteps move down Old Ryle Road.

"I'd want to know who my parents were," Shalaya Crump said, "and why they left when they did. And can I have two questions?"

"Yeah," Baize said and coughed nastier than she had all day. "Some people are the sky, though."

"I'd wanna know what I'm supposed to do now to help time and change in Melahatchie be less painful," Shalaya Crump kept talking. "I know that's so Agatha Christie, but I wanna do the right thing. It's hard when time and people keep on changing, though."

"I don't get it," Baize said.

Shalaya Crump didn't say a word. I raised my head off the ground and looked over at her. She was looking right at Baize, who was looking up toward the sky. "I just never meant to hurt you," Shalaya Crump finally said.

At that point, Shalaya Crump understood what I figured only parents could understand about their children. Baize was more than just sick. She could only be born if Shalaya Crump and I had her in 1999, but the longer we were in 1964, the more Shalaya Crump and I knew that Baize would have to eventually disappear.

I wanted to beg Shalaya Crump to save Baize's life and come back to 1985 with me. I wanted to tell her that we could go close the hole, go home, eat sardines together, dig in the dirt, and never travel again. We could do all the stuff we were supposed to do until 1999. Then we could kiss with tongue. And we could act like we were on HBO after dark. And we could get married. And we could have our baby.

Deep down, I knew it couldn't work like that anymore.

Shalaya Crump didn't say a word when Baize asked her, "What do you mean?" She seemed stuck in a long, lonely silence that, I figured, only pops up when a parent has to decide whether to save the future in a special way or save the life of the special child they never really knew.

Baize raised her head and asked Shalaya Crump again, "What do you..."

I interrupted Baize and tried to take the attention off Shalaya Crump for a second. "What does dot-dot-dot mean, Baize? You know, like when you write it on your computer, in those rhymes. What does dot-dot-dot mean?"

Baize didn't say anything, but Shalaya Crump answered. "It's what you use when someone is about to cut someone else off, right?"

"Naw," Evan said. "I think it's just a long pause."

"Ain't a period or a semicolon a long pause?" Shalaya Crump asked Evan. "Like long compared to a comma?"

"Maybe," he said. "You talking about them three periods in a row, I thought?"

Baize started coughing again and squeezed my hand. "If you could be any punctuation, City, what would you be?" It was the first time Baize called me by my real name, and it felt better than anything in my whole life.

"Um, I think I'd be a question mark," I told her. "Like if I had my own book, I want a cover with shades of maroon and blue and green like this forest right here on the front and back. And in strange places on the cover, I'd want there to be all these different kinds of eyes of people I love on it. And on every page, I'd want there to be one question mark. I wouldn't even mind if a Klansman was on the cover."

"But why?" Baize asked. "If every page is blank, ain't there a question mark kinda understood to be there anyway? Like that book I was reading, *Long Division*, the last chapter is just blank pages."

I thought about what she was saying and it made a lot of sense.

"I guess you're right," I told her. "What would you be?"

"I'd be an ellipsis."

"What's that?"

"That's the dot-dot-dot you were talking about." She let go of my hand and sat up while leaning on both of her hands. "The ellipsis always knows something more came before it and something more is coming after it." Baize started coughing and grabbing her chest. "It's hard for me to breathe, City."

I stood up and made sure *Long Division* was in Baize's backpack. I had the computer under my arms. "So you'd have pages filled with dot-dot-dot in your book?" I asked her.

"No," she said. "I'd have a front cover with the words 'Long Division' across the top and below 'Long Division' would be a blue-black ellipsis. We'd all be inside the book, too, with those other characters already in the book and we'd all fall in love with each other."

I got everything ready to leave and looked down at all three of them. Evan's left hand was in Shalaya Crump's right hand and Baize was nuzzled under Shalaya Crump's left arm. "Come on, Baize."

"Where we going?"

"We should be going home," I told her. "We can come back next week."

She laughed at me as I helped her up. Shalaya Crump and Evan started to get up, too. "Y'all don't have to get up," I told them. "We're fine."

Evan walked over and hugged my neck. "I'm sorry," he said in my ear. "I didn't think it would happen like this."

"Yeah. Me either," I said. "I'll see y'all soon, though. For real."

Shalaya Crump walked up to me when I was thinking of cussing Evan out and she had these humongous tears in her eyes. "We did it," I told her. "We changed the future by changing the past."

"City," she said. "It wasn't supposed to hurt. Not like this. But I can make it worth it."

"That's how we know we're changing the future in a special way, though, right?" I asked her. That was the best thing I'd ever said to Shalaya Crump. I didn't have to think about whether or not it was *GAME*. All four of us knew that special change, the kind that lasts, hurts.

I watched Baize and Shalaya Crump hug for what felt like ten minutes. Neither of them wanted to let go. But eventually Baize did. "I'll holler at y'all soon. Wipe away that stank face," she said. "I understand. I'll be back."

I took Baize's hand and walked toward the hole, away from Shalaya Crump and Evan. I wanted so bad not to turn around and watch them watch us leave.

"Bye," Shalaya Crump said. "Maybe we'll see y'all tomorrow. I'm sorry."

Baize started to turn her head, but I tightened my grip on her hand and pulled her toward the hole.

"Forget tomorrow," I said loud enough for Shalaya Crump and Evan to hear as we walked off.

When Baize and I got in the hole, I pulled out a book of matches I'd taken from Evan's brother. There were three matches left in the book. I struck one of the matches and gave it to her. Baize looked at me like we tied for last in the longest uphill three-legged race in the world. We slumped against the sides of the hole and both slid down to the ground. She leaned her head on my right shoulder.

"City?"

"Yeah, Baize."

Baize buried the left side of her face in my shoulder so I wouldn't see the tears flooding the gutters of her right eye. All the tears that didn't fall onto her computer fell into her mouth. "What happens to us now?" she asked. "I'm so tired."

"Hold your face up." I looked up toward the top of the hole to keep my tears from falling. "It's gonna be okay. Open your computer. Let me hear one of your songs."

Watching Shalaya Crump love Evan smashed my heart, but lying to my daughter about what was about to happen to her made every living thing in my body just quit. I never knew my father, but Mama tried her hardest to be there for me. When we lived in Jackson, being there for me meant leaving me to stay with my grandmother when she couldn't handle being just a mother. I didn't hate on Mama or feel bad for myself because at least I had a Mama who cared, unlike Shalaya Crump, who never knew either of her parents. I loved Melahatchie and Shalaya Crump, but every time Mama dropped me off in Melahatchie, a part of me always expected her to never come back.

I wondered if Baize knew what was coming.

The computer made her face glow blue. She played some instrumental and started rapping the lyrics really low. *Not your everyday rapper but everyday is haze.* Then she stopped and closed the computer and talked to me in the dark. "I guess we can't go back to 1964 and all just stay together again, huh?"

"Nah," I told her, "We're right where we need to be. And your mama, she's where she needs to be. We'll come back one day and see her and she can come back and see us."

"You know I made the high honor roll every quarter since y'all left, right?"

"I figured," I said. "Hell, I make the honor roll every now and then and I ain't nearly 'bout sharp as you are."

Baize fake giggled to herself. "You wanna stay with me for a while when we get home?" she asked and found my hand in the dark. "I just need to take a nap for a few hours. Here," she went in her backpack and got out *Long Division*. "I think you should read this while I'm asleep."

"Why?" I lit a second match.

"It's just all starting to make sense now."

"It does?"

"Yep. You'll see. Read it from the beginning."

My match started to burn the tips of my swollen fingers too, so I held it with my fingernails and I looked at Baize's slick face until the match burned all the way down. I tapped Baize on her leg and let her know that I was about to get up.

"City?"

"Yeah, Baize."

"I love you."

"Don't say that. Not now. Please don't say that."

"Why? We took care of each other today, like a father and daughter goon squad are supposed to," she told me with her voice hollowing out. "I'm just keeping it one hundred. I knew y'all wouldn't disappear forever."

"I love you, Baize."

I turned my face from Baize, closed my eyes, counted to ten by twos, and pushed the door open. Then I climbed all the way out of the hole and, *slowly, slowly, slowly*, I turned back toward the hole in the ground.

Long Division was in the bottom of the hole, but Baize Shephard was gone. Forever. I made my daughter disappear.

OUR MESS.

I jumped off my knees with *I made my daughter disappear* still ringing and dusted myself off. Then I looked right in Pot Belly's crossed red eyes. "Is Baize dead?" I asked him. "How come the last chapter of this book is like 20 blank pages? Look." I showed both of them the empty pages at the end.

LaVander Peeler wouldn't touch the book and Pot Belly wouldn't nod yes or no to my question. "Is Baize really gone?" I got close to Pot Belly's mouth.

"Don't do it, City," LaVander Peeler told me.

I ignored him and pulled the rag out anyway. Pot Belly did this spitting thing before saying, "I ain't do it, man. I ain't do it."

I moved down by his legs and started trying to find a little key that looked like it fit the lock. "Is Baize Shephard dead?" I asked him again. "Is that what 'disappear' means?"

"Your grandmother took me down to Lake Marathon," he said, ignoring my question. "When we get out the car, she had some folks waiting for us."

"But is Baize really gone?"

"Some beat me. But most, they just watched."

I looked at LaVander Peeler. Pot Belly's story sounded too made up, even more made up than everything that had happened the past few days.

"I told them I'm already saved," he said. "Every time I say that, they beat me in my face until your grandmother made them stop and say something about a man named..." his voice trailed off for a bit. "...Tom Henry, they said his name was."

"That's my granddaddy."

I could see Pot Belly feeling the grit on his teeth with his tongue. "Wait, were you there when my granddaddy died too?" He looked down. "Please just tell me."

"That's what I'm saying. I ain't do it. I don't even know no Tom Henry. The folks at the lake," he started talking slower than before, "they said Tom Henry was the one who saved me from drowning back in the day."

"Wait. You're the white boy my granddaddy died trying to save?" I asked him.

"Please let me go, man. They blaming me for stuff I ain't do."

"You kicked me in my back and called me out my name," I told him.

"I did that," he said. "And I'm sorry. But I don't know nothing 'bout that little girl. And I don't know nothing 'bout no Tom Henry. They blaming me for everything wrong, but I ain't do it."

I looked as hard as I could into each of his eyes and tried to imagine my grandfather looking in those eyes as he was choking on water, running from death. "You been cross-eyed your whole life?"

"I swear before God, man, that I ain't do what they say I did. I ain't do it."

"Who did it then?" I asked him.

I wanted to feel more hate, but I figured that being saved and falling in love with Jesus was making me feel what I felt. And what I felt was the feeling you would have when you read a good mystery book and made that big connection a few pages from the end.

"Y'all mad at something more than me," he said. "I ain't do it."

"I don't know why," I told him, "but I don't hate you even if you were there when my granddaddy died. And right now, I don't even hate you for kicking me in my back and calling me a 'nigger.' For real."

"He kicked you in your back?" LaVander Peeler asked.

"Yep," I told him. "I already told you that. He kicked me in my back, and then he called me 'nigger.' But I don't think he even knows what a 'nigger' is." I looked back at Pot Belly. "I just want you to be honest with me. Do you know where Baize Shephard is? Did you kill Baize Shep—"

"No," he said before I could finish her name. "Hell naw."

"You know where she is?"

"I ain't do it. I don't know nothing about that little girl."

"You know who killed her?"

Pot Belly closed his eyes. "You serious?" he asked me. "That story you reading, it said that little girl disappeared, and the man responsible for that disappearing is the man who wrote that story."

"I know what this book said, but it's just a book. I'm asking you where Baize's body is."

"You find the man who wrote that story, look to me like you find that little girl." Pot Belly's voice was cracking and he was sobbing.

"So she is dead, right? I know you didn't do it but I think you know who did."

"*You* killed that girl," he said through some quivering lips.

"Who?"

"You," he said, as calm as anything I'd heard in days. "You know what you did to that girl, and that's your business."

"How could I kill her? I wasn't even here."

"You did it, man. You did it. You wrote it in your book. Please let me go."

I heard him. I saw him. Whether I believed what he said didn't matter. I saw that he believed it. LaVander Peeler, without a tear in his eye, walked closer to Pot Belly. He got on his knees, wiped off his mouth, got a few inches from Pot Belly's face, and said, "All things considered, I don't believe you can use 'nigger' in a sentence."

"What in the devil is wrong with y'all?" Pot Belly asked. "Why are y'all doing this?"

"You can't use it," he said. "All things considered, I bet you can't even spell it, much less use it. Am I wrong?"

"Please," Pot Belly said, "Y'all making this personal. I'm so sad and I just want to go home. I'm sorry for calling you out your name."

"Can you at least spell it?"

"N-I-G-G-E-R," he said.

"That ain't right," LaVander Peeler told him.

"N-I-G-G-E-R," he slowed it down this time.

"Nope," LaVander Peeler said. "All things considered, I don't think that's right."

I got up to pull LaVander Peeler out of Pot Belly's face when he cocked his arm back and jabbed Pot Belly in his left eye. Almost in the same motion, Pot Belly reared his head back and butted LaVander Peeler right in the middle of his face. LaVander Peeler grabbed his face with both hands, made these snorting sounds, and wobbled out of the shed.

Even though I was saved, I reckon I react like a demon when a grown white man head-butts LaVander Peeler in the face. I gripped *Long Division* and started smacking Pot Belly in his face as hard as I could, when, all of a sudden, Grandma burst in the door of the shed breathing loud as hell. "What is wrong with you?" she asked me. I didn't say a word. I just handed her *Long Division*. She wiped blood off the book and handed it back.

Pot Belly was calling Grandma all kinds of "black bitches" and "niggers" and he kept saying, "I ain't do it! I ain't do it!," when Grandma said to me, "Gimme my keys."

I gave her the keys and watched her pull out the butterfly blade. "Leave, City. Both of y'all both go get in the car. And lock the doors!"

Pot Belly's angry yells of "I ain't do it!" slid into screams, which slid into gurgly moans by the time I got to the car. LaVander Peeler was already in the backseat, covering his ears. I'd never heard anything like the moans coming out of that work shed.

And then the moans stopped.

Passing Tests...

I couldn't tell where I was because the air was as thin as it had been in 1964 and the forest was only a little less lime green than it had been in 2013. Before heading to the Freedom School, I looked across the road where the Co-op and Mama Lara's house were. There were sidewalks where the ditches were and lots of black folks and Mexican folks of all ages walking down the sidewalks talking and laughing out loud. Across the road were these cool-looking trailers on wheels. Each trailer had a different shape and a huge garden in the front yard. Down the road was a huge grocery store called Shephard's Co-op.

I looked toward the Community Center and there was a woman out in front. She motioned for me to come in the building, then disappeared in the door.

The building had changed. It wasn't a church and it wasn't a community center. It was actually a museum. At least that's what the sign said. It read, "The Lerthon Coldson Civil Rights Museum." It made me kind of mad that the museum was named after a grimy drunk dude who called a girl "baby," but I figured lots of museums were named for part-time losers.

In the middle of the room were two desks that were bolted to the ground. All around the walls of the room were glass cases holding sheets, rifles, and books, between doors that went to other rooms. The bird's nest at the top was still there, too.

I walked right to the middle of the room and sat in one of the desks. On the desk was a sheet of paper. It looked like a test that had already been taken. It didn't make sense to me, though, because the name on the test was mine and it was actually written in my handwriting. Only the year was blank.

Name __City Coldson__ Year ____ True/False —Underline one

1. Desperation will make a villain out of you.

<u>True</u>/False

2. Only fools would not travel through time and change their past if they could.

<u>True</u>/False

3. You were brought to this country with the expectation of life, liberty, and the pursuit of happiness.

True/<u>False</u>

4. If you push yourself hard in the direction of freedom, compassion, and excellence, you will recover.

<u>True</u>/False

5. Loving someone and loving how someone makes you feel are the same thing.

True/<u>False</u>

6. Only those who can read, write, and love can move back or forward through time.

<u>True</u>/False

7. There are undergrounds to the past and future for every human being on earth.

True/<u>False</u>

8. If you haven't read or written or listened to something at least three times, you have never really read, written, or listened.

<u>True</u>/False

9. Past, present, and future exist within you and you change them by changing the way you live your life.
<u>True</u>/False
10. You are special.
True/<u>False</u>
Bonus
11. You are innocent.
<u>True</u>/False
Score: 80%

I put the test back on the desk. *When did I even take this test?* It was super annoying to see a test you don't remember taking, but it was even more annoying when you missed some of the answers and whoever was grading the test didn't tell you which you missed. I knew there were more important questions on the test, but right that second I wanted the answer to the easiest one. And the easiest one to me, right there, was, "Loving someone and loving how someone makes you feel are the same thing."

Mama Lara walked out from one of the rooms while I was thinking. She looked exactly like she looked back in 1985.

"You're a witch, ain't you?" I asked her. "You watched it all happen, didn't you, just like the sky? Please just tell me what's going on. Is any of this real?"

"Do I look like a witch to you? Even after all you been through today, does my baby still believe in witches and magic?"

I didn't answer her question. All I said was, "I'm not a baby." I held my head right there in that desk and tried to listen to my heartbeat. "I don't understand, Mama Lara. If we changed the future, how come I'm still here? How come you look the same in 2013 that you did in 1985? Say something. Why would my mama and daddy still have me if we changed the future? It just doesn't make sense."

Mama Lara had what looked like Baize's laptop computer in her hand.

"Where'd you get that from?" I asked her.

"People disappear, City," she said, ignoring my question. "We live, we wonder, we love, we lie, and we disappear. Close the book."

"Are you for real? That's it?"

"And sometimes we appear again if we're loved," she said. "Accept it. Which answer did you get wrong on the test? I know you know."

"I don't even know when I took that test, Mama Lara," I told her. "I'm not trying to be disrespectful. I'm just so tired."

"The test ain't going nowhere," she said. "When you're ready to find out what you got wrong, you will. Close the book."

"Close the book? Then what? Then can Baize come back? Is that Baize's computer?" I asked her again. "Is she here somewhere?"

"Take it," she handed me the computer. "You're so close."

"I know she's here. I can feel her. Where is she?" I asked.

"Wait." I looked up from the computer. "Is Shalaya Crump the governor of Mississippi, or is she like the president or something?" Mama Lara just looked at me. "How old is she now?" I did the math in my head. "Damn near 65? I bet she's still fine as all outdoors, though. Did she marry that dude, Evan?"

Mama Lara stood there smiling with her hands folded across her chest. Honestly, I didn't know what it took to be a good president or governor, but I knew Shalaya Crump had it. I knew it from the first day I met her. In her own way, she was as compassionate and thoughtful as a girl could be, but her mind was stronger than yours and no one could ever really break her heart. You could sprain her heart, and her heart would bruise a lot, but it could never ever be broken. Never. I figured that there were probably 27 people like that in the world at one time and they were the only people who should be running for president of anything that mattered.

With all the windows in the museum open, and the lightning bugs outside winking like it was going out of style, I looked at Mama Lara. "So this is it?" I said loud enough so she could hear me.

"No," Mama Lara said. "This ain't it. You know how movement works now. You know how love and change work. And you know that sometimes, just sometimes, when folks disappear, they come back, don't they?"

"I hear you, Mama Lara, but you don't get it. Right now, all that goofy talk don't help me. I just need something to hold on to. I need to know what's gonna happen tomorrow. Don't you see what I'm saying? If you can't help me get Baize back, can you just stop talking for the rest of the day? You ain't got no stories to watch on TV? Please just stop talking."

"Think about what I'm asking you, City," she said and sat in the desk next to me. "The book is open. Close it and get to work. How else do people disappear?"

I looked down at the desk and thought about everything I'd experienced in the last few days and, I guess, the last 50 years. "Water," I told her.

"What else?"

"Um, fire?"

"What else?"

"The wind...and um, words?"

"Who uses words to make folks disappear?"

"People."

"And who makes people disappear?"

"Um, people make people disappear," I told her.

"That's it," she said. "And everything that makes people disappear can make people what?"

"Reappear?"

"It's all in your hands now. They're waiting for you."

I sat there in the desk looking at my actual hands and thinking about water, fire, wind, words, and people. Both sides of my hands looked so worn, so bloody and smudged and ashy. From typing on a laptop computer, to brushing my hair at the Spell-Off, to tying the hands of a fake Klansman, to reading the first chapter of *Long Division*, to holding my daughter's hand, my hands had done things I'd never imagined wanting them to do.

I wanted to walk out of that museum ready to explore, knowing that I'd done new things with my hands and new things with my imagination. Maybe I could find Shalaya Crump and Evan tomorrow, I thought. There was so much I wanted to explore. But before I could go forward, I had to go back under.

Again.

So I grabbed the computer, told Mama Lara thank you, and headed back toward the hole. I loved the slice of the new Mississippi that I'd seen and I respected Shalaya Crump's decision to stay and fight for us, but I needed Baize back. I didn't care if it was right to anyone else but my daughter and me.

When I got in the hole, I opened the computer. A revised version of the paragraph I'd written when I first took Baize's computer back to 1985 was on the screen:

I didn't have a girlfriend halfway through ninth grade and it wasn't because the whole high school heard Principal Jankins whispering to his wife, Ms. Dawsin-Jankins, that my hairline was crooked like the top of a Smurf house. I never had a girlfriend because the last time I saw Shalaya Crump, she told me she could love me if I helped her change the future dot-dot-dot in a special way.

I reread it. And I wondered. And I wandered. And I wrote. And I reread that. And I wrote more. And I erased some lies. And I wrote more. And I erased some truth. And I thought about Honors English teachers and librarians. And I forgot about them. And I thought about what people like Shalaya, Baize, Evan, and me needed to read in school to prepare to fight, love, and disappear. And I forgot about that. And I wrote more. And the more I wrote and erased, the more I felt Baize and other characters slowly—word by word, maybe even sense by sense—coming back.

Meow

That fat-head black cat, with the "Red Naval" collar around its neck, appeared and started meowing right outside the hole. I grabbed the cat and brought it down in the hole with me. "Don't call me an asshole, okay?" I told it. "You were right last time, but still...I ain't in the mood for that. Man, I lost my daughter and my half-wife and now I'm stuck in 2013. You hear me? Ain't you supposed to be old and dead?"

The cat licked its paws and pawed at something in the shadows of the hole.

I reached over toward the shadows and saw that it was pawing at *Long Division*.

"Wait," I told the cat. "Can you tell me who wrote this?"

Meow

I opened the book to the last chapter. With the cat lying on the side of my lap, the top of the hole open, and the light blue of the computer screen cupping my greasy face, I closed the book and wondered if I was the reader or somehow, actually, the writer of the book I had in my hands.

"Wait," I said to the cat. "Did I write this? When?"

The cat ignored me and kept scratching its ears.

"I know this is supposed to be all dramatic," I told the cat, "but can you just help me understand what this book has to do with me? Somebody knows and I'm just tired of not knowing."

It just kept licking its paws.

"Thanks a lot, homie," I told the cat and sucked my teeth. "Where would I be without you? Did you ever really talk to me?"

The cat yawned and started licking its own ass.

Making Baize really reappear was going to be harder than making her disappear, harder than anything I'd ever imagined in my life. And I was going to have to do it all with a book without an author called *Long Division*, Baize's computer, a fat-head cat, and a hole in the ground.

That's one of the only things I knew. I also knew that "tomorrow" was a word now like the thousands of other words in that hole. I closed my mouth, pulled down the top of the hole, and imagined more words in the dark.

But someone else was in the hole with me.

I heard more breathing and more fumbling around, so I walked toward the noise until I was close enough to smell dried sweat, pine trees, and ink.

"Who is that?" I said, sounding scared as hell. "How'd you get down here?"

I gently reached and rubbed my hands up, down, and all around their noses, their eyelids, their dry lips and ear lobes. I found their thighs, their flimsy T-shirts, and finally all of their crusty hands. I had one more match left from the book I'd taken from the 1960s, so I went in my pocket and struck the match.

"*You!?*"

Slowly, we opened our red eyes in the dark and taught each other how to love. Hand in hand, deep in the underground of Mississippi, we all ran away to tomorrow because we finally could...

COVERED IN INK.

Out in the Bonneville, LaVander Peeler sat in the back and I sat up front with Grandma. She sat there not saying a word for a few minutes, with one hand on my thigh and the car running. She took her hand from my thigh and cupped her face with both hands before massaging her temples with her thumbs. I placed my left hand on the back of her neck and rubbed it like she'd do to me when I couldn't sleep.

I sat there, waiting for Grandma to say something and, really, waiting to hear from her how being in love with Jesus was going to help us out of whatever situation we were in. I didn't want no silly voices pass-interfering when Jesus decided to let me know what to do next. But even if you put it on strong leash, and even if you're saved, the imagination makes more noise than a little bit and takes you wherever it wants to go.

And my imagination did exactly that. It took me right across the road in those Magic Woods and it had me stepping on dead catfish and brittle monkey bodies and the blue crossed eyeballs of white folks. All the while, all I could hear around me was Uncle Relle saying, "Gotdamnit. Gotdamnit. Gotdamnit."

Jesus, I thought to myself, *if you're there, I'm not trying to cuss you. I swear I'm not.*

Then, it took me back to a bed on a stage where Mama, Troll, Shay, Gunn, and MyMy were there and they were all kissing me all over my stretch marks and showing stretch marks I never knew they had. Without warning, my imagination calmed down and took me right back to my baptism and that Halona King song was blasting on level eighty trillion.

I pulled *Long Division* from my bag. "Grandma, I'm fine," I told her. "Really."

"Your face," she said.

"What?"

"It looks like my baby done aged fifteen years in two days. Lawd, have mercy. Please have mercy. This wasn't supposed to happen like this."

"Oh, naw. I'm fine, Grandma. I'm just waiting, but it shouldn't be long now." I sat there with *Long Division*, trying to get situated in the passenger seat of the car. "In a way, everything is right here." I handed her the book. "I think Jesus wanted me to find this book. You should read this one day. There's another one in the shed."

"I picked it up," she said.

"You did? Good. You should read it."

"I love you, City," she said and put the book back on my lap. "Galatians 6:9 say, *Let us not become weary in doing good, for at the proper time we will reap a harvest if we do not give up.* I ain't giving up, but I didn't do good this weekend and I reckon they 'bout to come for me. I want you—"

"Grandma," I interrupted her, "I'm gonna miss you. You know that, right? I am. And I'm gonna miss Melahatchie so much. And you ain't even got to tell me; I already know I can't say nothing about what happened in that work shed. It didn't really happen, right? I think I know where Baize Shephard is, Grandma."

I reached for Grandma's waist, smashing my head against her chest as she hugged my neck. Her heart was pounding so hard, so fast. The smell of the shed and Pot Belly was still strong on her chest. "You scared, Grandma? We didn't kill that man, right? Even though you think he killed Granddaddy and Baize Shephard, we didn't kill him, did we?"

I could feel tears from Grandma's face dripping onto my head. "Grandma, I have another question." I pulled away from her so I could see her eyes. "What does Jesus say is the difference between the fiction in your head and the real life you live? You know what I mean? It's like there's two of everybody, the one in fiction and the one in real life. But what's the difference?"

She squeezed my hand tighter and looked me right in the eyes. "Really, it ain't no difference, City," she said. "Because unless you use both of them the right way, they just as bad or just as good as you want them to be. But you lead both of them," she whispered in my ear. "And don't take no ass-whupping or no disrespect from no one in your own house or your own dreams, you hear me? Do whatever it takes to protect you and yours," she said. "Especially in your dreams. Especially in your dreams, because you never know who else is watching."

"Grandma," I looked behind me at LaVander Peeler, who was looking out of rear window, "that's what I did at the contest. That's all I was trying to do. You think I did the wrong thing to protect me and mines today?"

Grandma tapped me on the forehead with my pencil and ignored my question. She told me to read and write when I got bored and needed to make sense of it all. She said I should never show anybody what I wrote, "…unless you really feel like Jesus forgot you and you're trying to save your own life, or the life of somebody you love." Then out of nowhere she said, "What I did to protect me and mines was wrong, City. I shoulda gone underground. I knew better."

"But you were just cleaning up our mess, right? You were doing what Jesus would have done."

"Naw." Grandma looked at her hands. "I was cleaning up my own mess. Or I reckon I was punishing that man for his part in some mess that can't never really be cleaned the right way. I don't know, City."

"It can be cleaned, Grandma. That's the thing." I wasn't sure what I meant, but I knew I meant what I was saying. "It's cleaner than it would be if folks didn't fight back. We can make it even cleaner."

"We can make it dirtier, too," Grandma said and kissed me right on the mouth and reached across me and opened my door. "You should go, City. They gon' be coming for me directly, so I should probably go to them first. Don't ever go back in that house or that shed. You understand me?"

In all the years I'd known my grandma, I never imagined her as someone's sad child. But there she was, looking like some kind of rotten blue loss was swallowing her whole, like she'd just lost 50 contests in a row in front of her parents, the boy she liked, and all the black folks to ever live in the state of Mississippi.

LaVander Peeler and I got out of the car and stood in front of the woods. While Grandma's Bonneville slow-crawled down the road and all these other cars were blowing their horn and passing her, I put my hand on LaVander Peeler's shoulder and walked him into the Magic Woods. I remembered where the rusted handle in the ground was. I didn't have to explain anything to LaVander Peeler. He wanted to come with me.

I reached down and pulled open the hole in the ground. We both looked at each other and walked down the steps. "This wasn't supposed to happen to us, City."

"Yeah, it was," I told him. "Like you always say, all things considered, we didn't really have no other choice or no other story to tell, so we had to make one." I waited for him to say something back but he didn't, so I looked right in his face and said what I should have found a way to say to him after the contest.

"I love you, LaVander Peeler. I do, man, and I don't care what you say about that homosexual stuff. I know you love me, too. You ain't even gotta say it. Just treat this like the best video game ever made and act like we just beat the game together."

LaVander Peeler looked at me, not like I was crazy, but like we just tied for last place in the longest uphill three-legged race in the world. The hole was huge once you got in and so much colder than I expected.

"Should we leave the top open?" I asked him.

LaVander Peeler just stood next to me, ignoring my question and resting his head on my shoulder.

"Listen," I told him. "You hear something? Sounds like someone breathing."

"City, all things considered," he said, "I'm so scared. Can we read that book?"

In that hole, right in that second, I felt as far away from Melahatchie and I felt as close to a real character as I had ever felt. And the craziest thing is that I wasn't sure if that was a good, bad, or sad thing. With LaVander Peeler's head on my shoulder, we started rereading *Long Division* from the beginning, knowing that all we needed to know about how to survive, how to live, and how to love in Mississippi was in our hands. The sentences had always been there

...

ACKNOWLEDGMENTS

I want to thank my father and mother for patience and life. I'm sorry I was so bad for so long. I just want you to be proud.

Thanks to my Aunt Sue, Aunt Linda, Nichole, and Mr. and Ms. Simmons for sharing their God, their healing voices, and their homes with me when I was homeless. Thanks to my little brother, Tommy, and my little sister, Jeanne, for the short time we've shared.

Thanks to Amie, Assefash, Kleaver, Danielle P., Sharon, Rachel, Tanay, Abby, Lauren, Catherine, Robyn, Amielle, Kendall, Leona, Ocasio, Akil, Evan, Cordelia, John, Nate, Rosa, Emma C., Brianna, Amanda, Adam, Safy, Parker, my agents David and Robert, and she who has next, "Nephew Jessie," for reading or listening to early drafts of this book and believing when there was little to believe in. Thanks to Kara for embracing this book like I was family. Thank you for opening your heart to these characters and me at a time when we were so afraid and most in need of magic, music, and time.

Thanks to Raymon for showing a draft to his little brother and needing to teach it to his students.

Thank you to Amitava, Imani, Paul, Michael, and Hua for real talk and modeling innovative literary excellence up close. To Leslie, Peter, Paul, Judy, and David for mentoring and advising me not to sell out.

Thank you, Millsaps College, for a peculiar kind of freedom. Thank you, Jackson State University, for always being home. Thank you, Oberlin College, for a second chance at life and art. Thanks to the Indiana University MFA program for time to learn from some great ones.

Thanks to Lerthon, David, Terry, Henry, Roy, Brandon, Kareem, Stacey, Baraka, Madra, Hasinati, Leighton, Shonda, Robyn, and Shirley for making thousands of Mississippi memories and keeping me alive.

To Andrew, Lila, Bob, and Joanna for welcoming me, and Cappy for keeping Vassar College's doors open to brilliance.

To Carlos, Luis, Prescott, Kisha, Torrie, Mona, and the one and only O.G. Raymon "Gunn" Murph for the kind of service, brotherhood, sisterhood, and love that saves lives.

To Bama, Magtoto, Adam, Paulsak and the rest of that first Writing the Underground class I taught at Vassar for holding me accountable to ride-or-die integrity.

Thanks to Morrison, Baldwin, Salinger, Butler, Jesmyn Ward, Natasha Trethewey, Rich Santiago, Ava DuVernay, Outkast, Big K.R.I.T., Ani, Jigga, Kanye, Joni, Maxwell, Scarface, 2pac, Spike Lee, Tyler, Crooked Lettaz, Frank Ocean, dream, Kendrick, Halona King, Brandon Green, Noel Didla, Adisa Ajamu, Marlon Peterson, Mychal Denzel Smith, Darnell Moore, and Killer Mike.

Thanks to Ron, Luke, Mia, Andy, Kim, and Lisa for your willingness to fight and collaborate. Ron, you took a chance on me when you didn't have to. I will never forget your courage.

I want to also thank 2010–2011 Senior Composition for creating and sustaining a rigorous, emotionally dense, innovative writing community when I was really unhealthy and ready to quit.

Thanks to Doug Seibold and the Agate Bolden crew for trust and putting innovative and soulful literature first.

Thanks are not enough to Professor Eve Dunbar for an intellectually demanding friendship while this book was being revised, for slapping blax and posing two questions about black regional literature that changed the narrative's trajectory and my writing life forever. Thank you so much for your care.

Grandma, thank you for teaching me how to pray, listen, laugh, and fight to the end. Blues.

ABOUT THE AUTHOR

Kiese Laymon is a black Southern writer, born and raised in Jackson, Mississippi. He graduated from Oberlin College and earned his MFA from Indiana University. A contributing editor at Gawker.com, he has written for numerous publications, including *Esquire* and ESPN.com. He is an associate professor of English and Africana studies at Vassar College. His collection of essays, *How To Slowly Kill Yourself and Others in America*, will be published by Agate Bolden in August 2013.

Q&A with Kiese Laymon, author of
Long Division

What inspired *Long Division*?

Like most of the kids I grew up with, I wanted to spend most of my time outside playing football or basketball, or wrestling. Unlike most of the kids I grew up with, I had a mother who wouldn't let me go outside unless I read "classic" books—*A Tale of Two Cities*, *Treasure Island*, and later, *Absalom, Absalom!* Then I'd have to write essays about what was so great about those books. I got good at it not because I liked those books but because I wanted to go outside and play with my friends.

By the time I was 18, I'd read all those classic books my mother made me read, and I'd also read a ton of books by black Southern writers. I loved some of those books but I was also hypercritical of them. I had a professor, Calvin Hernton, who said the best way to critique art was through the creation of alternative art. The book was born from this impulse. I had started two different stories, both of which were ultimately concerned with the limits of love and history. I wanted to create a book within a book that was really two love stories, possibly told from the same consciousness. I also wanted to create a book that was in conversation with *Kindred*, *Invisible Man*, *The Adventures of Huckleberry Finn*, *The Bluest Eye*, *The Catcher in the Rye*, *The Color Purple*, *Black Boy*, *The White Boy Shuffle*, and all those "classics" my mother would make me read before I was allowed to go outside.

What does being a Southern writer mean to you?

Being a Southern writer means that I write to and from a group of people that a lot of other American writers neglect. I feel a responsibility to the richest artistic region on Earth. In my opinion, Southern literature and Southern music have shaped America more profoundly than work from any other region.

Who are your heroes, on the page and elsewhere?

B.B. King, Alice Walker, Mahalia Jackson, Richard Wright, Jesmyn Ward, Outkast, William Faulkner, Catherine Coleman, Fannie Lou Hamer, James Baldwin, and all those kids who died fighting for my freedom in Mississippi.

Your 2012 *Gawker* essay "How To Slowly Kill Yourself and Others in America" received a huge amount of attention when it was first published. Why do you think it struck such a chord among so many people?

I thought a lot of people would enjoy the essay because of its musicality, content, and pace, but I didn't think it would stick with so many people. I knew it was something that we haven't seen a lot of on the Internet, especially in terms of my decision to write it in present tense. I also think that people were really ready for a different expository approach to the American gun and race narrative.

How much of your own experience is reflected in the novel?

My mother had me when she was pretty young, and I was sent to my grandmother's house in rural Mississippi whenever I was too much for my mother to handle. I spent a lot of time at Grandma's just watching, listening to her interact with the craziest, most amazing folks I'd ever met. I also spent a lot of time playing in the woods across the road from her house. One summer, I found this hole that I convinced myself was a time tunnel. I was too afraid to really explore the hole, but I was sure that it was my portal to the future. The grandmothers in the book are really different from my own grandmother, and I'm really different from the City characters we meet, but the woods in *Long Division* are the same woods I played in as a child.

What was the most difficult part about writing *Long Division*?

The most difficult part was finding the right way to distinguish the 1985 City from 2013 City. The narrative voices needed to be similar but they also needed to differ due to changes in pop culture, technology, and the passage of time. I wanted their relationships to the language of love and heartbreak to be fairly distinguishable. There's a point early in the book where City says to the reader, "That felt like love to me." Simple sentence. The 1985 City, who's much less rhetorically sophisticated, just isn't capable of that kind of absolute earnestness, at least not initially. The second most difficult part was writing the final scene with Baize. It scared me. I didn't want to write it.

What role does humor play in the novel and in your writing in general?

I don't trust people or writing that are afraid of laughter. I think this book is dark in many ways, filled with critiques of race, gender, geography, and the nation as a whole. But I also hope people will think it's a crazy funny book. Some of the humor is "look at me" stuff, but most of it, I hope, grows organically out of the character and narrative. There's this really serious part in the book where Coach Stroud says to City, "You act like a li'l head-buster, but don't never forget, City, that you got a head, too." Coach is so sincere. And in that moment, City is genuinely afraid Coach is about to chop him in his esophagus. I've reread and rewritten that section hundreds of times, and it's still funny to me, though neither of the characters think it's funny at the time.

Who is this book for?

This book is for Americans who were teenagers in 2013, 1985, or 1964. It's a book for lazy writers, ambitious readers, and all those people who feel like they've never been written to before.